UNDER A MAUI MOON

**Center Point
Large Print**

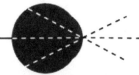

**This Large Print Book carries the
Seal of Approval of N.A.V.H.**

UNDER
A MAUI
MOON

Robin Jones Gunn

CENTER POINT PUBLISHING
THORNDIKE, MAINE

This Center Point Large Print edition
is published in the year 2010 by arrangement with
Howard Books, a division of Simon & Schuster, Inc.

The text of this Large Print edition is unabridged.
In other aspects, this book may vary
from the original edition.
Printed in the United States of America
on permanent paper.
Set in 16-point Times New Roman type.

ISBN: 978-1-60285-793-3

Library of Congress Cataloging-in-Publication Data

Gunn, Robin Jones, 1955–
  Under a Maui moon / Robin Jones Gunn.
    p. cm. — (Hideaway ; 1)
  "Center Point Large Print edition."
  ISBN 978-1-60285-793-3 (lib. bdg. : alk. paper)
  1. Self-actualization (Psychology) in women—Fiction. 2. Maui (Hawaii)—Fiction.
  3. Large type books. I. Title.
PS3557.U4866U53 2010
813'.54—dc22
                                                    2010009468

For Bob and Madelyn, two of God's children.
Thank you for inviting us to Maui
to water your banana trees for a month
while you visited family on the mainland.
I returned from our time at your peaceful home
and robust garden with the seeds of this story
tucked in my heart.
We'll house-sit for you again anytime.

Ke Akua Hemolele,
ua piha ka honua i kou nani
a ke ho'omaika'i nei ia 'oe.

Holy God,
the earth is full of your glory
and so we worship you.

ACKNOWLEDGMENTS

MAHALO TO SOME VERY special people who have shown me their generous *aloha* and *kokua* over the years.

Dr. Norton, who during a deep, dark season of life, once pressed a key to a hideaway cottage into my weary hand.

Kahu Kordell and Kahu Cathy Weaver who invited me to speak at the Kamehameha Schools and offered valuable insights and a few giggles while I was writing this story.

Some of my favorite touch points on Oahu: Hawaiian Islands Ministries, Logos Bookstore, Daniel Kikawa and Aloha Ke Akua Ministries, Daughters of Hawai'i, Calabash Cousins and Mission Houses Museum.

A special thank-you to Tutu Lucy Siu and her friend for their generous assistance in translating the lines from the hymns into Hawaiian.

Bob Greenwald, artist and lifelong friend who has spent more than sixty years composing poetry such as "A Touch of Paradise," which he agreed to let me incorporate into this tale.

My ever-supportive husband and children, with many sweet memories of all our camping trips to Kipahulu over the years. I'm ready to go back with all of you anytime.

Dave Lambert, Becky Nesbitt, Janet Grant, and Rachel Zurakowski, my friends and skilled editorial geniuses who face each challenge I throw at them with grace and kindness.

"God's my island hideaway,
keeps danger far from the shore,
throws garlands of hosannas around my neck."

(Psalm 32:7 *The Message*)

1

"E ka Makua e; he nani kou.
He kupanaha kau mau hana a pau."

"Abide with me; fast falls the eventide.
The darkness deepens. Lord with me abide."

L OADING THE LAST CUP into the dishwasher,
Carissa decided to run the noisy old machine
in the morning. She much preferred the calming
sounds of the Northwest summer night that
sneaked through her open windows—crickets
with their friendly fidgets, frogs trying to outdo
each other with persistent one-note wonders.
Across the lawn a blue jay perched on the top of
the hammock frame and tilted his head as if to
say, "Are you coming out?"

Carissa reached for the small book of poems
she had bought in downtown Portland during her
lunch break that afternoon. Making her exit from
the empty house, she traipsed barefoot across the
warm grass and crawled into the hammock. With
her feet up and ankles crossed, she drew in a deep
breath and pressed the book against her stomach
with both hands.

Above her, a tribe of starlings rose from the tall
pine tree in the north corner of the yard. Moving
as one, the birds darted across the sky, writing

their own invisible lines of poetry with sharp, black movements. She watched them disappear over the rooftop while in her nostrils lingered the dusty fragrance of the towering cedar trees that stood shoulder to shoulder along the back fence. Their proud chests were gilded with the golden medals awarded by a commanding August sunset.

A softness hung in the air. It was just the right balance between the mossy dampness that greeted them nine months of the year in the great Northwest and the feathery dryness that rose from the earth on an Indian summer evening in September. This was the sort of magical summer night meant for lingering.

Carissa adjusted her position and twisted her warm brown hair into a small fist of curls at the base of her damp neck. She should be content. She knew that. She should feel much more of a sense of peace. Yet a disagreeable restlessness clung to her.

Exactly when the slow-burning melancholy had arrived and marked her spirit like a bruise, she couldn't remember. All she knew was that the discontent was with her—on her—following her everywhere, the same way Murphy, their aging black Labrador, shadowed her around the house. The loyal Lab had joined Carissa at the hammock and was resting his chin on the sagging edge, awaiting an affirming pat or scratch on the head.

"Just you and me again, isn't it, Murphy?" She

tugged his ear and scratched where the old dog liked it most, beneath his collar.

Richard should be here. He should be the one lingering with me. This is a night for reminiscing over the past and dreaming about the future.

Carissa tried to remember the last time she and her husband had shared such a night or even sat outside together and gazed into the twilight sky. What happened to those luxurious nights a few summers ago, right after their son moved out? They would take their time enjoying dinner on the patio and then together climb into this hammock made for two. Here they whispered their affection for each other, with fingers intertwined. They spoke of their future with eager anticipation.

But here it was, the future, and she and Richard had become little more than two roommates sharing a bed, a stack of bills, and a growing discontent with their life together.

Murphy nuzzled her hand, prodding Carissa for more scratches.

With one hand on Murphy's head and the other on her unread book of poems, Carissa closed her eyes and cried just a little. But then, unfortunately, a little bit of guilt joined her as well. Richard had a good job. What he did was important. He helped people in significant ways. Lives were being changed. Over the twenty-four years of their marriage, Richard had made many sacrifices for her.

Why was it so hard for her to concede to this small sacrifice and find a way to keep content the three nights per week that Richard worked late? Her life was far too good for her to feel sorry for herself over this.

So the guilt came back to sit beside her. She knew she should be grateful for her husband and his job.

Yet loneliness isn't something that can be blown away with a breeze of logic. If it could, I would have been over this months ago.

Drawing in a deep breath, followed by another even slower and more consoling breath, Carissa drifted off. Lulled into a weightless half-sleep accompanied by Murphy's calming presence and his rhythmic breathing, a dream came and rested on her. Carissa imagined she was afloat on a vast ocean, heading effortlessly to an inviting cove. Overhead a brilliant full moon illuminated the sea. She felt safe. Protected. Not alone.

Murphy moved, rousing Carissa from the vivid half-dream. She closed her eyes and tried to return to the soothing image of the moon on the sea, but Murphy became restless. His ears lifted, and his head turned toward the house.

"No, it's not your master. He won't be home for a while." Carissa tried to read the face of her watch, but the night had closed in around them. She had dozed longer than she had thought. Now it was too dark to see. As she shifted in the hammock, the poetry book slid off onto the grass. Reaching for the book, she tried to remember if she had read any of the poems before falling asleep. No, she knew she hadn't opened the book. How was it that the lyrical image of the ocean and the moon had been so clear? Where did that impression come from?

Murphy turned toward the side yard, his ears perked up. A low growl came from the faithful watchdog, and then with uncharacteristic spunk, Murphy took off and bounded toward the side of the house by the garage. He let out a bark and then growled at the closed gate, barking in a long succession the way he used to bark at the UPS man years ago, when the dog was still young and suspicious.

"What is it, Murphy?" Carissa rolled out of the hammock and headed for the nearby gate. "Did a rabbit slide under the fence?"

The security light blinked on. Carissa froze. Rabbits and squirrels didn't create enough motion to set off the security light. Something larger was out there, just on the other side of the unlocked gate.

Then she heard it. The unmistakable sound of feet crunching through the gravel along the side of the house.

Carissa lunged for Murphy's collar and pulled him with her, dashing to the back door. She yanked the rigid dog inside the house with her, quickly turning the bolt and rushing to the front door to make sure it was locked. Murphy stayed at the back door, growling, while Carissa stood in the darkened living room, cautiously peering out the front window.

A car was parked in front of their home. Cars never parked in front of their home. They lived on a dead-end street with only one other house nearly half an acre away.

Carissa tried to quell her panic as she reached for the phone. Reason told her to dial 911 but instinct prompted her to call Richard. He picked up on the first ring.

"Someone's here, Richard. A prowler. The security light went on."

"You sure it wasn't a squirrel?"

"No! There's a car out front."

"In front of our house?"

"Yes!"

His tone changed. "Is it a Toyota?"

"I don't know."

"Is the car white?"

"Yes."

"Carissa, call the police right now. Hang up and call the police. I'm on my way."

Her hands shook as she dialed 911 and spoke rapidly to the dispatcher. He asked for specifics, and Carissa listed how the dog barked, the security light went on, she had heard footsteps, she couldn't think of any reason for a car to be parked

18

in front of their house. Then she suddenly felt self-conscious. What if it was only a large rabbit that had triggered the security light? What if it had been several rabbits, and their shuffling in the gravel sounded like footsteps?

Before she could talk herself into calming down, the pulse of a flashing blue light seeped through the closed shades, indicating the police had arrived. Two officers with long-handled flashlights approached the parked car. Through the corner of the front window, Carissa could see the outline of a man in the driver's seat. He handed his wallet to an officer who then returned to the patrol car with the ID in his hand. The other officer remained standing beside the car, apparently asking the man more questions.

With her heart pounding, Carissa unlocked the front door, slowly opening it just a few inches in an effort to hear what was being said. Their voices were too low.

Murphy arrived at her side. He poked his nose out the door and growled. Carissa pressed her leg against him. "Shhh! Don't bark. Stay here."

The first officer got out of the patrol car and strode toward the suspect with purposeful steps. He ordered the man out of the car and told him to lean against the hood while the other officer placed him in handcuffs.

A moment later, the first officer was at the front door.

"Good evening, ma'am. I'm Officer Roberts. Were you the one who made the call to 911?"

"Yes."

"May I ask you a few questions?"

She repeated the details in response to his questions, and then the officer asked, "Your husband is Dr. Lathrop, is that correct?"

"Yes."

"He's a psychologist, is that right? A professional counselor?"

"Yes, he is. Do you know my husband?"

"I do. He assisted our department a few years back." Hesitating, the officer added, "He helped with the Sellwood case."

An involuntary shiver shot through Carissa. Her grip on Murphy's collar tightened, and the compliant dog took the action as a command to sit.

Just then a Mazda with squealing brakes peeled around the corner and screeched as it turned into the driveway. Six-foot-tall Richard Lathrop lurched from the car, leaving the door ajar. Instead of rushing to the front door, where Carissa stood with the officer, he went to the handcuffed man at the curb.

"You can go back inside now, Mrs. Lathrop. We'll take it from here." Officer Roberts started to walk away but then seemed to have a second thought.

He turned toward Carissa. "Listen, if you ever

hear anything suspicious or have any cause for concern, anything at all, you call us right away. Don't hesitate. Make the call."

Carissa nodded.

He gave a respectful dip of his chin and walked away.

Carissa felt her chest compressing. All her earlier hammock dreams of floating on a tranquil sea beneath a bobbing moon had vanished. It felt as if she had stepped into a nightmare. The soft fragrance of the honeysuckle blossoms on the twin vines that arched over the front door seemed out of place in light of what was happening in their front yard.

At the street, Richard was talking with the officers. His posture and gestures gave the impression that he was making a plea on the suspect's behalf.

Richard, what are you doing? Tell me you're not defending that man. He was prowling along the side of our house! Let the police take him in for questioning!

As Carissa watched with her teeth clenched, her persuasive husband apparently convinced the officers to uncuff the man.

No!

The suspect stood beside his car rubbing his wrists while Richard walked with the two officers back to their patrol car. He spoke with them privately for a few more minutes before they all shook hands and the officers got into their car and drove off.

No, don't leave!

Richard returned to the man. With his arms folded, Richard leaned against the car casually and tilted his head the way he always did when he was listening to someone with whom he disagreed.

Staring across the wide front yard that had turned dark now that the patrol car was gone, Carissa tried to burn her anxious thoughts into the back of her husband's head.

Richard, tell me you're not trying to counsel this guy. Not now. Not in front of our house.

With a shove, Carissa slammed the front door loud enough to send her husband a passive-aggressive message. She hated that she even knew what such behavior was. She hated that she knew anything about Richard's world of counseling. It terrified her to think about the Sellwood case and what had happened to that innocent woman. The predator who had attacked her in her home late at night had been a client of Richard's. True, he had been a client for only one counseling session and that session took place a year before the man carried out his heinous crime. But Richard's notes from that one session aided the police in their arrest and eventual conviction.

While Carissa knew how much her husband had helped a lot of people rebuild their lives, all she could think of in this moment was, *What about the ones who don't respond to counseling? How many unstable clients has my husband met with that I don't know about? How many is he meeting with now?*

She stopped in the middle of the kitchen and allowed herself to ask a question she had never faced head-on before. *How many of his clients know where we live?*

Carissa suddenly realized why Richard had installed a security alarm system in their house the same day the Sellwood case hit the news. She understood more clearly why he had put a small canister of mace on her key chain and tested her to make sure she knew how to use it. Their unlisted home phone number now made sense.

Why hadn't she seen this before? She was vulnerable. Here, in her own home, she was at risk. Richard had never come out and told her so, but his actions indicated that she was in danger.

Counting back the months and years to the day the Sellwood case broke, Carissa realized that was the day that a silent fear had entered their home and their marriage like an invisible gas. It had been slowly smothering her. Was that the heaviness she had been carrying around for so long? Or was it that Richard kept so much of his world hidden from her?

As soon as Carissa looked the unspoken fear-phantom in the face, it morphed. She was no longer silently afraid. She was furious.

Stomping over to the kitchen sink, she poured herself a glass of water and drank it quickly, as if the cool liquid could douse the embers that now burned inside her.

I'm not safe here. In my own home I'm not safe. That's not okay. That's wrong. Just then she heard the front door open. For a moment she didn't move. A sharp pain shot through her jaw. She unclenched her teeth.

Her broad-shouldered husband entered, rubbing his forehead and looking agitated. His thinning blond hair needed attention. His blue, button-down shirt was crumpled, and his khaki trousers showed blotted evidence of a stain from whatever it was he had eaten for lunch. Richard lowered himself onto the couch and said nothing.

Carissa took a seat opposite him and started with a question to which she already knew the answer. "He was a client, wasn't he?"

"Yes."

"One of your dangerous ones?" She tried to keep her words slow and even.

"I wouldn't call him dangerous."

"But they handcuffed him. Obviously he has a record. What did he do?"

Richard glanced over at her, barely making eye contact. "He's not a predator, if that's what you're worried about. He's just in a bad place right now. His wife left him. She took the kids and cleaned out the house. He's frantic. He called me earlier, but I didn't take his call. That's why he came here. He was trying to see if my car was in the garage and didn't want to bother you if I wasn't home."

While Carissa felt a slight twinge of sympathy for the man, it wasn't enough to quell her fears. "Why did she leave him? What did he do?"

Richard hesitated. He stretched his neck from side to side, as if trying to release the tension, but didn't respond to her question. That infuriated Carissa. She knew her husband could be trusted to keep the confidences of his clients, but now she was the one who needed to be trusted, and he was shutting her out.

"Richard, what was he convicted of?"

"Voyeurism and domestic violence."

Carissa felt her heart pounding and her anxiety elevating. "And you dismissed him from any charges? A convicted Peeping Tom, who comes to our house and looks in our windows?"

"The domestic violence was dismissed, and the voyeurism conviction was more than five years ago. He hasn't had another incident since—"

"You wouldn't call tonight another incident?"

"He's really a level one, Carissa. No human contact. He's not dangerous."

"How do you know that? What about the predator from the Sellwood case? Did you know for a fact that he wasn't dangerous?"

Richard sat up straight, as if her comment had

25

sent a shock through the couch. "There is no comparison. You're making this into more than it is. Nothing happened."

"Nothing happened?" Carissa leaned forward, her patience gone. "Richard, I can't believe you're taking this so lightly. Our home, our private space, was violated tonight. I was sleeping in the hammock when Murphy heard this client of yours on the side of the house. Do you know how terrified I was when the security light went on and I heard footsteps in the gravel?"

Carissa didn't give him a chance to respond. "No, of course, you don't know. How could you know how terrified I was? You didn't even come in the house to check on me when you got home. You went to him! You defended him. You're still defending him! Do you see the problem here? I'm your wife. You're supposed to defend me and protect me, not your volatile clients!"

"You're overreacting, Carissa. I told you, he's not volatile."

"I can't believe you're still defending him! Will you listen to yourself? Richard, I'm telling you, I don't feel safe in my own home. What happened tonight is not okay. I am not okay."

Carissa hadn't expected the tears to come the way they did, fast and hot, racing down her cheeks. The tears angered her. But Richard angered her more. *Why wasn't he seeing the severity of the situation?*

26

Leaning back and turning his steady gaze toward her, Richard said with calculated inflection in his voice, "I can see how you would feel—"

"No!" Carissa shot to her feet and put her hand up to stop him. Her enraged voice trembled, and her tears stopped immediately. "Don't you dare start with that soothing tone and that concerned-counselor look. Not with me. You can go be the big savior to all the lost men in the world and tell them you understand their pain. But don't pretend to understand what I'm feeling. Not like that. Not when you won't even hear what I'm saying. All you really care about is your clients and their demented issues! You're losing touch with reality."

Richard was suddenly on his feet with a stern finger pointed at her. "Don't ever say that to me! You're the one who is out of control here!" His eyes were wild, and he looked as if he might throw something.

Stunned by his unexpectedly intense reaction, Carissa gave into her instincts and fled to their bedroom, slamming the door.

The white heat of her fear and anger inciner-ated her tears before they could leak out. She couldn't believe this was happening. Trying to calm her spirit, she waited for Richard to come to her. She was certain that once he cooled off he would open the door and diplomatically suggest they sit down and talk things through. That's what he did. He repaired broken relationships. He restored order and brought understanding. He initiated forgiveness.

But not tonight. Richard didn't come to her to make things right. And Carissa didn't open the door and go to him.

2

"A hele akua, A luhi no, a uhi mai kapo
Maluna o'u
Ku'u mele 'oia mau
E pili E ku'u Iesu ou la wau."

"Though like the wanderer, the sun gone down,
Darkness be over me, my rest a stone;
Yet in my dreams I'd be
Nearer, my God, to thee."

CARISSA SPENT THE NIGHT curled up in the overstuffed corner chair in their bedroom. As the morning sun stretched its long fingers of groping light in through the small spaces between the shades and window frame, she recoiled from its grasp.

Stumbling into the bathroom, she cast a critical glance at her sallow reflection in the mirror. The cinnamon highlights in her shoulder-length brown hair gave off the impression that even her head was still smoldering after last night's battle.

Her intense, pale blue eyes had turned the shade of a bottomless sea. All the lines around her mouth appeared dark and deep. Nausea accompanied each bend and turn, as she showered and dressed for work.

Delaying as long as she could, she finally opened the bedroom door. She didn't know what she would say when she saw Richard. They had crossed into unfamiliar territory last night. Anything could happen next.

But nothing happened. Richard wasn't on the couch where she expected to find him. Nor was he in the guest bed.

Murphy was stretched out on his rug by the back door. He opened his eyes, raised his head, but made no effort to come to her.

"Come on, Murphy. Outside. Move." Not a hint of kindness accompanied her commands. With his head lowered, the stiff old dog stepped out on the back patio. The freshness of the new day rushed in through the open door, reeking of warmth and beauty. Carissa wanted none of it. She shut the door, locked it, and checked inside the garage. Richard's car wasn't there.

Carissa told herself she didn't care. She backed her car down the driveway and pressed the button to close the automatic door as she drove down the street. With a glance at the front of the house, seeing the doors all locked and the shades pulled, she felt a second wave of sadness come over her.

I love that house. But I'll never feel safe here again.

The same churning thoughts that kept her tossing in the chair last night returned. *What's going to happen to us? To our marriage? We've never had a fight like this. Can a couple as disconnected as Richard and I are ever recover from what happened last night? Why didn't he try to fix things? Has he given up on us?*

A single tear marked her painful thoughts with a straight, clear line down the left side of her face. One tear. That was all. Twenty-four years of marriage, one grown son, a thousand memories, yet only a single tear.

And that, she decided, was Richard's fault.

He should have come to her last night. He should have fought for her. That was the real problem in their marriage. He no longer cared about her. Because if he cared, he would have come to her last night. The Richard she married would have broken down the bedroom door, if he had to. They would have talked things through for hours, and he would have made her cry, cry so hard that this morning her eyes would be swollen and red. Her closest colleagues at work would immediately know something was wrong, and they would extend silent nods of understanding, the only solace she would accept from them.

Instead, her tear ducts were dry. And she was alone. Solitary.

Carissa didn't turn into the Coffee People Drive-Thru, as she usually did on her way to work. Her stomach couldn't handle coffee. If this had been any other morning when she felt this miserable, she would have ordered a chocolate-filled croissant to go with her medium, extra-hot Velvet Hammer. Today she was neither hungry nor thirsty. She was numb. And she knew she couldn't fix numb with pastries or mochas.

Pulling into the back lot of the medical offices, Carissa tried to compartmentalize what had happened last night. This was work. She was a professional. Whatever she and Richard needed to resolve, that would happen later. Not at work.

With her choice of parking places, Carissa noticed that Dr. Walters's car was parked in its usual spot. This was early for him. At sixty-nine years old and the senior M.D. among the six physicians in the group practice, Dr. Walters kept fewer hours than the other doctors. He usually came in after ten and took off Thursdays. Here it was, Thursday, and he was at the office a little after 8 A.M.

Carissa parked next to Dr. Chan's car and realized all six doctors were there early this morning. As the office manager of this small medical practice, Carissa always knew about staff meetings. Had she forgotten today's meeting? She didn't think so.

Rushing from her car, as if she were late, she

found she didn't need her key to enter the back door of the Hillside Family Physicians' office. It already was open. Carissa kept her footsteps soft, listening to see if she could hear the doctors gathered in the front waiting room.

The scent of freshly brewed coffee wafted from the break room. *Who is here doing my job?*

"Molly?" Carissa stood in the doorway to the break room.

Dr. Garrett's twentysomething niece nearly dropped the glass coffeepot. "Carissa, you freaked me out! I didn't see you come in."

"I'm early. I didn't realize a meeting was scheduled for this morning."

"I think it was sort of a last-minute meeting, you know? You probably didn't have reason to know about it."

In the eight months Molly had worked in the office as a part-time receptionist, she consistently went beyond her required job description. It didn't seem that out of the ordinary for her to be there this early, yet Carissa couldn't figure out why she didn't know about the meeting but Molly did.

"Would you like some help with the coffee?"

"No, that's okay. I have it covered. Do you want some? I was going to make a second pot."

"No, none for me. Thanks."

Molly turned her head so that her jet-black hair picked up a bluish sheen in the fluorescent lights. "Are you okay?"

Carissa turned away. She opened the refrigerator, busily looking for something. As casually as possible she said, "I'm fine."

"You look . . . you look sort of tired."

"I guess I am a little." Carissa pulled a bottle of water from the back of the refrigerator and made her way to her office without grilling Molly on why she knew about the meeting. A low echo of the doctors' voices filtered down the hall from the front waiting room. As curious as she was to know what the meeting was about, Carissa knew the doctors' discussion would be tag-team-tattled through the office before lunch. All she had to do was wait. The details would come to her soon enough.

Turning on her computer, Carissa glimpsed the picture frame next to the monitor. The photo was of Richard and their son, Blake, at his college graduation. She gazed a moment at the image of these two men in her life and then took down the picture and put it in her top drawer. She couldn't handle their smiling faces looking at her. Not this morning.

Carissa went through a stack of folders on her desk. At least half of her workday was spent organizing the aging Dr. Walters. He had come to depend on her, as if she were his personal assistant. Every time she found a file he had misplaced or she managed to decipher one of his scrawled notes, she felt a personal sense of accomplishment because he always thanked her heartily.

Carissa was in the midst of a hunt for a prescription dosage in the file of one of Dr. Walters's patients when a tap sounded on her door.

"Come in."

She turned to see Richard standing only a few feet away with a ragged but determined look on his face. He was wearing the same clothes he had worn last night. He quietly closed her office door behind him.

"We need to talk." This was not his counselor voice speaking.

"I agree."

He didn't reply. It seemed he was waiting for her to speak first, as if she owed him an apology.

Carissa blurted out the question foremost in her mind. "Where did you go last night?"

"Back to my office. I had paperwork to finish up."

"Then where did you go?"

Richard lifted his chin. "I stayed at my office."

His crumpled clothes backed up his claim.

"Why didn't you come home and try to talk things through?"

"You weren't ready to talk. Not after the way you walked off and slammed the door."

"I was mad."

"You're still mad."

"So are you."

Richard crossed his arms and tilted his head just right. She knew that no matter what she said now, he would disagree with her.

A tap sounded on her closed office door. Before she could say, "Come in," the door opened, and Dr. Walters entered. His white lab coat was buttoned crooked.

"Well, hello, Richard." Dr. Walters extended his hand. "Good to see you. How is everything with you these days?"

Richard responded with an automatic and almost believable, "Fine. How are you, sir?"

Dr. Walters leaned back. His lower lip protruded slightly, as it always did when he was thinking through a list of symptoms and was about to offer a diagnosis. "Well, I guess I could say I'm doing all right, all things considered. Do you mind if I borrow your wife for a few minutes? I need to give her an update on our meeting this morning."

"I was just leaving." Richard's voice sounded cordial to Dr. Walters, but Carissa could still hear the sharp edge just under the surface. Richard moved to the open door of Carissa's office without turning back to look at her.

In frustration she tossed out, "If you're going home, Murphy's in the backyard. I didn't feed him before I left."

"I'll take care of him." Richard's words were firm and even. As he exited, Carissa felt her face warm.

You'll take care of the dog, but you won't take care of me.

Dr. Walters closed the door almost all the way and looked at Carissa over the top of his glasses. "Everything okay?"

"I forgot to feed the dog this morning." She shrugged, as if that would help him to believe that the obvious tension between Richard and her was over something petty.

Dr. Walters closed the door the rest of the way. Carissa had the feeling he was about to give her one of his rare fatherly lectures, the way he had several years ago when she came to work with strep throat and wouldn't agree to go home until he made her take a throat culture and then walked her to her car.

"Carissa, I need to tell you about some decisions we've had to make here. I'm afraid this will not be good news for you."

"What sort of decisions?"

"I have decided to retire."

Carissa let out a breath of relief. She had heard these same words from Dr. Walters many times before. Each time he announced his retirement, he ended up reconsidering based on his abiding love for his patients. He always ended up going back on the roster but scheduling himself for fewer hours and fewer patients each time.

As it was now, Dr. Walters saw patients only

seven months of the year. The other five months he spent with his wife at their vacation home on the island of Maui.

"So, does this mean you're cutting back to only being in the office for six months a year?"

His half-grin acknowledged that she was on to his predictable ways. However, a somber sadness clung to the corners of his mouth. She could see that this time it was different.

"No, I'm making my retirement official this time. It's not fair that the other doctors have to carry so much of my patient load in the months when I'm not here. I need to hang up my stethoscope. Most importantly, Betty wants me to be home with her. She has a Honey Do list that reaches all the way to the ceiling."

"I can't believe you're really going to retire."

He nodded and took on a more serious expression. "We discussed the details at the meeting this morning. It was agreed that Dr. Garrett would take over here as the head physician."

Carissa wasn't surprised. Dr. Garrett was the logical choice. She wondered if she now would be asked to take on more duties as Dr. Garrett's personal assistant. He was a quiet man and far more organized than Dr. Walters.

"Dr. Garrett asked that I be the one to let you know about the decisions he's made for staff changes in light of my leaving."

Carissa appreciated getting a heads-up whenever there were staff changes or schedule changes. It made her job easier.

Dr. Walters removed his glasses and looked at Carissa straight on, his brows lowering like flags at half-mast. "I'm afraid the decision is to let you go."

She didn't move. Then blinking, she repeated, "Did you say, let me go?"

"Yes. I'm very sorry, Carissa. I know you didn't expect this."

"I don't understand. Why?"

"As is the case with most business decisions, finances were a determining factor. You know how challenging it has been to remain within our operating budget for the past year or so."

"Yes, but I . . ." Carissa knew she was the highest-paid support staff in the office. She wasn't prepared to justify her position.

Dr. Walters raised his chin. "Finances aren't the only reason, though. The new operating system is now covering many of the responsibilities that originally were part of your job description. And the new billing and insurance procedures have improved greatly since you first came on staff."

"Yes, that's true, but . . ." Bravely rounding back her shoulders, Carissa tried to think of something brilliant to say. "Wouldn't all the doctors agree that an office manager still is needed?"

"Yes, they do. All the doctors agree there is need. However, they see the position in a more limited capacity with fewer responsibilities."

Dr. Walters shifted his position. "And that's why it's been decided that Molly will take on the office manager position. In a greatly reduced role, of course."

"Molly?" Carissa felt her face going pale. "Are you sure the doctors all agreed to this?"

"Yes, they did. I no longer have a say in the final decisions around here, and for that I am sorry, Carissa. Very sorry."

Carissa stared at him.

"The layoff is immediate. You'll receive your compensation, of course. I expressed my confidence to the other doctors that you would stay on long enough to assist in a smooth transition. Dr. Garrett believes Molly is prepared to start immediately."

"What does that mean?"

"That means you have today and tomorrow to get Molly up to speed on everything she needs to know. Tomorrow, Friday, will be your last day."

Carissa could barely breathe. In a whisper she said, "And you agreed to this?"

Dr. Walters lowered his puppy dog eyes. "As I said, these decisions are out of my hands now. I know this comes as a deep disappointment to you, Carissa. I never expected my retirement to affect your position. I realize how much you've done for me here, especially over the past few years. You single-handedly kept me going at a productive level, and I'm very grateful. I want you to know you can depend on me for a top-notch reference wherever you decide to go next."

Her throat was beginning to close. Carissa had no idea where she could go. She hadn't applied for a new job in more than fifteen years. This was where she belonged.

"There is one more thing." Dr. Walters reached into his coat pocket.

Carissa didn't think she could handle "one more thing." Not after all the life-altering news he had just given her. For a moment she wondered if he was going to pull out his pad and write her a prescription for a sedative to help her recover from the shock.

Instead he pulled out his key ring. Without saying anything, the aging gentleman worked at removing one of the keys with his short thumbnail.

"Hold out your hand."

She did and was embarrassed to see that her hand was trembling. Dr. Walters placed a single key into her palm. The top of the key was painted white. Carissa looked at him for an explanation.

He smiled one of his pleased smiles. She had seen that look a number of times over the years. It was the smile that came to him when a patient's blood work returned negative for diabetes or when he opened a biopsy report from the lab and saw the word "benign." This was his life-giving grin, and he was giving it to her in the midst of her grave loss.

"What's this for?" Carissa still held the key in her open palm.

"I'll tell you tomorrow. Keep it in a safe place, and before you leave tomorrow, I'll tell you what it's for."

For a long time after Dr. Walters exited her office, Carissa sat staring at the wall. The key remained in her clenched hand. None of what had just happened seemed real. She never expected to lose her job.

An overwhelming sense of grief crept up from her gut and seemed determined to wrap its clutches around her heart. It was the first time in her married life that she didn't call Richard as soon as she had important news. How could she tell him anything right now?

It was also the first time in the past few years that she felt like crying out to God. Not that she knew what she would say to him either. Her drifting away had been slow and not obvious to others. But Carissa knew. She knew how it used to feel at moments like this when she could easily run to the deep, holy corners of her heart and cry out to God. He always met her there and calmed her in mysterious ways.

The portal to that quiet place now seemed a thousand miles away, across a treacherous ocean. Carissa felt very much alone.

Molly appeared at her partially opened door. "Is it okay if I come in?"

"Can we wait until later for this, Molly? I'm not quite ready to start your training."

"Oh, I know." Molly entered the office anyway. "I just wanted you to know that I didn't realize this is what Dr. Garrett was going to decide. I didn't ask for this, you know what I'm saying? I mean, I hoped I'd eventually get hired on full-time here, but not like this. This wasn't my idea. I'm really sorry you're leaving."

Carissa felt herself soften a little with a twinge of compassion for Molly. In a low voice she said, "Don't worry about it."

"Well, I'll try not to worry about your losing your job, but I can't guarantee I won't still feel bad about everything. I mean, I understand it's going to be gruesome for you to have to train me, but we have only today and tomorrow; so if you can help me out a little here, it would be great. I'm available whenever you are."

Carissa glanced at the key in her palm and then back at Molly. "We might as well start now. Why don't you see if you can bring in another chair."

Molly paused. "Oh. Okay. Sure. I can do that."

Reaching for her purse, Carissa tucked Dr. Walters's key into the coin pouch of her wallet. It was the safest place she could think of at the moment. She came to work numb. Now she was on autopilot.

The remainder of the day Carissa provided Molly with thorough direction and felt secretly amazed that she was coping as well as she was. At around four-thirty, though, Carissa felt as if her brain had stopped. All her synapses had gone on strike.

"Molly, how about if we stop and call it a day?"

"Are you kidding? That would be totally fine with me. I don't know about you, but I'm on overload. This is a lot to learn."

They agreed to come in at eight the next morning to start early. Carissa shut down her computer and realized she had an even bigger challenge facing her now. Would Richard be home when she got there? Or did he have clients again tonight?

Her office phone rang just then. It was her younger sister, Heidi.

"Hey, I'm glad I caught you. Would you like to meet up for coffee around seven tonight at Francine's?"

Carissa hesitated. This was the worst time in her life to come under her sister's scrutinizing eye. She did like the idea, though, of having plans so that she had an excuse not to go home. At least not right away.

"Okay. Sure."

"Really? Great! Is seven o'clock good for you?"

"Actually, I think I'll go there for dinner. Do you want to have dinner with me, or meet me there at seven?"

"I can go now," Heidi said. "As a matter of fact, I'm about three blocks from your office. That's why I thought to call you. Do you want me to pick you up, and we can go together?"

"Sure. I'll meet you out front."

Carissa knew she couldn't delay the inevitable forever. She had to go home eventually. She had to tell Richard she had lost her job. The two of them had to talk through their unresolved issues.

But before she faced all those difficult moments, what could it hurt to have a night out with her perpetually upbeat sister? Especially when Francine's served the best chocolate hazelnut torte in all of Portland.

3

"Palupalu anei 'oe, ane ma'ule ahina no?
E ho 'oho a nonoi,
Mai mumule noi mau
Ku kokoke maia Iesu,
Makukau e kokua mai."

"Do thy friends despise, forsake thee?
Take it to the Lord in prayer!
In his arms he'll take and shield thee;
Thou wilt find a solace there."

STANDING IN FRONT OF the medical office while waiting for Heidi, Carissa pulled out her phone. She typed a text to Richard, stating she would be home after nine.

Why am I telling him? If this had been last night, I wouldn't have thought twice about letting him know I was going to dinner with Heidi. Last night it wouldn't have mattered what time I was getting home.

She erased the text without sending it just as Heidi pulled up in her slightly battered Volvo station wagon. Heidi reached over to unlock the passenger's door. "Hey, cute shirt. I don't think I've seen that one."

Carissa slid in and closed the door. "I'm sure you've seen it before. It's not new."

"What do you think of my earrings?" Heidi fingered the dangling beads and smiled at her big sis.

"Cute."

Heidi's blond hair was pulled up in a twist of chaos that somehow managed to look stylish. Like Carissa, Heidi had their father's fair skin, thin nose, and pale blue eyes. His Scandinavian genes were, according to their mother, the only good thing he ever gave his two daughters.

"Don't you recognize them?" Heidi asked.

"No."

Heidi's chin dipped, and her mouth opened in mock shock. The view revealed her scar from a tongue piercing gone bad.

"What?" Carissa asked.

"I can't believe it. You forgot already. These are the earrings you bought for me a few weeks ago when we went to the Saturday market. Remember? I was looking at them and walked away, and then you told me you had to go to the bathroom, but you really went back and secretly got them for me. Do you remember now?"

Carissa nodded.

"Well, I absolutely love them. I've worn them practically every day since you gave them to me. In case I never thanked you, thank you. You're always doing little sweet things for me. So tonight, I'm buying our dinner."

When Carissa didn't protest, Heidi looked at her more closely. "Are you feeling all right?"

"Yeah, I'm just tired." Carissa tried to force a lighthearted expression.

"Well, I don't know about you, but I'm famished. I've been craving chocolate all day, which is why Francine's is the perfect choice. I need something with ganache. I'm counting on them having raspberry gâteau on the dessert menu tonight. This is not a crème brûlée sort of night, if you know what I mean."

Carissa didn't know what her sister meant, but it didn't seem to matter. Heidi kept chatting about dessert options as Carissa tried to calm the rumble in her stomach. She wondered if subconsciously she had agreed to meet Heidi tonight because she knew she could elicit sympathy from her sister if she wanted it. Yet now that the opportunity was before her, Carissa knew she didn't want sympathy. She didn't want dessert either. She didn't know what she wanted.

As Heidi steered the car back into the traffic flow, she glanced over at Carissa. "Are you sure you're okay?"

"I'm fine."

"Did I tell you about that old skating rink off Belmont? The one we used to go to when we were kids?"

"What about it?"

"I read in *The Oregonian* that it's being looked at by Whole Foods. Can you imagine how thrilled my husband would be if an organic grocery store were available within walking distance? He would be there every day, oogling the eggplants and caressing the cabbages."

Carissa knew she should be grinning at Heidi's quip, but her mind was too numb. Her sister's marriage was in full bloom while hers was dying. *Why? How did we get to this place of disconnect?*

Heidi kept chatting, carrying on a one-sided conversation, as they drove across the Burnside Bridge. Carissa gazed out the lowered car window and watched the bikers weaving through a stream of strolling pedestrians as they all headed to downtown Portland on this mild August evening. The dark waters of the Willamette River hosted an assortment of motorboats as well as sailboats that appeared to be picking up their pace with the vibrant evening breeze.

How can the rest of the world so effortlessly be rolling along when my life is in the midst of such upheaval?

As they drove past Powell's Books, Heidi rambled on about her new Pilates class while Carissa thought of all the times she had visited Powell's on her lunch break. She especially loved to go on rainy days, which prevailed nearly nine months of the year in Portland. It lifted her spirits to prowl around the three-story labyrinth that covered a square city block and carried every new and used book imaginable. Was it only yesterday when she had come here and picked up the small book of poems?

I won't be coming here like I used to, will I? After tomorrow, I won't have lunch breaks to spend at Powell's because I won't have a job.

The realization sent another tremor through her fragile system.

"Do you mind walking?" Heidi asked.

"Walking?" Carissa tried to focus on her sister.

"To Francine's. Parking is so difficult to find anywhere near Twenty-third Avenue."

"I don't care."

Feeling Heidi's scrutinizing gaze as they sat at a stoplight, Carissa decided she couldn't do this.

"You know what? I changed my mind."

"Okay. No big deal. I'll drop you off in front of the restaurant and then go find a place to park."

"No, I mean I changed my mind about going to

dinner." She tried to hide the wobble in her voice. "Can you take me back to the office?"

"Okay." Heidi pulled into the parking lot of a Goodwill Store and made the turn to go back down the hill. "What's going on? Something's obviously bothering you. What is it?"

Carissa paused. While Heidi was commendably sympathetic, she was also quick to share personal information with others. If their mother got ahold of the news about Carissa's job loss before she told Richard, it would be a mess. Saying anything to her sister now wasn't a good idea.

Heidi reached over and gave Carissa's hand a squeeze. "Hey, hello! Are you still with me?"

"Yes. Sorry. I'm just too tired to do this tonight."

"That's okay. What do you think it is that's making you so spacey? Hormones maybe?"

"No, it's not hormones."

"Are you sure? Because my mother-in-law went on some sort of estrogen therapy a few years ago. She said she was spacey all the time and felt like she was going insane before she started the treatment. It's worked well for her."

"It's not my hormones," Carissa repeated, more firmly this time.

Heidi wouldn't let it go. "Are you starting to have hot flashes? You could be premenopausal. You are in that whole empty-nest phase of life right now. I have a friend at work, about your age, and she gets vitamin B shots every two weeks. She says it makes a world of difference in her energy level."

"Heidi, I don't need shots of any sort. I'm just under a lot of stress right now. That's all. I don't want to talk about it."

"Okay. That's fine."

To her credit, Heidi remained quiet for the next two stoplights. Then she said, "You do know that extra vitamin C is good for stress, right?"

Carissa bit the inside of her lip. But she didn't say anything she later would regret. She was prepared for Heidi to start suggesting one of her thirty-day herbal cleanses, as she had in the past. This time Heidi seemed to pick up on the hints from her sister and managed to stop with all the advice. For someone who was nine years younger than Carissa, Heidi sure enjoyed stepping into the role of firstborn whenever Carissa was out of sorts.

Heidi pulled into the back parking lot of Hillside Family Physicians. With faux-finality, she said, "Sorry if I was bugging you with my suggestions. I was just trying to help."

"I know."

"I understand that you don't feel like talking right now, but would you promise that you will call me when you do feel like talking?"

"I will." Carissa reached over and gave her sister's arm a "thanks for trying" squeeze. "I'll call you in a few days."

Heidi looped her arms around Carissa and cleverly managed to slide in one more piece of advice along with her closing hug. "I hope you can go home, take a long bath, eat something, and sleep. Get some good sleep."

With a wave, Carissa climbed into her car. She drove straight home even though she still wished she had someplace else to go. As much as she didn't want to go home to an empty house, even more she dreaded going home to find Richard there.

As she pulled into the driveway, she saw him in the front yard, mowing the lawn. He stopped and let the mower engine idle while the two of them exchanged noncommittal glances. This was so out of the ordinary for both of them—the cold stares, the inability to bounce back from a disagreement. She hated it. All of it. How was she going to tell him she had lost her job?

Richard returned to mowing, and she drove into the garage, closing the automatic door behind her. *So what am I supposed to do now?*

Heidi's final bit of advice seemed to have more of an effect than Carissa wanted to admit because all she wanted to do when she walked into the house was fill the bathtub with water as hot as she could stand and soak until she turned wrinkly.

Locking the bedroom door, Carissa ran the water as high as it could safely go and then inched her way into the tub until the water was up to her shoulders. Her soft brown hair dangled in the water. Beads of perspiration streamed down her forehead. She stretched out her toes, and her breathing slowed to a less erratic pace.

If there was a sensation just past numb, this was it. She hadn't felt this way since right after her miscarriage almost sixteen years ago.

As she let the steamy bath relax her, Carissa thought back on how Richard had insisted after the miscarriage that she get some help. He said he saw her spirit sinking into a deep, dark place. His idea of help, of course, was counseling.

Carissa went to two sessions and decided she was over it. Opening up to a stranger, no matter how qualified that counselor was, just didn't feel right to her. She felt like such a hypocrite. Here she was, telling her husband she fully supported what he did and encouraging others to go to counseling. But when she had the opportunity, it didn't work for her.

Instead, she ended up talking to her closest friend from church, who also had had a miscarriage. Together the two young mothers mourned, and somehow they both slowly were healed in the process.

Carissa tried to think of another woman she could open up to now about the conflict in her marriage and the loss of her job. No one came to mind. While her mom was supportive and caring, just like Heidi, Carissa didn't want to open that family box of chocolates. Too many hidden fruits and nuts.

Fed up with her self-reflective session, Carissa climbed out of the tub and wrapped herself in a plush towel. From the closet she pulled out her most comfortable, airy summer dress. Then she stretched out on her bed and waited out the light-headed sensation that often accompanied her hot baths.

As exhausted as she was, Carissa knew that a nap would elude her. She had to talk to Richard. She couldn't go another night curled up in the bedroom chair with nothing resolved between them.

Padding her way into the kitchen, she saw that Richard was seated at the kitchen table in his grass-stained jeans. The toaster was dismantled in front of him. All the main pieces were belly up on two dishtowels. Why was it that even in his off-duty time, the man had to "fix" something?

He looked at her. "Are you ready to talk?"

"I need to eat something first." Carissa opened the refrigerator door in search of anything that would settle her stomach. Dry toast was the only item she thought she could handle. Some black tea with lots of warm milk might go down, too.

Pulling out the loaf of bread, Carissa untwisted the tie and took two slices. Then she realized where the toaster was—on the table in pieces. Just like the rest of her life.

In frustration, she threw the slices into the

trash and stuffed the loaf of bread back into the refrigerator.

"What's wrong?"

"I'm hungry!"

"Why don't you make some scrambled eggs?"

I don't want scrambled eggs. I want toast!

A sickening heaviness pressed in on her chest. After not eating all day, the only thing that sounded good right now was not toast but a milk-shake. A Burgerville vanilla milkshake.

Grabbing a sweater and her purse, Carissa headed for the garage.

"Now what are you doing?"

"I'm going to get something to eat."

"I'll go with you." It wasn't an offer or a question. Richard was already on his feet, ready to go.

"I'm just going to Burgerville."

"Fine. I'll go with you."

Carissa had no steam in her left to protest. She slipped her feet into a pair of sandals by the back door, and the two of them headed off to the local hamburger stop, just as they had done many times over the years, starting with when they were teenagers.

As they drove together in silence, Carissa thought of how different the summer night had felt only twenty-four hours ago, when she had stretched out in the hammock in the backyard, thinking she was going to leisurely read through her poetry book.

Then she thought of how different a night like this felt twenty-four years ago, when their love was fresh, and she thought she was living a poem. Back then they couldn't keep their hands off each other. Everything Richard said intrigued her and melted her heart. Every look she gave him softened his expression.

That was then.

Richard pulled the car up to the drive-through speaker and ordered his usual Tillamook cheeseburger with extra tomatoes. Carissa ordered a vanilla milkshake. After two sips she felt better. Stronger.

As Richard pulled the car back onto the main street, Carissa decided she might as well get the inevitable over with. "I was let go today."

Richard glanced at her and then back at the road. He looked at her again. "What did you just say?"

"I was let go today. Fired."

It took a moment before he seemed able to respond. "You were fired?"

"Yes."

"Why?"

As she gave him a condensed rundown, Richard pulled the car into the parking lot of a used-furniture store and turned off the engine. Facing her, with his eyebrows dipped precariously, he said, "Why didn't you tell me?"

"I'm telling you now." Carissa sipped her

shake. The chill numbed her insides. She wished she had ordered the larger size and then realized how detached she was from the reality of this moment. It felt as if she were watching a play from the front row, rather than actually being the one involved in the conversation.

Richard's response wasn't what she expected.

"This isn't right. This isn't right at all." None of his usual calm, cool, confident counselor demeanor remained. His expression clouded. His make-it-happen, fix-it list began. "Did you talk to Dr. Garrett? Did you remind him of your seniority?"

"No, I didn't talk to him."

"You need to talk to him. First thing in the morning. He can still reverse his decision. You haven't signed anything, have you?"

"No."

"You need to set up a meeting with all the doctors. Make sure Dr. Walters is there. Remind them of all you do for them. See what sort of adjustment can be made. Do they need to cut you to thirty hours a week until a new doctor is hired to take Dr. Walters's place?"

"I don't know if they are going to hire anyone else."

"Find out. See what their plans are. You need to find a way to stay on there. Carissa, we can't make it on my income alone."

"I know that."

He rubbed his forehead and stared out the windshield. She was fully aware that they couldn't live on just Richard's salary. Part of the reason was because Richard charged clients much less than the going rate. He also paid far too much for his shared office space, and he met with a number of clients at no charge "just to get them back on their feet," as he had said more than once.

Carissa knew it would be of no value to pick apart his business practices. They had talked that topic to death over the years and nothing had changed. The conclusion was always the same. He was doing what he loved. He was having a dramatic impact on many lives. This was his "ministry" as much as it was his job.

Therefore, Carissa always took the high road. She acquiesced to carrying the larger portion of the financial load.

"I guess we'll have to move," Carissa said flatly. She hadn't expected those words to pop out of her mouth. It was a fleeting thought, not one she had considered long enough to suggest with confidence.

"Move?" Clearly, it wasn't the solution Richard was considering.

"I don't see how we can stay where we are. How can we afford it? Even if they kept me on for fewer hours or if I got another job tomorrow, my salary isn't going to be what I'm receiving now.

Besides, I don't feel safe in our house. Not after last night."

"Carissa, nothing detrimental happened to you last night. You are taking one benign incident and expanding it into a global life issue. You are not in danger in our house."

"How can you say that? You still don't see the problem, do you?"

"I see the problem, all right. The problem is that you don't trust me. For some reason, you've stopped respecting me."

Carissa couldn't believe he was saying these things. "Richard, you know that I respect you. You know that I trust you."

"No, you don't. You used to stand with me and support what I do. This is what I've worked for. All the years of school, all the hours I had to log before I could get my license. You agreed this was the door God opened. Why are you shutting me out?"

"You're the one who has been shutting me out! You're more involved in your clients' lives than you are in my life. I'm the one who lost her job today, and you're sitting here telling me I should support you! I have supported you. Don't you see that?"

"You don't support my decisions. You made that clear last night."

"I was frightened. We had a prowler at our home."

"I took care of it."

"No, you didn't. Not permanently."

What followed was a volley of foul accusations that no two people who ever claimed they loved each other should speak. They kept at it for ten minutes, locked in the car's confines in the vacant parking lot of the used-furniture store.

Exhausted and having gotten nowhere in their debate, Carissa leaned against the car door with nothing more to say.

In response to her silence Richard said, "You've given up, haven't you?"

She didn't know if he meant she had given up on fighting or if she had given up on him and on their marriage. Instead of answering, she just stared at him. Who was this man beside her in the car?

"We're done." Richard turned the key in the ignition. He backed out of the parking lot and drove home way too fast. Again, Carissa didn't know the extent of the intended meaning of those words.

Are we done, Richard? Do you see our marriage coming to an end? Is that what you're trying to say?

As soon as he pulled into the garage, Richard strode into the house. Carissa sat alone in the car, trying to make sense of what was happening to them. The engine pinged. Feelings of betrayal and confusion caused her to tremble.

Drawing up the small portion of courage she had left, Carissa went inside the house and headed for their bedroom. She was prepared to make peace at any price. More than anything, she wanted to feel strong again. She wanted to work things out with Richard and find a way to pull herself together. Then they could make clear-minded decisions about what to do next.

Carissa stepped into the bedroom and saw that Richard had tossed an open suitcase on the bed. He was standing in the closet, yanking his clothes from the hangers.

4

"E maliu mai, e Iesu
I kela keia la me 'Oe
Pela no e ku'u Haku e."

"If I falter, Lord, who cares?
Who with me my burden shares?
None but thee, Dear Lord, none but thee."

CARISSA FROZE. RICHARD IGNORED her and shoved a pair of jeans into his open suitcase. *No!* The word caught in her throat and wouldn't escape in a sound.

A flashback came over her, covered her, and consumed the room around her. She was twelve years old, cowering in the hallway of her childhood home with her toddler sister in her arms. Through her parents' half-open bedroom door Carissa and Heidi had watched their father—their hero—jerk his clothes from the closet and storm out of the house while their mother shrieked and threw his shoes at him. He left without even looking back at Carissa or Heidi.

And he never returned. He never contacted his daughters again. Just like that, their father erased himself from their lives.

Carissa shook as she stepped into the walk-in closet with Richard. Her voice trembled, but she managed to form the words, "No. Richard, don't do this!"

He gave her a stern look. "Don't do what?"

"Don't leave. Not like this."

"I have to give my presentation at the ACFI conference on Saturday." Richard's words were firm and authoritative. "My flight goes out at two-thirty tomorrow, and I have two clients in the morning." He shifted his weight. "You forgot, didn't you?"

Carissa shrunk back, her heart still racing.

Richard tilted his head. "Wait a minute. What did you think I was doing?"

Carissa stammered, trying to come up with a way to hide her intense reaction. "I . . . I thought the Denver convention was next week."

"It is. That's the NWCA. This weekend it's the ACFI in Sacramento. You thought something else was happening here, didn't you? You thought I was leaving you."

She was too upset to reply.

"Why won't you be honest with me? You keep clammed up inside yourself all the time now. You don't come out and tell me what's going on. I have to try to guess or find out at Burgerville that you lost your job. You didn't use to be like this."

Carissa realized that, in all the years Richard had been her closest friend as well as her husband, she had never related to him what happened the night her father left. It had always been a memory too painful to bring up. And here she was, feeling the same emotions that had paralyzed her as a twelve-year-old, and she still couldn't speak about them with the one person who could be trusted with her soul wound.

At least he used to be the one she felt she could trust with her soul wound. Now she didn't know. Maybe Richard was right. Maybe she didn't trust him.

When she couldn't manage a reply, he said, "See? Even now you're shutting me out. If you're not willing to talk to me, then we can't resolve anything."

He stood waiting impatiently for her to explain herself. But she couldn't.

"That's what I thought." Richard brushed past and pulled open his dresser drawer so forcefully the entire drawer came out. He let out a string of foul words, and Carissa turned to flee down the hall. This wasn't like Richard at all. She didn't know what to do, what to say. In the chaos of her crashing emotions, a single thought came to her.

You should leave.

Carissa heard the thought as clearly as if she had spoken it aloud. Such a solution to her pain went against everything she believed. Throughout their marriage, Carissa and Richard had studied the Bible together, listened to sermons, attended marriage-improvement conferences, and agreed at every turn that, since they both came from divorced families, they would never go that route.

Yet here they were, physically divorcing themselves from each other for the second night in a row while still under the same roof.

Carissa shut the door to the guest room and stood with her back pressed against it. She realized that she and Richard had been divorced emotionally for quite some time. That separation would explain the dull loneliness that ached in her last night when she was alone in the hammock. It was all coming into focus now. For the past year and a half, the two of them slowly had been pulling apart from each other. In all the ways that really counted, weren't they divorced already?

If you moved out, you would only be making

official something that's already happened between the two of you.

Her logic made sense. Another empowering thought came.

You should leave him before he leaves you.

For the first time in many draining hours, Carissa felt as if some relief, some form of freedom, was within her reach. A strange sense of strength engaged her spirit and filled her with a new purpose. Self-preservation.

She curled under the covers of their son's old bed. No tears came. Only sleep. Her exhausted body barely moved until she woke the next morning. When she got up, Carissa felt oddly rested. Maybe the war had ended. No more battles needed to be fought today.

Opening the guest-room door, Carissa pattered down the hall to the bathroom. She could see that their bedroom door was open. Looking in, she saw that Richard wasn't there. The bed was made, and his suitcase was gone.

Carissa no longer had a place to put her torn-up feelings, so she didn't try to process the look and feel of the vacated bedroom. All she could think about was that she had to get to work by eight. She had to train Molly today. Then she was going to leave the job that for the past fifteen years had been the primary source of her income, her daily purpose, and for that matter, her identity. What she would do after that, she had no idea.

But she was beginning to feel as if she had options.

Just then she heard the coffee bean grinder. Richard was still there. She took her time showering and getting ready for work and then made her entrance into the kitchen. Richard was sitting at the kitchen table, eating scrambled eggs.

He kept his back to her as he spoke. "There's more in the pan, if you want some."

Things were back to normal. This was how their lives had been for more than a year and a half. They were roommates sharing the same space. None of the smoke from their fiery arguments of the past two days seemed to hang in the air. Richard had gone back to his efficient self, without even questioning why she had slept in the spare room. Maybe what he had said last night was how he truly felt. Maybe he also knew that they were "done."

Carissa pulled a plate out of the cupboard and stood by the sink, eating the rest of the scrambled eggs.

"I'll be back on Sunday. I'm leaving my car at the airport because right after I return I'm going out to Gresham. One of my clients, a separated couple, are renewing their vows."

The irony punched her in the gut. Her husband had once again saved a marriage. Not their marriage, but someone else's marriage.

This wasn't the first time Richard had participated in a vow-renewal ceremony. She had gone with him to two others and had felt so proud of her husband. At each ceremony Richard had lit up like a young boy who had just received his first bicycle. Both times he cried. Such ceremonies were the fruit of his labors, but this time she wouldn't be with him to enjoy the moment. He didn't even ask if she wanted to meet him there.

Carissa let her plate clang as she dropped it in the sink.

"Are you going to have Heidi come stay here while I'm gone?"

"No."

"Does that mean you feel safe enough to stay here alone?"

Carissa had put that part of the stressful events of the last few days out of her mind. She didn't know how to answer.

Richard came over to the sink. Looking at her he said, "It takes two people, willing to communicate, to make a marriage work."

At first she gave him no reply. Silence seemed her only ammunition. Then, as he turned to go, she shot out, "I did communicate, Richard. I told you what I was feeling Wednesday night, how frightened and vulnerable I was. You weren't even willing to validate my feelings. Instead, you tried to shame me for having a strong reaction when my private space was violated by a Peeping Tom, who has a police record for violence and for who knows what else!"

"Why are my clients such a problem for you all of a sudden? I've had unstable clients off and on for the past ten years. You knew that. Why are you going into such a tailspin?"

"Because this is the first time one of them came to our house! And when it really mattered, you chose that client and his well-being over me. That's why this is a problem. It's a huge problem, and I don't see you showing any interest in fixing it. You can fix everyone else's injured marriage, but when it comes to ours, you don't care! Can you tell me why that is, Richard?"

Instead of his face turning red, as it did when he was about to blow off steam, Richard turned a pale shade of gray. "I'll tell you why. My clients respect me."

"I would respect you, too, if you cared for me the way you care for them."

Carissa felt the uncommon strength from the night before filling her up. *You can leave him. Now. Just go.*

Following her impulse, she picked up her purse, strode to the garage without a good-bye, and backed her car out before the tears fogged her vision.

Why did I have to say all that? Why couldn't I just let it go? He doesn't see it as a problem. He's not going to change.

Wiping her eyes, Carissa was washed with the memory of when they first met at church summer camp. Under the soaring evergreens of Camp Maranatha, Carissa spotted tall, good-looking Richard Lathrop with his sensitive eyes and golden-blond hair. He noticed her, too. Before the week was over, Carissa had given her heart to both God and Richard in a package deal. Richard made the same decision.

They nurtured their budding affection with prayers and promises. They protected it with purity. They worked steadily toward the goal of their wedding day, which came on the heels of Carissa's nineteenth birthday. Marrying Richard was the fulfillment of every dream Carissa had for her young life. She knew he would never leave her the way her father had.

Now, here they were, twenty-four years after vowing to "love, honor, and cherish," and Carissa knew it was over. They both had changed. A lot. They weren't the same people they were then.

Reaching deep inside, she found some leftover courage in the rubble of the past few days. She rallied her thoughts and focused on what waited for her at work. She could do this. She was good at compartmentalizing.

On her way to work Carissa's phone beeped. She thought Richard might be texting her. At the stoplight, she checked her cell phone and saw that the beep was a reminder on her calendar. Today was her friend Ruthie's birthday. Ruthie was Dr. Chan's assistant, and she had been out yesterday on a personal day. Carissa wondered if Ruthie knew yet that Carissa was leaving the office. In the chaos of the day before, she hadn't thought to call her close friend and tell her the depressing news. Especially since Ruthie was at the spa for the day, celebrating her birthday with her cousin, who was in town.

Making a U-turn, Carissa drove to Le Petite Sweet and bought two dozen éclairs since she was the one who signed up a month ago to bring treats for Ruthie's birthday.

When Carissa arrived at work, Molly was already there, sitting at Carissa's desk inputting her preferred music into Carissa's computer.

"I'm going to be in the break room," Carissa said.

"Okay. Take your time. This is going to take me awhile."

Let it go. Don't say anything you'll regret later. All you have to do is make it through today. It's Ruthie's birthday. Be happy for her if you can't find anything else to be happy about.

Setting out the éclairs and pulling together some impromptu decorations, Carissa was glad she could do this for her friend. Over the years Ruthie had always been there for her, and now it was Carissa's turn to do this small thing.

Just as Carissa affixed to the table the last paper flower she had made from a napkin, Ruthie walked into the break room. She stopped and looked at the lovely table and at Carissa. Then her eyes misted over.

"Carissa, what are you doing?"

"I'm celebrating you. It's your birthday."

"But you're leaving."

"I know. I'm sorry I didn't call to tell you last night. Did you have fun with your cousin?"

"Yes, we had a fantastic time." Petite Ruthie stepped closer and put her arms around Carissa. "Don't leave."

Carissa rested the side of her face on top of her friend's fragrant, dark hair. In whispered words she knew her friend would understand, Carissa said, "I don't want to leave. This is really, really hard. I'm not doing well, Ruthie. I'm not doing well at all."

Ruthie pulled back and looked at Carissa with her intense green eyes, still misty. "Oh, Carissa. This is awful. I'm so sorry."

In an even lower voice, Carissa confided to her friend, "Things are horrible right now with Richard. Really awful. This is the worst possible time for me to be let go."

"Can you fight the decision?"

"I'm scheduled to talk to Dr. Garrett at nine-thirty, but from the impression I got yesterday, I don't think I'll be staying on."

"This is so awful." Ruthie gave Carissa a big, consoling squeeze just as Ginger from the reception desk entered the break room.

"Ooo, did you bring cupcakes, Carissa?" Ginger asked. "As soon as I saw that you were the one bringing birthday treats, my mouth started watering for your daisy cupcakes."

"I didn't have time to make cupcakes last night."

"She brought my favorite, éclairs," Ruthie said, quickly picking up the pace. "I'm going first, since I'm the birthday girl."

Carissa joined her, picking up one of the éclairs and raising the decadent pastry toward Ruthie. In keeping with her desire to celebrate her friend, she said, "Happy birthday, Ruthie. You are one in a million."

Ruthie smiled warmly and sympathetically at Carissa. "Thank you. I'll miss seeing you every day more than you'll ever know. But we'll still have our monthly movie nights." Ruthie dabbed a bit of pastry crumbs at the corner of her mouth. "We'll just have more to talk about now when we see each other."

Ginger looked oddly at Carissa. "Are you leaving?"

Carissa nodded. She didn't know what to add.

Ruthie came to her rescue, saying, "Dr. Walters is retiring."

"He is? How did I miss all this? You guys always have the inside scoop in the back office. We never know what's going on out front."

A few others entered, delighted to find birthday

goodies. Ginger stepped over to Carissa and gave her a hug. "I'm going to miss you, too."

"Thanks, Ginger." Carissa made a quick exit to her office and got to work with Molly. At nine-thirty she had her brief conversation with Dr. Garrett. When he made it clear that her employment at Hillside Family Physicians was over, Carissa returned quietly to her office and cleaned out her desk.

Ruthie popped her head in twice during the day to offer encouraging smiles. Others from the office came in throughout the day and offered their awkward good-byes. Through it all Carissa tried to keep strong.

At five o'clock, Carissa pulled out the key Dr. Walters had given her and headed to his office at the end of the hall. Her guess was that the key belonged to a file cabinet. Most likely he had some personal items tucked away that he feared he might forget about after Carissa was no longer there to remind him.

Extending her open palm to him, she said, "You wanted me to hold this for you. Here you go."

A wonderful grin rolled across his lips. His eyebrows rose. "Actually, I wanted you to hold on to it until I checked with Betty. She agreed with me. We want you to take that key and make good use of it."

"Okay," she answered slowly. "And what does the key go to?"

"A very important door." This statement seemed to delight him for some reason. Plunging his hands into the large pockets in the front of his lab coat, Dr. Walters dipped his chin and peered at her over the top rim of his glasses, as if he had a scrumptious secret he was just dying to tell her.

"A door?"

"Yes, a door. You know how Betty and I spend the winter months on Maui?"

"Yes."

"This key unlocks the front door of our cottage."

Carissa wasn't tracking with him. "Do you want me to make duplicates of the key for you?"

He chuckled. "No, I have enough duplicates. I want you to take that key and go open that door and stay there as long as you can. This is my farewell gift to you."

The reality sank in. "You're offering me your place on Maui? I can go stay there?"

He grinned and nodded, rocking back and forth on his heels. "Betty and I don't plan to go back over until the rain starts up here again. I'd say that gives you a stretch of about three months to decide when you want to make good use of that key. Go as soon as you can. Stay as long as you can."

Carissa stared at the key and back at Dr. Walters. "Are you sure?"

"Very sure." He reached over and curled her

fingers atop her open palm so that the key was securely in her grasp. "Take that hardworking husband of yours and go have yourselves a vacation. More than a vacation. A second honeymoon. Do you think you can get him over there with you before the summer is out?"

Carissa scrambled to compose an appropriate answer. "I . . . I don't know. Richard is in Sacramento this weekend and has another conference coming up in Denver."

Dr. Walters examined her expression briefly and then made his diagnosis. "Then you go. The sooner the better. You need to come apart before you come apart. The Lord will meet you there. Actually, he's already there waiting for you."

Carissa gave Dr. Walters a courteous smile. He was a deeply spiritual, God-fearing man. While she would say that her beliefs were in alignment with his, it had been quite some time since she had "met with the Lord" anywhere.

"I appreciate this more than I can say. Please tell Betty thank-you for me, too. This is unbelievably kind of you. Of both of you."

"Our pleasure. I'm sure you've heard me talk about my brother, Dan. He and Irene live just on the other side of the row of banana trees at the front of our cottage. If you need anything, they'll be there to help you. Betty will give them a call, once you decide when you're going. I'm sure my wife will have a few things she would like you to take over with you in your suitcase, if you don't mind. Some new towels, I think she said. Why don't you give her a call? You two can decide on a time to meet up."

Wasting no time, Carissa phoned Betty and made plans to stop by Saturday morning.

"I should warn you," Betty said over the phone. "The place is small. Only one bedroom. It has a full kitchen, a nice living room area. Some patio furniture out back. Not much of a view to speak of, but the palm trees we put in make for some good shade in the afternoons."

"Sounds like paradise to me."

"We think so."

Carissa drove straight home. She couldn't believe she had been offered a hideaway. A safe place to go where she could be on her own. None of Richard's clients would be there.

Richard wouldn't be there. She wanted to go immediately.

The sting of leaving her job was overshadowed by the rush of plans Carissa made as soon as she arrived home. She found a last-minute flight online for a fantastic end-of-summer price. The flight left Portland on Sunday and went directly to Maui. With a breath of courage, she hit enter on the keyboard. Less than a minute later the confirmation e-mail appeared in her inbox.

A small detail she had been avoiding remained. She needed to call Richard and tell him what she was doing. She had justified the trip, telling herself that Richard was usually the one jetting off to conferences. He didn't seem to feel the need to clear his travels with her ahead of time. Why did she feel she had to receive his blessing for her trip? It was a gift. A bonus compensation for the loss of her job.

Despite all her reasoning, Carissa still felt nervous when she pressed Richard's cell phone number into her phone. She hated that he had left with the two of them not speaking. While she knew she shouldn't have raged at him the way she did in the kitchen, she still felt he should have done something more to unravel their problems. The unsettledness between them felt torturous.

When Richard's voice mail picked up her call, she made a quick decision to leave a short message. "It's me. Umm, I . . . I guess I want to say I really wish things between us weren't the way they are. I know we need to talk more sometime. But I, uh . . . I have something I should tell you so if you have a chance to call me after your workshop, I'd appreciate it."

After she hung up, Carissa made sure the alarm system was set on the house and then went to work organizing and packing. She did all the laundry and took out the trash. It hardly concerned her that she was home alone. She made sure everything was locked up tight and that

Murphy was with her inside the house when she went to bed.

Saturday morning she met with Betty to pick up the towels and a list of details. Saturday afternoon she finished packing.

Saturday evening Richard called.

He sounded buoyant. "Thanks for calling last night. Sorry I couldn't call back sooner."

"That's okay. How's the conference going?" Carissa felt as if they had slipped back into their familiar cordial mode that had marked their relationship over the last eighteen months. At least that was better than arguing.

"Good. Very good, actually. I found out I received high reviews for the workshop I gave this morning. This was a practice run for the Denver conference next week. I'm feeling a lot of weight off me."

Carissa realized the pressure from the two conference presentations must have been causing him a lot more stress than she knew about during the past week. Why hadn't she factored that into the tension level on his side? Probably because he hadn't said anything about the stress he was feeling.

And he's the one telling me I should do a better job of communicating.

"What happened at work yesterday? Did you talk to Dr. Garrett? Did you convince him to keep you on staff?"

"No."

"You didn't talk to him?"

"I did talk to him. He told me his decision was final. Yesterday was my last day."

Silence followed on Richard's end of the phone. "I thought we agreed you were going to try to stay on there at least part time."

Carissa squeezed her eyes shut in frustration. "You arrived at that solution, but you don't understand. That wasn't an option offered to me. I asked Dr. Garrett if I could be considered for future part-time employment, and he flat out said no."

"Okay, don't get upset. I'm only going by what we talked about. So, what are you going to do?"

Carissa hesitated. She knew she had to tell him. All this independence was so new to her that she didn't know what to do except make an announcement.

"Well, to start with, I'm going to Maui tomorrow."

Nothing went well in their phone conversation after that. It didn't seem to matter to Richard that Carissa had been given the key to "a very important door" or that the flight was a bargain.

"If you wanted a vacation, why didn't you arrange to go with me to Denver next week?"

An acrid memory came back of one of the conventions she had attended with him a few years ago in which she had spent the first day sitting through a series of workshops on addictions and psychotic behaviors. While Richard hobnobbed with renowned specialists and got his therapist batteries recharged, she was miserable.

"Going to a conference with you in Denver wouldn't be a vacation for me, Richard."

"And going to Maui by yourself would be?"

She couldn't deny it. The answer popped out. "Yes."

Richard hung up on her. She couldn't believe it. He had never done that before.

His line about marriage taking two people willing to communicate came back to her with a sardonic twist. This time he was the one pulling away. If he wasn't willing to communicate with her, she couldn't do anything about it. That was his problem, not hers. How many times over the years had she heard him say she couldn't fix other people's problems? They have to arrive at their own realization of what they are doing wrong and be willing to work on changing.

Well, this time that was the position she was going to take with her husband. She couldn't make him change. In the morning she would fly to Maui, where she was looking forward to a real vacation with time to rest and refocus. All she could hope was that the time she and Richard spent away from each other would help both of them think through what should happen next.

Carissa was thinking she already knew what the "next" was going to be. She just didn't want to think about it. Not yet.

5

"Ha mau! He le o lani
Ke mele 'ia mai.
Ma o mai a pu'u nani, ma kela ao mai ka'i."

"Hark! 'Tis the voice of angels
Borne in a song to me.
Over the fields of glory, over the jasper sea."

A S THE FLIGHT ATTENDANTS checked to make sure the passengers were ready for the plane's descent, Carissa adjusted her seat to its upright position and gazed out the window. Below her stretched the vast Pacific Ocean, a deep turquoise blue blanket dotted with frothy white caps in a wide, irregular pattern.

"You going home?" The man beside Carissa leaned over and looked out the window. He had been friendly and helpful with her overhead luggage when they first boarded the plane, and she thought his accent was charming. Australian was her guess. For the majority of the flight, he had snoozed or watched the movie.

"No, I don't live on Maui," Carissa answered.

"I used to. Met my wife there. She's coming to meet me at the end of the week for a bit of a holiday. I'm set to put on two weddings. Both couples are old friends who happened to plan their big days close to each other. Convenient, right? Makes for a nice reason to come back."

"Are you a wedding coordinator?"

He laughed. "No, I'm a pastor. I guess I should have explained that I'm officiating at two weddings, if that's the right term."

Carissa could see why this guy had been requested to officiate. His demeanor was cheerful and kind.

"You have any friends on the island?" he asked.

"No, I'm on vacation."

"Well, you have a friend here now." He extended his hand and shook hers. "Gordon McAllistar. If you need anything during your stay, the mates at Hope Chapel will know where to find me. You just call them and say you're trying to get ahold of Gordo. They'll track me down."

"Thanks. I'm Carissa, by the way."

"Nice to meet you."

Gordon leaned closer, his sight set on something outside the window. "Aww, there she is! Hello, beautiful. Did you miss me? I missed you, Maui girl."

Carissa tried to visually drink in all the rich colors as the island came into clear view. *I'm really here.*

"Make sure you go to the top of Haleakala to see the sunrise." Gordon pointed to a magnificent volcano that rose from the center of the island wearing a halo of clouds. "Better yet, do what my wife and I did. Take a hike inside. It's not an easy hike but definitely worth the effort."

Carissa had no intention of hiking or doing anything strenuous while she was on Maui. She came to relax—to sit on the beach, swim, read, and eat fresh pineapple, among other delicious things.

As the plane curved around and came in closer to the flat center of the island, Carissa noticed fields of waving, silver green stalks.

"What crop is that?"

"Sugarcane. And that's the old sugarcane mill."

A tall smokestack issued a continuous, elongated cloud of dull white smoke from the burning of the sugarcane stalks. The runway came into view, and with a bump and a hop, the landing plane slid to a stop at the terminal gate.

Gordon helped her to pull down her suitcase from the overhead compartment and struck up a conversation with a scruffy-looking young man standing in the aisle. They were talking about a surfing spot called "Slaughter House." Carissa wondered how it got its name.

As she waited her turn to slide into the aisle, she noticed a pervasive sense of excitement yet contentment among the passengers. The group feeling was different from what she had experienced on flights to Chicago or Dallas. It was easy to believe that every passenger wanted to be here, and they all expected something wonderful to be waiting for them.

The minute Carissa exited and stepped into the open-air terminal, a rush of soft, warm air touched her face and teased her with its gentle fragrance. She knew she was in a place like no other she had ever been in. Her heart told her, *You are safe.*

Everything was exactly as Betty had described it to Carissa, the tropical feel of the airport and baggage claim, the greeters in floral print shirts and muʻumuʻus, with strings of purple orchid leis over their arms.

Carissa spotted her large suitcase coming toward her on the conveyor belt and moved into position to retrieve it. Apparently Gordon saw her movement as well because he stepped over and asked, "Would you like a hand with that?"

Carissa stepped back, giving Gordon room to grab her luggage. The poor man somehow lost his balance and tumbled onto the moving conveyor belt. Instead of releasing his grip on her suitcase, he awkwardly stood and trotted alongside it, plowing past other awaiting passengers as if his hand were permanently attached to Carissa's suitcase. He managed to ram his way nearly halfway around the turning carousel before releasing his grip and letting the bag go.

She tried hard not to laugh. He gave her a hands-up shrug from the other side of the baggage claim and called out so all the observers could hear, "I have a message for you from your luggage."

Carissa felt her face warm, as everyone was now looking at her and then back to Gordon. "She said she wanted one more turnabout on the carousel, and then she would like to go for an ice cream, if you don't mind."

Everyone laughed, including Carissa. It felt good.

When her bag came around the second time, she reached for it without any assistance. A woman standing next to her chuckled. "Are the two of you off to get ice cream now?"

Grinning, Carissa maneuvered both of her suitcases out to the curb where Betty had told her to wait. Carissa pulled out her information sheet but didn't have to wait long before a large white truck pulled up, and an equally large brown man wearing sunglasses leaned over and called to her through the open passenger's window. "Eh! You Carissa?"

"Yes." She checked her information sheet. "Are you Mano?"

"Ya, Mano, like da' shark." He laughed a high-pitched, childlike chuckle, as if he had made a joke. Carissa had no idea what he was talking about.

The man jumped out of the truck's cab while the engine was still running and came over to her, cradling a dainty floral lei in his large hands. His Hawaiian print shirt flapped open in the breeze, revealing his belly button. The image of his big paunch peeking out at her was engagingly child-like and unattractive at the same time. He had on crumpled shorts and flat, rubber flip-flops that looked as if they might fall apart at any moment.

"E komo mai o Maui." He looped the fragrant lei over her head and kissed her on the cheek. *"Aloha."*

"Oh! Thank you." His gesture and kiss caught Carissa off guard, especially because the action was surprisingly gentle coming from such a large man and because he made the greeting all in one motion. None of it seemed foreign to him, as if the action flowed out of his heart and over her head as naturally as the breeze.

"You got jus' da' two?"

"Excuse me?"

"Da' kine suitcase. Jus' da' two?"

"Yes. I have only two suitcases."

With that, he effortlessly chucked them into the back of his truck as if they were a couple of throw pillows he was tossing onto a couch.

With his sandals flip-flopping, he trotted over to his side of the truck, and Carissa figured out she was to climb up into the passenger's side. It was easier said than done, since the step up into the wide cab was a big one. She held on to the inside door handle, and once she was in, Mano took off before her seat belt was fastened.

The radio apparently was set to a local station because the song that rolled past them and out the open windows had the distinct sound of a ukulele and all the words were Hawaiian.

"You okay if we stop fo' sum grinds?"

She didn't know what he meant but said, "Okay."

Mano drove through several stoplights in a heavily trafficked area. He turned into a strip mall where he parked next to a windsurfing store.

"You comin' in?"

Carissa had no idea where they were, why they had stopped, or where she would be going if she went with him.

"No, I think I'll wait here."

He left her in the big truck with the keys in the ignition and the windows down. Carissa quickly pulled out her phone and checked the folded-up papers in her purse that had her extensive notes from her conversation with Betty. Dialing the number Betty gave her for her sister-in-law, Irene, Carissa swallowed her confusion and put the phone to her ear. A woman answered on the fourth ring.

"Hello? This is Carissa Lathrop. Is this Irene?"

"Oh yes. Wonderful! You're here. Dan, Carissa's here. No, on the phone. I'm talking to her now. I don't know. I'll ask. Where are you?"

"I don't know exactly. I'm in a white truck with a man who knew who I was, so I got in . . ."

"Yes, that's Mano, our neighbor. She's with Mano, Dan. At the airport?"

Carissa guessed that last question was for her and not Dan. "No, we left the airport and now we're at a shopping mall."

"Oh, good. They're at Da' Kitchen. Did Mano say he was getting the *kalua* pig?"

"Pig? I don't know. The only animal he mentioned was a shark."

Irene chuckled. "That's because his name, Mano, is Hawaiian for 'shark.' The pig is what he's bringing home for lunch. Yes, Dan, he's picking up lunch for us now."

Carissa was beginning to question this adventure altogether. If Mano was taking a pig home to Dan and Irene, where did they live and what sort of cottage would Carissa be staying in on the other side of the banana trees? Betty had said it wasn't much of a place, but she hadn't mentioned pigs. What if there were chickens? Carissa didn't care for chickens at all.

"So should I just wait here in the truck?" Carissa dearly hoped the pig was going to ride in the back and not up front with her.

"Yes, you wait right where you are. Mano will bring you to our house. We'll see you very soon."

"Irene, wait. Before you hang up, I was thinking. Since we're still near the airport, it might be a good idea for me to go ahead and rent a car after all."

"No, that's not a good idea. Renting a car, Dan.

She said she could rent a car. Yes, that's what I told her. Here, you tell her."

The three-way phone conversation turned to just two people when Dr. Walters's brother, Dan, got on the line with Carissa. "*E komo mai o Maui.* Welcome to Maui."

"Oh, thank you." She realized then what Mano's earlier greeting meant.

"You may not rent a car." Dan's voice carried the calm, authoritative tone she had come to know and love in Dr. Walters's voice.

Still, she had to protest. "It's not a problem for me, really. I think it might make things easier."

"No. We told Betty and Norman we would take care of you, and that's what we're going to do. You don't want to get me in *pilikia* with my sister-in-law, do you? No, you may not rent a car. You're going to borrow our car whenever you need it. That's what we decided. Therefore, you may not rent a car."

"Okay." Carissa leaned back, feeling put in her place.

"Mano is a good driver. You're not worried about his driving, are you?"

"No." It was an honest answer. Mano's driving was the least of her concerns at the moment. She was trying to figure out if she might need to rent a hotel room if this setup turned out to be a disaster.

"Well, then we shall see you by and by."

With that he hung up.

Carissa looked around. She tried to relax and get her bearings. By the comings and goings of the people in the parking lot, this was a place where locals gathered. She could hear some of them greeting each other using the same clipped sort of dialogue Mano used. Their conversations had a rhythmic cadence, the questions rising and receding like the ocean tide. The warm air flowing in through the open windows kept her from perspiring even though it had to be in the mid-eighties. She heard a low rustling sound and realized it was the tall palm trees across the way, shaking out their shaggy manes.

So this is Maui.

In her excitement and packing flurry of the past two days, Carissa had dreamed up many images of her first visit to the Hawaiian Islands. Not one of her dreamed-up visions looked like this—a parking lot at a strip mall.

With her lips pressed together, Carissa punched in Richard's cell phone number. A trickle of perspiration slid down the back of her neck.

"Carissa?"

"Hi. I just thought I'd call to let you know I arrived. Are you back from Sacramento?"

"Yes."

A pause hung between them before she asked, "How was the wedding?"

"Vow renewal. I'm on my way there now."

"I hope it goes well. I know how much you enjoy those."

"Thank you."

By his polite responses, she knew this conversation wasn't going to go anywhere. She didn't know why she had called him. Maybe because, whenever she had stepped out of her comfort zone in the past, Richard was the first person she talked to, so she could process the situation. Yet, here she was, trying to make small talk with him while sitting in a truck with a stranger named "Shark," who went to get a pig and left her to stare at a window sticker on the windshield that read "Got poi?" How could Richard relate to any of this? Their two worlds weren't going to intersect here.

"Listen," Carissa said. "I want to tell you I'm sorry things are in such a bad place for us right now, Richard."

"I'm sorry they are, too." He offered no further apology nor any words that would lead them out of the pit they were tumbling into once again.

"Do you want me to call you while I'm here? Because I'm getting the impression that I'm bugging you."

"It's up to you. You're making your own decisions now, apparently."

The next few lines back and forth weren't kind. Carissa wanted to hang up on him, but she resisted. She closed the conversation saying, "I can see this was a bad idea. I thought I should call you, but I wish I hadn't. I won't bother you again."

"If you want to take the martyr position, that's your choice. I can't change you."

Carissa picked up some steam. "No, you can't change me. And I think that's what's bothering you the most." With that she did hang up.

She didn't have time to process her feelings after their short interaction because Mano strolled toward the truck with several plastic bags in his hands. She didn't see a pig anywhere. He hopped in and handed her the bags. Something smelled delicious. Her appetite, which had eluded her for the last few days, seemed to be back in full force.

Blocking out Richard and the disconcerting conversation, she asked, "What is this? It smells wonderful."

"*Kalua* pig."

"Oh. This is the pig. Is it like pulled pork?"

"I dunno. It's *kalua* pig to me."

He drove with one arm out the window and one hand on the top of the steering wheel. He seemed so relaxed. He asked her a few questions, and she understood about 50 percent of what he said, so her replies included a lot of simple yeses and noes whenever she picked up a key word and thought she knew what he was asking.

They drove less than half an hour on mostly two-lane roads along with lots of other cars. She hadn't expected the island to be so populated or to have so much traffic. Turning onto a residential street, Mano made another right and then a left and stopped in front of a normal-looking, single-story track home in a moderate neighborhood. No chickens were in sight.

Carissa slid out, being careful with the big step down from the truck's cab since she had the bags of food in her hands. Mano retrieved her luggage, and they went to the front door. The landscaping was lush and green with exotic-looking bushes and trees. It was the most intricately landscaped home on the block.

Above the doorbell was a plaque etched in cursive letters.

"Dan and Irene,
Two of God's Children"

Before either of them could ring the doorbell or knock, the door swung open. A round-faced man, who looked to be of Asian heritage, greeted her with a wide smile. "You're here. Good. Come in. Hey, Mano, you have the food. Even better. Mo' betta', as they say here. Come in!"

The man's voice matched Dan's voice she had just heard on the phone, but Carissa was confused. How could this man be Dr. Walters's brother? Her expression must have showed her puzzlement because the man at the front door laughed.

"He didn't tell you, did he? My brother still likes to surprise people. I'm the adopted one."

Carissa tried not to look surprised. She glanced down and noticed an assortment of flip-flops and canvas shoes lined up by the front door.

"Irene!" He called out. "Where is she? Here, hand me those bags. She must be over at the cottage. I'll put the food inside, and we'll go on over. Are you going to eat with us, Mano?"

"You know it, *brah*."

The three unlikely amigos made their way along a pathway that bordered Dan and Irene's house. Once again, none of this was how she had pictured her arrival and settling in on Maui. When Betty said Carissa would be picked up by one of Dan and Irene's friends, Carissa never conjured up an image of Mano. She also expected to be dropped off at a little cottage and left alone for her secluded time of rest, reflection, and restoration.

Now these people were including her in their lunch plans. What else did they have planned for her?

As the three of them came upon the open backyard, Carissa's eyes widened. In front of her was a tropical garden paradise, private and unexpected. She noticed stalks of corn growing in straight rows and orange trees as well as an extensive raised garden with perfectly round watermelons and green zucchini growing like long noses poking out of the ground and having a sniff of the rich earth.

Interspersed around the yard and along the borders were an assortment of tropical trees and shrubs; tussled palm trees; and skinny, tall papaya trees with their clusters of barely yellow fruit hanging far too high to reach. She stopped and tried to take it all in, amazed to see exotic orchids growing right out of the side of the coconut trees in what looked like small cradles fashioned of bark. A butterfly flitted past her, as if welcoming her to the best playground on the island for all things winged and wiggly.

"This is your yard?"

Dan looked pleased. "It is. This is the place. We call it the Garden of Eatin'. Are you a gardener?"

"Yes, a little. Not like this. This is really something. It's beautiful."

"It's yours." Dan swept his arm in a gesture of grand invitation. "Anytime you want, you come and enjoy it, okay? Or, better yet, come over and help me to pull weeds."

Mano laughed. It was still surprising to hear such a giggly, high-pitched laugh come from such a large man. "You give Dano sum *kokua*, he be yo' friend fo' life."

"What's 'ko-coo-ah'?"

" 'Help.' Mano is always offering me his *kokua*. He's such a good neighbor. Sadly, I can pay him only in bananas." Dan pointed up as they continued around to the garden's back side. A small yet imposing gathering of banana trees divided the property.

Carissa noticed two clusters of unripe bananas hanging from two of the trees. The pudgy fingers of green fruit pressed themselves close together and stayed tucked safely under the lazily flopping banana leaves. She lingered a moment, awed to see real bananas growing on a tree.

"This way," Dan called. She followed him, and there, at the end of the path, was a fairy-tale cottage, Hawaiian-style.

A smile came. Despite that she hated being unsettled with Richard and that she had lost her job and didn't know what was going to happen once she returned home, Carissa felt as if, for right now, she was safe. She didn't have to struggle.

This set-aside time was a gift. Everything else in her life was in upheaval. But here, she could rest. This was a place of peace. Peace and safety.

The plantation-style bungalow was painted green with white trim on the shutters and around the door and windows. On the porch that graced the cottage's front, two high-backed rocking chairs kept time, nudged along by the comforting breeze. An enormous fern hung from the center of the porch.

"Irene, our guest is here." Dan reached for the doorknob, but the door opened before he got to it.

In front of them stood a diminutive woman in a pair of baggy pink walking shorts topped with a white gauze shirt. She wore a pair of glasses. Her short, salt-and-pepper hair was tousled every which way. Irene was leaning on a colorfully decorated cane complete with zebra print ribbons and several dramatic feathers.

"Welcome, welcome. Come in, Carissa. Are you thirsty? I put some iced tea in the fridge. The windows are all open. Would you like to look around? You must be tired. Dan, did you invite her to eat with us?"

"I did."

"And is she? Mano, you're eating with us, aren't you?"

If Irene's form of conversing was birthed from nervousness, it would have been irritating. For some reason, coming from her, it flowed with a sweetness that Carissa found endearing.

"Did you sleep on the plane? It's not such a bad flight, is it? Five hours from Portland. We've taken that flight a number of times, haven't we, Dan?"

"We have."

Irene moved to the side and let Mano enter with the suitcases. "Do you want your things put in the bedroom? Mano can put them in the corner for you. I set up the luggage rack. Are you sure you're not thirsty? You must be hungry, though. We can all go eat first. How would that be?"

Carissa was actually more interested in exploring the tidy, brightly decorated guesthouse, but she followed Dan and Irene back to their home. Mano was right behind them, as they retraced their steps. Only this time, they cut through an opening on the side of the yard with the banana trees and followed steppingstones in a diagonal pattern that took all of them to the large covered patio at the back of the house.

"We'll eat outside here, on the lanai." Irene tapped the patio table chair with her revved-up cane, while Mano slid the back screen door open and went inside as if it were his own home.

"Go ahead and sit, Carissa. We'll bring the food out," Irene said. "You're our guest. You're on vacation. I always say that, on the first day of vacation, you shouldn't lift your fingers for any unnecessary reason. Or your toes. After the first day, you can put your fingers and your toes anywhere you like. But on the first day, you should sit. Yes, just like that. Sit and breathe. That's all you have to do. Breathe."

"And eat, of course," Dan added. "Wait until you have a taste of this *kalua* pork. And the macaroni salad. You bought macaroni salad, didn't you, Mano?"

"You know it." He stepped out on the patio with the white plastic bags. As he opened them on the table, it appeared everything they needed was there, including paper plates, forks, small packets of soy sauce, and lots of napkins.

"Do you like sticky rice, Carissa?" Dan opened one of the plastic containers. "Oh, good! We have some chow fun noodles, too. Have you had that before?"

"I don't think so." She didn't know what sticky rice was either, but she was about to find out.

"Good grinds," Mano told her, taking off his sunglasses. He had the happiest eyes, round and glistening like two pieces of polished obsidian plucked from a mountain stream.

Carissa sat there like a queen as Dan dished up her plate for her. Without moving her fingers or her toes, she smiled while the friendly little luau began around her. This also wasn't what she expected to experience when she arrived on Maui.

But she had no complaints. None at all.

6

"Ho'omana'o kakou iaia la
E ha'i a'e i na lu'ulu'u
Ina 'eha na kaumaha
Lohe ia a ho'opau no."

"O what peace we often forfeit,
O what needless pain we bear,
All because we do not carry
Everything to God in prayer."

PROPPING HERSELF UP IN bed the first
morning in her island hideaway cottage,
Carissa felt like a queen. She smoothed the quilt
around her legs and took in the details of the
lovely room.

The bed was made of dark wood with four
spindle-style posts that rose to hold up a white
gauzy canopy. The tails of the sheer canopy fabric
tumbled over the spindles like waterfalls cascading to the aqua blue bedspread. Hand-stitched
pineapple appliqués were arranged systematically
across the queen-size quilt, completing the feel of
tropical luxury.

Everything about the small cottage felt right.
The bathroom that adjoined the bedroom had a
wide mirror that helped to make the space feel
open. On the towel rack hung bright-colored,

striped towels that matched the equally bright-colored, striped shower curtain.

Carissa could spot Betty's influence around the cottage in the strategic use of island colors, particularly the blues, oranges, and greens. The upholstered furniture, the floors, and the walls were all neutral colors, which made the colors pop in the tropical floral-print throw pillows, the paintings on the walls, and even in the pot holders hanging from a magnet on the refrigerator.

Waiting for her on the kitchen counter was a package of coffee. Irene made a point to tell Carissa several times that the coffee came from a plantation right on Maui. During their picnic on the patio the day before, Dan suggested Carissa go there, if she wanted to see how the coffee grew and was roasted.

They also recommended a number of other things for her to see and do during her visit. According to them, Maui had it all—beaches, waterfalls, volcanoes, snorkeling, sunset sailing, lavender fields, an aquarium, and museums. It was much more than Carissa had expected and far more than she wanted to do.

All she wanted was to be alone.

Now that she finally was alone for her first morning in this peaceful place, she took her time thinking, moving, and deciding. There was no rush. She could sleep all day, if she wanted. When was the last time she rose on a Monday morning and didn't have to go to work?

What would it be like to live in a place like this?

Beside her on the bed stand rested five books she had gathered the night before from the extensive collection on the shelves in the living room.

She got up and used the small French press in the cupboard to make an aromatic cup of coffee. Returning to her queenly bed, she was all set for some slow sipping to accompany her leisurely reading.

Then she thought about Richard. Her reading mood went on pause. Ever since she was sixteen, Richard was the one with whom she shared everything that mattered to her. If their relationship were what it used to be, she would be on the phone with him right now, and he would be eager to hear all the details of her visit so far. He would want descriptions of the people, the food, and the scenery. He would ask questions and evaluate. He loved to evaluate. But now that they were floating in this undefined place of autonomy and had closed off their thoughts and feelings toward each other, Carissa realized she would have to process all these new experiences by herself. She could do that. She was strong and capable. As much as it felt natural to want to talk to him, she knew that after their dead-end conversation yesterday, another call was pointless.

Just breathe. Isn't that what Irene told me? Just breathe.

Carissa tried breathing deeply in and out. She pushed the onslaught of the past week back, way back, far from this place of peace. Yet in the shadows she could feel the deep sorrow creeping in closer.

"I'm being too reflective. I need to get up. I have to go do something. I have to work my way into relaxing."

She had no idea why she told herself that or what she was going to do. All she knew was she refused to sit there and slip into depression.

The only persistent thought she had was that she should go pull weeds. She had no other plans or schedule for the day. If she went and did that now, at least she would feel that she had offered her *kokua* and could use the gardening time to think about what else she wanted to do that day.

Her shorts were wrinkled, but it didn't matter for garden work. Pulling up her hair in a clip, she washed her face, applied a quick rub of sunscreen to her face and bare arms, and headed out the front door.

The sensation of warmth and golden light startled Carissa as she stepped out on the front porch. The breeze from the day before was missing. Instead the air was still. The shaggy palm trees stood their post, undisturbed.

In place of the trade winds was a chorus of tropical birds. Some cooed, some tweeted, some trilled. Blended all together, their song was magnificent and unlike anything Carissa heard at home.

With flip-flops on her feet, Carissa stepped through the small break in the foliage that linked the bungalow grounds to Dan's paradise garden. The morning sunshine covered the garden with full light, and like the sun, Dan was already up and going strong. He had a well-worn straw hat on his head and an equally well-worn hoe in his hand.

"Good morning." Carissa stood back, waiting to be properly invited to enter the Garden of Eatin'.

Dan didn't seem to have heard her. He was working the earth around the base of the orange trees.

"Hello!"

Dan turned and smiled when he saw her. He waved for her to come over, and she made her way toward him, gingerly picking her way on the steppingstones.

"How was your sleep?"

"Very nice. It's such a comfortable bed."

"Quiet enough for you?"

"Yes, very quiet."

"Good." His deeply creased face glistened with perspiration. The old T-shirt he was wearing had a logo on the front of an outrigger canoe.

"I came to help," Carissa explained when he didn't add any more small talk. "What was the word? *Kokua*? I'm here to *kokua*."

Dan looked surprised. "This is your vacation. You should be out seeing the island and enjoying your free time. Yesterday I was only making a light comment about helping with pulling the weeds. I didn't mean for you to take me seriously."

Carissa shrugged. "I'd like to help. I love being outdoors, and I don't have any other plans; I thought this would be a good way to get in a morning stretch."

"Well, then, I won't turn down your offer. Do you need gloves?"

"Gloves? No. That's okay. Where should I start?"

Dan leaned on the hoe's handle and looked around. "Over there with the tomatoes would be a good place for you. Some of those straggling vines need to find their way up out of the dirt. More stakes and string are in the shed on the side of the house. All the weeds you pull can go in the compost pile over there behind the ginger."

Carissa looked around. She remembered Dan pointing out the ginger yesterday during their patio luau. She had asked about the exotic plants over in the corner of the yard, and Mano had laughed, saying none of the plants was exotic to them. Dan asked which plant, and she said, "The one that looks like giant red Qtips."

Dan kindly told her it was ginger while Mano laughed some more.

Now, getting her bearings, Carissa set to work, gently untangling the first wayward tomato vine. It seemed determined to crawl along in the dirt and tumble into the watermelon patch rather than stay the course and climb heavenward up the prepared ladder of string woven between the steady stakes.

The fragrance of fresh tomatoes was strong in the full warmth of the morning sun. Only two tomatoes were blushing red around the edges. The rest were still tight little green orbs, drawing all their strength and future from the well-supplied vine. Even in their preripened stage, though, they smelled like tomatoes. That intrigued Carissa. She sniffed her hands. They smelled like tomatoes.

For some reason the scent was comforting. At the grocery store, she always bought tomatoes that were sold in clumps still connected to the vine. She liked the fragrance. Even though the vines were shriveled and frail by the time they ended up in the grocery store, whenever she reached for a clump of ripe tomatoes, she could still smell the garden on them.

She dug her hands into the rich, moist soil at the base of the tomato plant. The earth felt different than the soil in her simple flower garden at home. This earth seemed to be deeper in color and more porous in texture. The soil was richer and darker than she was used to. She held up her palmful of earth and let it slide through her open fingers. The dirt shone with hints of volcanic red in the full sun. This was beautiful dirt. To her novice gardener's hand, it felt like mink.

Dan had stepped closer. She hadn't realized he was watching her until he spoke. *"Aloha 'aina."*

Carissa looked up at him, squinting against the brightness of the sun. "Is that Hawaiian for tomatoes?"

"No, that's Hawaiian for what you are experiencing."

"What I'm experiencing?"

"You're connecting to the land. We call it *aloha 'aina*. Love of the land. Can you feel the richness of the earth?"

Carissa stood and gave Dan a cautious nod. She emptied her hands and brushed the dirt off. While Portland was full of enthusiastic environmentalists who would love to discuss the "richness of the earth" with him, she didn't see herself as a tree-hugger.

However, she did love nature and was always the one who noticed the sunsets or the first baby bird chirps in the nests tucked into the honeysuckle vine that arched their front door.

Richard never notices small beauties in nature. I always have to point them out to him.

It bothered her that Richard had once again

106

come to the forefront of her thoughts. She was surrounded by newness, beauty, and peace, and yet she felt all the same heaviness she had felt at home. Why had her anxiety followed her here?

I don't want to spend my entire getaway time feeling like this.

Dan tapped the end of his hoe on what Carissa thought was a patch of green ground cover. "You see these weeds here with the long arms? These grow very fast. Any of them that you see starting up, pull them out. Be sure you get the root."

Glad for a refocusing of her thoughts, Carissa went back to work, pulling the fast-growing weed clumps. They actually looked pretty. She hadn't seen this sort of weed before and would have thought the trailing green arms speckled with tiny white flowers were supposed to be there. It was pretty and looked healthy.

"I see what you mean about the roots," she said to Dan as she gave one of the more stubborn clumps another tug.

"Yes, some of those would have been easier if I'd pulled them up sooner. Once those runners get entwined with the tomato vines, they take over in no time. All the fruit is lost."

"I know how it is with vines." Carissa thought about the honeysuckle at home. The extravagantly blossoming vines were a stunning focal point of their house, but they hadn't started out that way. She told Dan about how her husband had planted two unassuming bushes on opposite sides of the entryway when they first moved in.

"He was obsessed about both plants being cared for so they would grow at the same pace, but, of course, they each seemed to have a mind of their own. It took almost three years before either honeysuckle stalk grew significantly. But when they did, I'm telling you, those vines lost no time in crawling up, around, and over the entryway. It's really beautiful now the way it arches over the front of the house. You can't tell where one ends and the other begins."

Dan grinned and leaned on the hoe, lacing his fingers together. "This is how vines grow strong. Woven together. This is what makes a good marriage."

Carissa began to nod in agreement and then stopped. *Marriage? I thought we were talking about plants here. The earth and vines and . . .*

Gathering up the pile of extracted weeds and heading to the compost pile, she knew she needed to make a quick exit before Dan went any further in his marriage analogy. Or worse, started to ask questions.

Returning from the compost, Carissa said, "I need to make a trip to the grocery store. When would be a good time for me to borrow your car?"

"Anytime. We rarely use it. Irene doesn't drive, and most days I have no place to go." Dan grinned.

"Would you like me to bring you anything from the store?"

"Yes. Irene has a list ready for you."

"Oh, okay." Carissa hadn't anticipated his reply. It gave her the feeling they were expecting her to make a run to the store for them that day.

She slipped into her hideaway cottage to take a refreshing shower before dressing in a skirt and fresh top. Adding laundry soap to her mental list of grocery items, she made her way to Dan and Irene's back door, cutting through the garden. The sun had climbed higher in the sky, and the air was noticeably warmer. The trade winds definitely were missed. Even the birds had gone silent.

Carissa tapped on the side of the sliding screen door, trying to see inside. Even though Dan and Irene had insisted yesterday that she come to this door, it felt awkward. She didn't have neighbors nearby at home, and she wasn't used to this sort of community connectedness.

"Come in, Carissa. It's okay. Come on in. You don't need to knock." Irene's sweet voice sounded close even though Carissa couldn't see her through the screen.

Sliding the darkened screen door to the side, Carissa stepped into the house for the first time. The decor surprised her. All the furniture was made of a dark, highly polished wood. The floors were covered with deep green shag carpeting, and on nearly every space of available wall hung large, framed paintings. The effect was lovely and calming.

Carissa spotted Irene seated at a long dining room table that was covered with papers and open books. But Carissa's eyes immediately went back to the walls and all the paintings, displayed like a folksy art gallery.

"What beautiful pictures." She stepped closer to a rectangular painting of the ocean with an immense, imposing wave. Inside the curl, an intrepid surfer on an orange surfboard bent just right, as if he were determined to ride the screaming silver-blue monster all the way to shore. To the side an intricate palm tree leaned in at an angle of agreement with the spray of water off the top of the wave.

Irene came to stand beside her. "That one is from Sunset Beach. On Oahu. Dan went over there a few years ago to take pictures of the big waves. He liked that one surfer. Doesn't remember his name. He was from California, and he told Dan that wave was the ride of his life. Dan still talks about watching him. Are you thirsty? I have some guava juice. Fresh, of course. Have you had breakfast?"

"Yes, I had breakfast earlier." Carissa realized all she had consumed was the coffee, but she wasn't hungry. "Thanks for the coffee. It was delicious. You said Dan took the photo of this wave. Who painted it for you?"

"Dan."

"He painted this?"

Irene gave a general sweeping gesture with her hand of the open dining, kitchen, and living room space. "He's been painting for so long, I'm afraid we've run out of wall space. If you find one you like, be sure to tell him. Make sure you truly love it because he'll want to send it home with you."

"I'm so impressed. I've never met a painter before."

Carissa moved over to a display of three smaller paintings hung one above the other. All of them were close-up paintings of tropical flowers against a black background.

"These are beautiful."

"You're an artist, aren't you?"

"Me? No. Not at all."

"But you have such a poetic spirit."

Carissa turned and looked at Irene, surprised at her comment.

"Well, wouldn't you agree? You have a genuine appreciation for everything you've observed since you've been here. Yesterday, when you asked about the heliconia growing along the side of the cottage, you said the flowers looked like origami birds on a tall stick. I would say those are words that spring from an artist's heart."

Carissa felt deeply touched. No one had ever likened her to an artist before. She didn't know what to do with the affirming words, so she quickly changed the subject. "Dan said you had a grocery list?"

"I do. It's right here along with some money in this envelope." She gave Carissa directions, handed her a stack of neatly folded, reusable cloth grocery bags, and told her where the keys to the car were hung by the back door.

Carissa was just about to be on her way when Irene said, "Did Dan tell you that he's leaving?"

"No." She turned to give Irene her full attention.

"He's going to the mainland on Wednesday to settle some business with a piece of property we used to own there. Our son, Kai, was planning to take him to the airport for his afternoon flight, but we might need to call upon you for the favor, if Kai can't get here in time. He's on the Big Island at the moment and might not be back by then."

"Sure, I'd be happy to take Dan to the airport."

"Good. I'll let him know. Mano is working that morning. Otherwise we would ask him, of course."

"Of course."

Carissa backed the red compact Saturn out of the garage and easily found the grocery store. As she strolled down the aisles, trying to find the items on Irene's list, she noted the prices were shocking, as Betty had warned her. But everything else about the store felt familiar.

Since Carissa didn't have a list, she took to filling her cart with anything that caught her eye. Anything she wouldn't normally buy or prepare at home sounded good, for some reason. The vacation foods in her cart included fettuccini, corn dogs, and fresh coconut cream pie.

About halfway down the soft drink aisle, her empty stomach protested, and she broke into a bag of peanut butter cookies she had added to her cart. The cookies were on Irene's list, but Carissa had picked up two bags since they sounded good. She knew it was a bad idea to shop for groceries when she hadn't had anything to eat. She also knew that addressing the hunger with three peanut butter cookies was an equally bad idea.

But she didn't care. This was her vacation. She figured she should do whatever made her feel like she was relaxing and getting what she needed out of this time. If that meant going for a fourth peanut butter cookie, then so be it.

Instead of loading the grocery bags into the car's trunk, where she was concerned the milk might get too warm on its way home, Carissa lined up the bags on the backseat like a group of toddlers off on a field trip.

In a way, she was taking them on a field trip. She wanted to drive around a little before going back to the house so she could see how far away the beach was and what other interesting spots were within walking distance.

She had to drive only a few blocks from the grocery store before the vast Pacific Ocean spread out before her. A road just below her paralleled the ocean and several impressive stretches of long, pale gold, sandy beaches. On the other side of the road, though, for miles, all that appeared were closely built apartments and condos. Interspersed between the old-style vacation rentals were several flat-roofed strip malls loaded with shops that catered to tourists.

And this area definitely had tourists. The vacationers were in the cars all around her, inching their way to the next stoplight. Tourists were on foot, clogging the pedestrian walkways. They were at the beach, stretched out in beach chairs, bobbing in the low-curling waves, and sitting under the palm trees in the public park areas.

None of the mayhem appealed to her, but the water looked inviting.

Carissa turned the car around and headed back to Dan and Irene's home. She formulated a plan. She was used to her life having a lot of structure; no wonder she had felt flustered this morning. She didn't know how to float around in oblivion. Having a schedule would help her to feel secure. That was important right now.

Her plan was to deposit Irene's groceries with her and Carissa's purchases in the refrigerator in her bungalow. Then she would make a big bowl of pasta with shrimp sautéed in butter. She would sit out on the back patio of the cottage and read until she dozed off. Then she would go inside and watch one of the many DVDs on the shelf next to the flat-screen TV. If she wasn't too tired, she might watch two movies. And she would eat another something wonderful from her shopping trip. Such a plan sounded sweetly decadent and just what she needed to relax. But there was more to her plan.

In the morning she would put on her bathing suit, walk down to the beach, and have the ocean to herself before the swarm of tourists showed up with their boogie boards and umbrellas. Then she would walk back, make some of the delicious Maui coffee, and decide if she wanted to spend another day reading, or if she wanted to drive into Wailea to visit the shopping center.

Carissa breathed in and breathed out. She loved having a plan. And an open bag of Nutter Butters within reach.

7

"He hemolele 'Oe! Iehova ke Akua!
Mele makou mai ke a lau la a pau kala."

"Holy, holy, holy! Lord God Almighty!
Early in the morning our song shall rise to thee."

CARISSA'S CLEVER PLAN PLAYED itself out nicely. At least in the beginning. She returned to the hideaway cottage, read, rested, ate heartily, watched two DVDs, and went to bed with a slice of coconut cream pie filling her up just above the top of her comfort level.

At 2:15 A.M. the coconut cream pie came back up, bringing a good portion of the sautéed shrimp and fettuccine with it.

For several hours Carissa twisted around in the queenly bed feeling miserable. She wanted to blame the pie for her aching gut. Or the shrimp. Maybe the shrimp were tainted when she bought them. Or that corn dog she popped in the microwave around nine-thirty before she started the second DVD. Perhaps that was the culprit.

No, her instincts told her that her body wasn't able to handle so much rich and heavy food on the heels of so much emotional stress. She knew food had never been an effective medication for her in times of anguish. Why she thought it would comfort her this time she had no idea.

The digestion aid she found in the sparsely stocked bathroom medicine cabinet seemed to be doing its work, but she couldn't sleep. Putting in another DVD, Carissa turned the television screen so she could watch it in bed and finally fell asleep to the sight of Mr. Darcy coming across a golden meadow at sunrise.

All plans for her own sunrise march to the beach were scrapped along with plans to read her way through at least one of the five novels she had selected. Carissa's second day in paradise was spent in bed and in shock.

Her life wasn't supposed to be like this. She couldn't stop thinking about her Mr. Darcy, who was just as valiant and infuriating as the one Jane Austen imagined. Yet, unlike in Ms. Austen's novel, Carissa's Mr. Darcy wouldn't come trouncing across a meadow or the ocean to be with her. He wouldn't even walk across the hallway of their own home last week when he had the chance.

The depth of Carissa's anguish frightened her. If there had been any liquor in the kitchen cupboards, she was pretty sure she would have given it a try. If she had found any painkillers in the bathroom cupboard, she wouldn't have hesitated to take enough of them to transport her out of her private torture.

As it was, all she had to take the edge off her fearful foreboding about the future were romantic comedy DVDs and coconut cream pie. She already knew how things turned out for Tom and Meg in all three of the unwatched DVDs on the shelf. She also already knew the disappointing abilities of the coconut cream pie to produce mood-elevating results.

Aside from more sleep, the only option Carissa could think of for comfort was the Bible she had seen on the shelf in the living room. She chose sleep.

By early evening, after much internal turmoil, Carissa was convinced that the next season of her life would be marked by change. Resolved, she decided her only route for survival was to bolster herself and be prepared for whatever was to come next. She wanted to be prepared for a new job, a new place to live, and possibly a completely different life, a single life.

If she and Richard continued on their current destructive course, she could very well be a divorced woman before her next birthday.

The onslaught of such an ominous future exhausted her, and so she sank back under the covers to dwell alone in her private cave. Some time long after the day was spent and the sun had set, Carissa got up.

She made herself a cup of tea, wrapped a throw blanket around her sagging shoulders, and padded out to the private, small back patio behind the cottage. From just above the roofline, a glow caught her eye. A streetlight?

No. She moved to the side and saw it was the moon. More accurately, it was a little more than half a moon.

"Cut in half," she whispered. "Just like me."

For a long while she stood, cradling the cup of tea with both hands and gazing at the moon. It felt to her as if she were having a stare-out with the One who could have prevented so much hurt in the world, including hers, if he wanted to. But there he was, looking on with only one eye, and even that eye was half open.

She knew her analogy was a stretch. But somehow it helped her to believe the reason things were going the way they were was because God had curtailed his care for her ever since she had withdrawn her trust in him.

Funny, that's what Richard said was the problem with our marriage, that I don't trust him. Well, maybe I don't. And maybe I don't trust God like I used to, either.

Carissa blinked at the unflinching moon. An ache of deep longing made her groan quietly in the night.

When did I become this person? I used to love God. I used to feel something wonderful when I heard his name. How did I get like this?

She sat on the padded lounge chair, her legs crossed, her back to the house, the roofline, and the peering moon. With slow sips, she felt the tea soothing her raw insides. The breeze was with her, shuffling the dried fronds on the palm trees, whispering in low utterings through the banana leaves.

Carissa lowered the teacup to her lap and lifted her chin to the stars. Adding her own whisper to the dark night sounds, she said, "Okay, come and get me. If you still want me, you know where to find me."

The intent of her challenge was that her whisper would find its way across the sea to the ears of her petulant husband. If he was so convinced that she had turned her back on him by going to Maui, then fine. But if he still wanted her and was willing to make the effort to pursue reconciliation, then her words would find their way to him on the trade winds, and he could make the first move. She wasn't going to call him again.

Downing the last sip of tea, Carissa pulled herself up from the lounge chair and caught sight of the lazy-eyed moon once again. She stared at it some more. The golden light against the velvet sky was unchanging.

If I were a poet, I'd try to write about you, O mysterious moon.

Carissa wondered if Irene was right about Carissa having an artist's spirit. It would explain her joy in spending lunch breaks at Powell's in search of books of unheralded poetry. More likely it was the influence of all of the romantic DVDs she had stuffed herself with during her waking hours that day. She had swallowed so much beauty, hope, and sweetness, it was bound to overload her system and find its way back out.

Somewhat calmed and strangely resolved, Carissa went inside and thought again about trying to write a poem. It would be a therapeutic way to express the intense feelings she had been processing all day. She only thought about it, though. She didn't search for paper or pen.

Instead, she decided to put her plan back into effect. Day two, take two. When the sun got up, so would she. It was time to introduce herself to the ocean and to the long sandy beach. This was Maui, after all. She was on vacation. In the morning she would start to act like it.

Leaving the bedroom windows open, Carissa anticipated that the morning song of the birds would be her alarm clock.

And they were.

Rolling out of bed, she still didn't feel well. Her head hurt.

Too bad. You're not staying in bed all day. Come on.

With renewed determination, she pulled on her bathing suit and shorts, slipped a T-shirt over her head, and reached for one of the plush beach towels she had brought in her suitcase. Her flip-flops were waiting at the front door where she had left them. Out into the freshness of the new day she went.

The shortest route to the sidewalk that led to the beach was through the garden. Carissa trekked past the banana trees and headed for the opening that would take her through Dan and Irene's backyard. But some movement made her stop and pull back.

There, in a long nightgown, was Irene. She stood barefoot in the dewy green grass. Her face was turned toward the east. Her eyes were closed. Both her arms were raised in a gesture of worship.

Carissa hung back, staying concealed behind the wide trunk of the banana tree. After Dan's comment the day before about "loving the land," she wondered if that was what Irene was expressing. Why else would someone rise at dawn and stand barefoot in the grass with her arms lifted to the heavens?

Then Irene's voice rose in harmony with the enthusiastic birds. *"Ke Akua Hemolele, ua piha ka honua i kou nani a ke ho'omaika'i nei ia 'oe."* Irene repeated the same words a second time.

Carissa watched, too intrigued to step away. The early morning light shed a soft glow on Irene's face, revealing an expression of loveliness, peace, and deep delight. She chanted the opening words one more time. And then again, the words rolling off her tongue like a softly sung lullaby. *"Ke Akua Hemolele. Ke Akua Hemolele."*

Carissa felt her soul stir at the sight and at the words. What did they mean? What was this little woman doing, standing there in her nightie, calling forth the new day?

Irene opened her eyes. She lowered her arms. Still smiling, she reached for her cane, which was propped up against a supporting pillar of the patio. Apparently unaware of Carissa's presence behind the banana tree, Irene hobbled back into the house, leaving the birds alone to finish the morning song.

For a few more minutes Carissa didn't move. If she cut through the garden, would Irene see her from the house? And if Irene saw her, would she wonder if Carissa had been watching her in her private actions there in the garden?

A disturbing thought settled on Carissa. *I'm a Peeping Tom!*

Not on purpose. And not in a way that was intended to compromise Irene's privacy. Yet, the facts couldn't be argued. She technically was standing on Dan and Irene's private property, watching Irene.

Putting her feet into motion and going the long way around the house, Carissa picked up her pace as she walked down the hill toward the ocean. If she admitted that she was out of line watching Irene in her private space, then she should correspondingly be merciful, yet cautious, with those who struggle at a much more dangerous level with the same defect.

No, that didn't settle with her at all.

In the past, Carissa would agree to such reasoning and find herself humbled by the reality of her failures. That humility gave her a sense of empathy for Richard's clients, who struggled with overwhelming, life-debilitating failures.

This morning, though, Carissa didn't want to be wrong. She didn't want to think about Richard or his clients or any of her own faults, even if they were innocent slipups. She wanted to be free. She wanted to be happy. She wanted to separate herself from everything she had left at home.

With determination, Carissa lifted her chin and strode down to the beach. She had to wait at the crossing signal to traverse the main, two-lane road she had explored on Monday. Even though it was early in the day, a number of cars and trucks waited as she crossed with the light along with a tanned young man wearing only a pair of ragged shorts. He was riding a rusted beach cruiser-style bicycle and balanced a yellow surfboard under his left arm.

"Hey, howzit? Nice day." He gave her a friendly nod.

Carissa was caught off guard by his tattered but sincere manners and didn't respond. A few more steps over a sandy rise, past a wooden lifeguard stand, and she was on the beach. As far as she could see in both directions, the pale yellow sand stretched out like freshly washed linens laid out to dry. Lapping gently at the shore's edges were drowsy waves dressed in the soft blue shades of the early light.

Beside her, a palm tree bent low like an aged wise one leaning toward the sea with an ear turned to listen to the mesmerizing ebb and flow of the endless tide. The palm cast a long, elegant shadow across the vacant beach.

This was the sort of tropical beach she had always hoped to visit. And here she was. Picture perfect paradise. Yes, this was the Maui she had imagined. This was the image she wanted to keep with her always.

To the right Carissa could see several more palm trees, all of them slanted at a right angle, stretching toward the shore. An older couple strolled along in the wet sand, holding hands. In the shallows, Carissa counted five paddle surfers. All of them stood on their boards with impressive balance and used their long-handled paddles to stroke their way into alignment with the gently unfurling waves. One of them caught the crest of a rising wave just right and lifted his paddle as he rode the wave toward the shore.

I think I'll do this every morning. I'll walk down here and go swimming. It's perfect.

Peeling down to her bathing suit, Carissa wedged her bare feet into the cool sand. The air was warm. Not hot. Warm and pleasant. She looked behind her at the great volcano that had filled her window on the plane. The morning sun seemed to rise up out of the volcano, as if invisible arms were lifting the blazing orb and setting it in place in the serene blue sky.

Striding into the water, Carissa stepped forward boldly until she was in up to her waist. Then she lowered herself, stretched out her arms, and made strong strokes toward the open sea. She could feel the determined rays of the sun on her back as she paddled about.

The rounded upper west side of the island of Maui looked as if it were far enough away to be a neighboring island; yet, at the same time, it blended so well with the blues and greens of the ocean, it all appeared to be a photo and not real at all.

Carissa remembered something her son, Blake, had said once when he was little. They were driving over a long bridge that spanned the wide Columbia River and linked Oregon to Washington. From the bridge, Mount Hood could be viewed clearly in the east. Set against the commanding blue autumn sky, the snowcapped peak had captured a tinge of the pinks and oranges of the sunset going on at the other end of the Columbia River. In either direction they looked, the view was magnificent.

"It's so pretty it looks like a picture," Blake had said. When he realized his declaration didn't sound quite right, he added, "I mean, it's so real it looks fake."

Richard and Carissa had laughed at their sincere son, and both of them said they knew exactly what he meant. Carissa felt that way now as she took in the 360-degree view. It was so real it looked fake.

Thoughts of Blake made her sad. She missed her son. She missed the way life had been for the three of them when they were all in sync. Blake's high school years had been the best season for them as a family. He was like his father, logical and systematic. He had no spurts of rebellion or teenage angst. He had gone through a bit of a phase in his preadolescent days, but by the time he was fourteen, he was a content young adult who enjoyed spending time with his parents and taking his mountain bike up the trails that edged Mount St. Helens.

She let the sadness bob along next to her in the rhythmic waves and thought, *That season of life went too fast. Why didn't I appreciate it more? Why didn't I love my son more while he was under our roof?*

Carissa continued treading water. Each color and detail around her seemed vibrant in the early light. She consoled herself with affirming thoughts about how Blake had told her she was a good mother and Richard was a good father. Together they had raised a strong, well-adjusted son. What would Blake say if he knew where his parents' relationship was headed? If they separated or eventually divorced, how would it affect him?

He would understand. Blake can handle this. It wouldn't affect him.

She knew better. Over the years, she had watched friends' lives be torn apart by divorce, and she knew everyone was affected to some extent. Yet, what could she do if Richard continued to push her away?

Determined not to dwell on such thoughts, she chose to enjoy the morning's beauty. She swam as if she meant it. With each kick and paddle, she imagined she was pushing herself away from her life at home and urging her thoughts and her spirit to move forward, to embrace the present.

It didn't take long before she needed to go back to the beach to catch her breath. Stretching out on the new towel, she could see why Betty was adamant about Carissa bringing these towels over here. The plush fabric, combined with the warm sun on her back, lured Carissa fully into the present. She felt strong and ready to focus only on what was in front of her.

Glancing around, she was surprised at the number of beachgoers who had arrived since she first had claimed her spot. Colorful umbrellas were planted in the sand, as couples and families claimed their territory for the day. Beach chairs were being unfolded to the right and to the left. A crying toddler protested the sensation of the unstable sand beneath her bare feet and raised her arms to her daddy, who scooped her up and then promptly handed the wailing wee one over to her mother.

Fifty yards from her a tall man with noticeably white legs carried a large ice chest by the two side handles. Behind him trailed a teenager with enough boogie boards and inflatable beach toys to start his own small beachfront rental shack. He was followed by a tall woman and three thin girls, all toting beach bags and lawn chairs, with beach towels draped over their shoulders. They plopped down their gear less than ten feet from where Carissa sat.

Time for me to go.

The uphill walk to the cottage proved to be a bigger challenge than she had estimated on the way downhill. When she arrived back at the cottage, she made coffee and then took it out to the back patio along with a bowl of cereal. Breakfast had never tasted so good.

The patio seemed like a different place each time she went there. Nothing of her mysterious whispering from the night before lingered in the light of day. The sun was now at just the right angle and felt wonderful on her salt-dotted legs. Closing her eyes, Carissa leaned back and sank into her morning sunbath.

Just as she was drifting off, she heard her name. Sitting up and catching the bit of drool that had begun to slide out of the corner of her mouth, she looked around. Dan was in the side yard, coming toward her.

"Am I interrupting?" he asked.

"No. I went for an early-morning swim."

"Good for you. Nice morning for a swim. Say, we didn't see you to tell you yesterday, but Irene wanted me to let you know I won't need a ride to the airport this afternoon. Kai returned last night, so he'll take me."

"Oh, okay. Good. Well, let me know if you or Irene need anything. I hope you have a good trip."

"*Mahalo*. Thank you." He turned to go and then clapped his hands and turned back. "Nearly forgot the most important part. We have fresh fish. *O'paka paka*. Kai brought it back from the Big Island, and we're having it for lunch. Are you interested in joining us?"

"No, that's okay. Thanks for thinking of me, though."

Dan didn't leave. He gave her a look, as if to say she was crazy to pass up fresh fish. "Are you sure? We have more than we can eat. And I picked tomatoes and zucchini this morning. Irene was hoping—"

"Okay." Carissa stopped him before he resorted to using his poor wife to influence her decision. Besides, none of the options in her refrigerator fell into the "fresh" or "healthy" category. With her stomach just returning to normal, it did seem like a good idea to go organic for lunch. "What time should I come over?"

"Eleven. We want to eat early, before my flight. Sound good?"

"Sure."

"Okay, then. See you by and by."

The lunch invitation was sounding more like a

brunch invitation. That was fine. She would use the afternoon to drive around and do some shopping since Dan had a ride to the airport.

At a few minutes after eleven, Carissa traipsed through the Garden of Eatin' and called to Irene at the screen door. Mouthwatering garlic fragrances wafted from the kitchen.

Instead of Irene responding to her greeting, a male voice called out, "Come on in. You don't have to knock."

Slipping out of her sandals, as she had come to learn was the accepted custom before entering the house, Carissa entered. Her bare feet were only a few steps inside when she saw the man who had invited her to enter. He was medium height and athletically built, and his head was shaved. Turning toward her with a spatula in his hand, he smiled broadly, showing off straight, white teeth and a good-looking, tan face. His eyes were striking and gave away the family resemblance to Dan and Irene.

"Kite?" she asked.

He looked at her funny. "Kite?"

"Oh, I'm sorry. I thought you were Dan and Irene's son, Kite."

He laughed, and the room suddenly felt brighter.

"Kai," he said. "My name is Kai. Take the 't' and the 'e' off of 'kite' and there you have it. It's Hawaiian for 'ocean.'"

She felt her face warming. "I'm so sorry. I misunderstood."

"That's okay. I'm guessing you're Carissa."

"Yes."

"Are you hungry?"

The true answer would have been "no," but she still felt caught off balance. "Yes, very. It smells good. Is there anything I can do to help?"

Irene entered with some fabric place mats in her hand. "Did you meet our son?"

"Yes, I did." Carissa offered another courteous smile at Kai and once again felt her face flush. At first she thought he must be in his thirties, but as she watched him, it seemed he was closer to her age. He was just in much better shape than most people in their forties.

Why am I feeling this way every time I look at this man? He's so good-looking. I had no idea their son would be a forty-something athlete. I wonder if he's married?

Then Carissa caught herself. All her fizzy thoughts went flat. *What are you doing? Why would you think such a thing? You're a married woman!*

She stood there, curling and uncurling her bare toes in the plush green carpet. A trailing afterthought sneaked in before her staunch resolve could catch it. *At least for now you're married . . .*

8

"A pi'i mai na nalu
Na 'ino ku'e
'A'ole lakou la e popo'I mai
Mai ku a maka'ua ha'alulu 'oukou
'O wau me 'oukou la."

"My grace, all sufficient, shall be thy supply;
The flame shall not hurt thee; I only design
Thy dross to consume, and thy gold to refine."

THE FISH WAS DELICIOUS. The conversation around the patio table was engaging. Dan's tomatoes and zucchini were undeniably fresh. And Carissa was a fumble of emotions and actions.

She dropped her fork under the table and then tripped on the track of the sliding screen door when she went inside to get a clean utensil. When Kai asked if she would like more iced tea, she answered, "Pwease."

If the others noticed her odd slip, they didn't let on.

She felt the same way she had in seventh grade, when she tried to hide her two-week-long crush on her science teacher. Fortunately, that crush wore off without anyone but her best friend catching wind of it. By then Carissa was over the puppy-love feelings and skated through seventh grade without her silly emotions causing any lasting damage.

She could only hope that would be the same conclusion this time around.

After they finished eating, Carissa asked if she might borrow the car again. Now she felt like a high-schooler, seeking permission to leave the house for the afternoon before she had done her chores. To ensure that those feelings had no basis, she started to clear the table and stack the dishes in the sink.

"I'll do those." Irene shooed Carissa away from the sink.

Kai, who had disappeared into the back of the house a few moments earlier, now emerged with his dad's suitcase in one hand and a piece of paper in the other. "I have the list, Mom. After I drop off Dad, I'll stop to pick up everything. Call me if you think of anything else."

Dan came from the back of the house just then, wearing a light sport jacket and a baseball cap. He gave Carissa a friendly wave good-bye and then headed out the front door with Irene scurrying along with her cane to see him off.

There. See? He's gone. What you felt was silly and childish and wrong. Kai didn't look at you twice. Get a grip on your thoughts and your emotions, Carissa! You're bouncing all over the place.

She was going to take off, but then she thought she should wait until the three of them had a chance to load up and say their good-byes out front. To give them that space, she went to work loading the dishwasher. She had just placed the last bowl onto the bottom rack when Irene returned with a somber expression on her face.

"Everything okay?" As soon as she said it, Carissa realized she shouldn't be probing. As gracious as Dan and Irene had been to her, she didn't have the right to insert herself into their family life. Especially when she was trying to drown all inappropriate first impressions of their son.

Irene looked at her wistfully. "I'm going to miss him, and he's going to miss out on the camping trip. It won't be the same without him."

Irene seated herself at the large dining room table that was still covered with reference books and an assortment of papers weighted down by a collection of flat rocks to keep from fluttering in the overhead fan's breeze. She glanced over her shoulder at Carissa. "Did I tell you about the camping trip? I can't remember."

"No, I don't think you mentioned it." Carissa's memory rippled back to past conversations but nothing about camping seemed to have been mentioned.

"We're leaving in the morning and will be gone until Sunday." With a twinkle in her eyes she added, "Although we could be back sooner, if my back doesn't agree with the sleeping arrangements in the tent. I've asked Kai to agree to chauffeur me home whenever I'm ready to return."

Now Carissa was impressed. Not only was this woman going camping, but also she was sleeping in a tent. The part of the information that appealed to Carissa most was that, for the next few days, she would have the cottage and the garden to herself. Kai would be gone, too, which was another distraction she didn't have to worry about. She could set her own schedule without surprise invitations to impromptu brunches.

"We're going to one of my favorite places on the island." Irene unfolded one of the maps in front of her on the table. "Would you like to see? Kipahulu. It's right here. Not far from Hana."

Carissa stepped over to the table and peered at the map. Irene picked up one of the pens on the table and circled the spot.

"Where are we now?" Carissa asked.

Irene drew a line and made another circle around an area labeled Kihei. It didn't look as if they were very far from the camping area, but then the whole island, which was shaped like a bottom-heavy figure eight, didn't appear to be very large.

Irene moved some of the papers around on the table and looked up at Carissa through her round-rimmed glasses. "Do you enjoy history, Carissa?"

Carissa gave her a sorta'-yes, sorta'-no gesture.

"I'm a bit of a nut about Hawaiian history." Irene blushed. "Dan calls it my excusable obsession. He says it's excusable because I've been invited to give a lecture next week on my research."

"What are you researching?" Carissa had a sinking feeling that she might be stepping into a trap.

"Ka'ahumanu."

Carissa had no idea if the word Irene just uttered referred to an animal, vegetable, or mineral. She kept standing as a ready escape plan so she wouldn't get swept up in boring details about whatever it was.

"Ka'ahumanu was the favorite wife of Kamehameha the Great, the powerful ruler who united all the islands in the 1790s. He had at least eighteen wives. The historians can't agree on the exact number. But she was his favorite."

Carissa grinned. She didn't mean to smile. It just struck her as funny that this darling little woman was surrounded by mounds of documents, and her important historical efforts started with a controversy of soap-opera proportions: How many wives did some ancient Hawaiian have, and which one was his favorite?

"She was quite a woman, six feet tall, tattoos on her leg, palm, and tongue. It's estimated that she weighed more than three hundred pounds."

Now Carissa did laugh. "Wow. She does sound like quite a woman."

Irene leaned forward, ready to defend her superhero. "Her hair was dark and wavy, and her eyes were compared to doves' eyes. Her skin was light, and her cheeks were as pink as the bud of a banana stem. She had a soft and tender voice."

Irene's passion for the subject was evident. In spite of Carissa's earlier hesitation, she was intrigued. She leaned against the side of one of the dining table chairs. She wasn't willing to sit down and get stuck there, but she did want to be comfortable and hear more.

"When Ka'ahumanu was only about nine or ten years old—again, the historians can't seem to agree—she was taken into Kamehameha's royal entourage. He was twenty years her senior; so she had to be kept entertained and cared for until she was old enough to be given to him as one of his wives. That's when she mastered surfing on the long boards off the Kohala Coast. On the Big Island."

Irene pointed to a picture in one of the open books. It was a sketch of Hawaiian men and women balancing on long surfboards wearing very little clothing.

Carissa didn't quite know what to say.

That didn't hinder Irene from continuing her story. "Ka'ahumanu loved to make kites out of *tapa* cloth. Her kites were fifteen feet by six feet and had to be tied to the coconut trees when the trade winds picked up. George Vancouver, the explorer, wrote about her when he sailed into these waters in 1778. She was fifteen when he met her, and he said she was 'an unexpectedly delightful and romantic young woman and one of the finest we had yet seen on any of the islands.' Mind you, he had been to most of the South Sea Islands on his explorations with Captain James Cook; so to say she was the finest was saying a lot."

"How did you become so interested in her?"

Irene tilted her head and looked off to the side as if trying to remember. "I think it was the story of the carriage that first captured my interest. It's hard to remember now. I know so much about her. Yes, I think it was the carriage."

"The carriage," Carissa repeated. Now she knew she couldn't leave until she heard the story.

A silly smile played on Irene's lips. "In the early 1800s, Ka'ahumanu had become the most powerful woman in the islands. So, to get into her good graces, a visiting sea captain gave her an extravagant gift. A carriage. Complete with seats upholstered in velvet.

"The problem was that, although horses had been introduced to the islands, no horses were broken that could be harnessed to such a carriage. So Ka'ahumanu harnessed ten of the strongest *kanakas*, that is, Hawaiian men, and they pulled the carriage. She made her second husband take a seat in the plush interior while she sat up front, holding the reins. The harnessed men pulled her through the most populated area of Honolulu so everyone could see her."

The image of the six-foot-tall surfer girl on the long boards had conjured up quite a picture for Carissa. But this mental image of a barely clothed, three-hundred-pound woman driving a carriage pulled by ten men was even harder to forget.

"Imagine what the Westerners thought when they saw her," Irene said. "They knew what a carriage was for and who should be sitting where. But for all the Hawaiians observing her actions, they knew who held the reins of the nation. And she certainly did, for many years. I believe Ka'ahumanu changed the course of the Hawaiian nation in many ways. Many profound ways."

Irene sighed and stroked the wrinkles folded into her quietly clasped hands. Her voice softened as she added, "And yet, near the end of her life Ka'ahumanu said, 'I had it in my heart to do something more.'"

Irene's eyes dropped gently. "I think that's why I love her so dearly. You see, I have the same feeling. I, too, have it in my heart to do something more for the Hawaiian people."

"Are you of Hawaiian ancestry?"

"Yes. Only a small percentage, and I have to go

back three generations to find it. I'm not connected to any of the *ali'i*."

"The *ah-lee-ee*?"

"Hawaiian royalty. My ancestors were commoners, but the records aren't reliable. I'm a mix of Japanese, German, Portuguese, and Filipino. That's how it is for many people in Hawaii. Somewhere in me there is an ounce of Hawaiian blood, and it is that ounce that calls to me to do something more."

Carissa wondered if the ceremony she had observed that morning when Irene was in the grass with her arms raised was part of her acting upon the ounce of Hawaiian blood or if perhaps she was going through the motions of some other tradition. It seemed that the words she had spoken were Hawaiian, but Carissa had no way to be sure. She didn't want to come out and ask Irene since Carissa didn't want to confess she had been observing Irene while in hiding.

"You said you were giving a talk next week. Where will that be?"

"On Oahu. At the Kamehameha Schools."

"I'm sure it will be fascinating."

Irene chuckled. "You're too kind, Carissa. I will be talking to junior high and high school students, and I don't know how fascinating they will think it is. I don't mind telling you, I'm already nervous. It's one thing to sit here and tell you these stories, but nearly all the students at the school are of Hawaiian ancestry. I don't feel quite adequate to the task."

"Maybe this is the 'something more' you want to do. You get to teach the students some interesting history. Their history."

"Yes. That's what Dan said, as well. He also said he would come be my support. But then this trip came up, and he'll still be on the mainland when I go to Oahu Monday." Irene looked at her watch. "You've certainly been patient. I didn't intend to take up your afternoon."

"That's okay. I liked hearing your stories." Carissa righted her posture, as she prepared to leave. "Thank you for sharing with me."

"That's what Hawaiians love to do. We call it 'talk story.' If you like listening to our stories, you should come with us to Kipahulu tomorrow and camp with us for a few days. I won't be the only one in the gathering with stories to tell."

"Thanks, but I'm really not much of a camper. Especially tent camping. I went tent camping only once. The outing was for our son when he was in the church youth group. It rained two of the three days, and we had a skunk and several raccoons that decided to join us."

Irene grimaced.

"Yes. Exactly. So you can see why that was my first and last tent camping adventure. I love nature, but I love a comfortable bed at night even more."

"So do I. That's why Dan and I invested in expensive air mattresses. And fancy fold-up chairs. I love camping at Kipahulu but only with my equipment."

"What is it that you love so much about Kipa . . ."

"Kipahulu."

"Is it a beach?"

"Oh no. The coast there is rugged from the lava flow. You have to go to Hana to find a sandy beach. But the waterfalls and the natural pools to swim in are glorious. One of my favorite chapels built by the Protestant missionaries almost two hundred years ago is there, and . . ." Irene straightened her shoulders, leading to her highlight. ". . . Ka'ahumanu was born in a cave not far from where we camp. Her birth occurred a few years before the outside world 'discovered' these islands. She died on a mound of scented pillows made of silk from China, holding a leather-bound New Testament in her hands—the first Hawaiian translation. Her life was a bridge, with one hand holding the ancient ways and the other hand grasping Christianity and the ways of the Western world."

Irene smiled warmly at Carissa. "But that, of course, is another story."

Carissa was genuine when she replied that she hoped she would get to hear the whole story sometime. For now, she was ready to head outdoors and not end up spending another day inside. Not when the weather was so perfect.

Her self-guided tour driving around the Kihei and Wailea areas included a stop at an upscale shopping center. The lovely fountains and rustling palm trees inside the open-air plaza invited Carissa to relax and just breathe in time with their unhurried rhythm. She strolled slowly past clothing stores and jewelers and took her time wandering around a gallery that sold original island art. This was the most soothing sort of shopping she could remember experiencing.

Smiling to herself, Carissa realized why that was. Her usual shopping pal was Heidi, and shopping with Heidi was never slow or contemplative. What Heidi enjoyed the most about shopping was providing a running commentary on everything she saw and making enthusiastic suggestions on what Carissa should buy or wear or at least try on. When Heidi was little it was impossible to keep her from touching everything her eyes fell on. Now that the two sisters were grown, Carissa still found herself wanting to take Heidi's hand inside shops that had lots of breakables on display. But that big-sister gesture had been rebuffed decades ago.

For the first time, Carissa wondered if her introverted and sometimes suspicious inner dialogue came from spending so many years of her life being the watchful companion of her irrepressible sister. Carissa was different when she went to lunch with Ruthie or shopped with other friends. Those times were more of an ebb and flow with an even exchange of ideas and comments.

I need more friends like that. Friends who bring out the best in me instead of making me apprehensive. I've become too closed off, and it's making me cynical. I don't want to be that way.

Carissa stopped in front of a gift shop and caught her reflection in the store window. *Is that how Richard sees me? Have I been closed off and cynical with him?*

As much as she hated to see the truth reflected in her expression in the store window, she knew that was the reality. It was right there, staring her in the face, and yet for so long she hadn't seen that tendency in herself. Over the past few years her life had narrowed to small, convenient circles, and her attitudes toward others had become narrow and controlling as well. Especially with Richard.

She let the epiphany settle on her the way the steady sun was quietly settling on her, warming her shoulders and back. She could make changes. She had to. Life was making changes on her. Why couldn't she start making some of her own?

To keep from dwelling too long on what those changes might be, Carissa entered the gift shop and looked at a display of books about local interests. She thought of Irene's extensive collection and wondered if there might be a book here that Irene didn't yet own. Flipping through the assortment on all aspects of the Hawaiian language, history, arts, quilting, and recipes, Carissa found a book on Captain Cook. Certain that he was the same historical figure Irene had just been telling her about, Carissa took the book to the register and bought it along with a box of chocolate-covered macadamia nuts.

It wasn't much of a thank-you gift for Dan and Irene to express her appreciation for their kindness to her, but it was a start. Giving was the way Carissa always felt as if she best connected with others. She wasn't effusive with words like Heidi. She wasn't a careful listener like Richard. But she liked to give.

Her shopping stretch was followed by a leisurely drive farther down the southwest coast of Maui and a visit to a big, beautiful beach where the sand felt like grains of raw sugar on her bare feet. She walked a long way down the shore, holding her sandals and just breathing. This felt right and good. This was what she wanted to experience.

Carissa sat in the sand for a while, watching kids play in the surf. She wondered if residents ever grew tired of the distinct beauty. Did they get island fever? What sort of job would enable her to move there? She realized that last thought was a big jump, but this was a place meant for dreaming.

Burrowing her bare feet in the warm sand, she wondered if Richard would like this beach. If he were here, would he want to rise early and go swimming with her?

Now, Kai . . . I'm sure he does get up every morning and go swimming in the ocean. Shaking that thought from her imagination and pulling her feet from their burrow, Carissa headed back to the parking lot. She watched a couple as they stowed their beach gear in their car's trunk and then paused to exchange a long, enthusiastic kiss. The two were still kissing as she walked past them, giving no indication that they even noticed her.

With a sigh, Carissa slipped into her car and slowly exited the crowded parking area. *I'm too young to be so old. Heidi thinks I'm menopausal and having a midlife breakdown. I feel like I haven't even lived yet. My life has been far too predictable. No, not predictable. Boring. I haven't done anything interesting or significant.*

She thought about what Irene had said concerning the Hawaiian woman having it in her heart to do something more. Carissa wanted to do something more, too. She just didn't know what that something was.

Trying a different route back to Kihei along a wide, well-paved upper highway, Carissa soon recognized the area and remembered her way back to the grocery store. She stopped in to buy a few more groceries and lingered in the makeup section. Into her cart went a handful of tubes of lip gloss and a new eyeliner. Then she pulled from the peg a pair of frivolous and flirty false eyelashes.

A few years ago Blake had brought some friends home from college for Thanksgiving. One of the girls—one that Blake had a strong interest in—wore false eyelashes. The lashes weren't obvious at first because she was so stunning that it appeared that they could be her own. But after the group left, Carissa found the packaging for the lashes while cleaning the bathroom. Ever since then she wondered what it would feel like to wear them.

Why not?

Carissa tossed the package of eyelashes in the cart and took a leisurely detour down the candy aisle. She felt like a teen trying to decide how to spend her allowance. If Richard were here, she knew that he would analyze her behavior. He would say that since her identity and purpose had shifted when she lost her job, her subconscious was trying on an assortment of alter egos from various seasons in life to find a place to reestablish her identity.

Carissa looked up, as if Richard were standing beside her, and scowled. She even looked up at just the right height for where his face would be. Aside from knowing she was role-playing by looking up at her invisible husband, Carissa detested the way the analysis had come to her so precisely. She was familiar enough with Richard's counseling that she knew how to analyze her own behavior and subliminal thoughts. *This is ridiculous!*

Plowing down the aisle to the checkout stand, Carissa put her items on the conveyor belt and read the headlines of the magazines lined up in the eye-level rack. Three of them in a row featured the bikini-clad body of a celebrity who had lost thirty-seven pounds on a dark chocolate diet. Supposedly, she ate two bars of dark chocolate per day, and the weight just melted off. *More ridiculousness!*

Carissa looked away. As a last-minute thought, she reached for a candy bar—then another—and tossed them on the conveyor belt as a final purchase.

Both bars were labeled dark chocolate.

9

"Mai hopo 'oe i na 'o nou, ke kia'i nei ke Akua
Malalo o Kona mau 'eheu Nana e ho'omalu mai
Na ke Akua mau 'oe e kia'i i na wa apau
Nana e ho'omalu mai Nana e kia'i ia 'oe."

"God will take care of you, be not afraid;
He is your safeguard through sunshine and shade;
Tenderly watching and keeping His own,
He will not leave you to wander alone."

ON HER DRIVE BACK to the cottage from the grocery store, Carissa started in on the first chocolate bar and had a strong urge to call Richard. She wanted to tell him she had analyzed herself in the grocery store. He would like to hear how his voice in the back of her head had explained why she was so shaken up last week. Her identity was being readjusted.

But then she remembered that when their slow-simmering conflict had come to a boil on the night of the prowler, she still had a job. Their disconnect was deeper than her job loss or his potentially anxious feelings about speaking at the Sacramento conference. They had been growing apart for months.

Returning to her moonglow-induced decision to let Richard be the one to seek her out, Carissa felt her gut tightening once again. She put the candy bar aside and said aloud, "Why is it so difficult for you to just call me, apologize for abandoning me, and say you want to make things right between us?"

Carissa suddenly had to stop the car and pull over. The nearest place was into the open parking lot of a large church. She was rattled because she realized her intense words weren't directed at Richard. They were an old, old wish. One she had repeated a thousand times since she was twelve years old. Those words originally were lined up in that exact order as an urgent thought directed to her absent father.

Letting out a slow breath, she conceded she was more messed up than she had thought. Maybe she did need therapy. Had she transferred all her disappointment from her father onto her husband? Had she been doing that their whole marriage? Had she kept Richard continually on trial for a crime of abandonment that he had never committed? At least he hadn't committed it until now. Was all this a slowly evolving, self-fulfilling prophecy?

If she weren't sitting in an idling car in a church parking lot right now, Carissa would turn off the engine and have a good cry over the mess that was her life. But the last place she wanted to be found crying was in a church parking lot. The odds were pretty good that someone caring, qualified, and in tune with God would just happen to come across her and offer her words of hope and spiritual insight.

And what would be so horrible about that? What's your big grievance with the church? Or is it against God? When did you stop turning to him and trusting him as your heavenly Father?

The answer paraded past as blatantly as the lined-up gossip magazines at the grocery store. *Heavenly Father. Father. Our Father.*

That title, "Father," was associated with the human who had abandoned her. Richard had told her years ago that this was a big piece of her soul wound. He told her she had held on to a false belief that all fathers showed up to get things started, but then they left. At the time, she didn't know what to do with that. But now she could see what that wounding had done to her. She assumed God had abandoned her as well. With no explanation, no connection to anything she had done or not done, her heavenly Father had started a relationship with her, but then he just had left.

Or was she the one who had left?

This was hard.

The answer was obvious, but she didn't want to speak it. She also didn't want to face those thoughts anymore. She didn't want to have to analyze herself or her problems one more minute.

Putting the car back in drive, she made a big circle in the parking lot and accelerated past the sign with the name of the church: Hope Chapel.

She drove another four blocks before she realized why the church's name was familiar. The guy on the plane had said he had friends there. If she needed anything, she could go to Hope Chapel and his "mates" would know where to find him.

Jutting out her chin and flipping on the car's turn signal, Carissa told herself she didn't need anything. She was here to relax. Not seek counseling—spiritual or otherwise. The insights that had come to her in the shopping center, on the beach, and now in the car weren't part of her agenda for this getaway time.

A few blocks later she reasoned that, once she returned home, she would seek out a therapist and give counseling another try. She could put all her insights on the table and let a professional tell her she was a mess. She didn't want to process those thoughts on her own anymore.

Turning down Irene and Dan's street, she resolved to shift back into holiday mode. She pulled into their driveway and saw that the garage door was up. Kai was inside the garage, lifting an ice chest from off the built-in shelves along the side.

"Should I park the car here in the driveway?" she called out.

Kai came over to hear what she said. His expressive eyes met hers.

"Should I park here?" she asked in a lowered voice.

"Sure. You can leave the keys in it." He went back to wrestling with the camping gear to get it ready for the trip the next day.

Carissa got out but hesitated a moment before stepping a few feet inside the garage. "Do you need any help?"

"No, I'm almost done. Thanks."

She went back to the car, retrieved her bag of groceries, and sauntered toward the cottage.

"Carissa?" Kai's voice echoed in the empty garage.

She scooted back around and entered his space a second time.

"Have you been to the other side of the island before?"

"No."

"Then why don't you come with us?" Kai asked.

"Do you mean go camping?"

"Yes, camping. You should come."

"Oh, I don't think so. Thanks anyway."

"You sure? You could see the real Hawaii. It's a good group of people who are coming. My parents have been friends with some of them for most of my life."

Carissa tried to picture this gathering of elderly folks, all pumping up their air mattresses and circling the campfire in reclining lawn chairs.

"I'm better off staying here, I think."

Kai shrugged, as if he were trying to be helpful and friendly, but she was giving him the brush-off.

"Thanks for inviting me, though."

"If you change your mind, you can always take my parents' car and come. We'll have plenty of food. We always do."

"Okay."

Now Carissa didn't know how to close off the conversation. He made her nervous, and she didn't want him to catch any hint of that. In an effort to appear carefree, Carissa gave her plastic grocery bag a swing and said, "Well, thanks anyway for the invitation."

"Sure."

"I hope you guys have a good time."

"Thanks."

On the second swing of the plastic bag, the small package of false eyelashes sprung from the partially opened top and flew across the garage, landing on top of the ice chest.

Kai picked up the package, took a look, and held it out to Carissa.

She couldn't form a response, so she took the silly things from him and made a quick exit.

The eyelashes made it as far as the cottage, where they were introduced to the bottom of the trash bin and there they stayed. Carissa spent the rest of the day exploring the nearby corners of the island and playing the role of the energetic tourist. Activity seemed her only hope for enjoying her time there and not getting pulled back down into the muck of her depressing thoughts.

While at the shopping mall in Wailea, she picked up some free tour brochures that came with loads of coupons, maps, and descriptions of all the interesting things to see. Later that day she went to a place described in the brochure as the best taco bar on Maui. After two tacos, she was ready to write her own review to counter-balance the one in the brochure. It was another downer of a day in paradise.

Carissa forced herself out of bed Thursday morning to make her trek down to the beach, where she swam for a short while in the calm water. Two paddle boarders bobbed on the water farther out. They stood on their surfboards and used long, flat paddles to move out to where the slow, curling waves began their dash to the shore. One of them managed to catch a wave for several yards before it hurried on ahead of him and tagged the sand first.

The refreshing swim felt good, but the morning seemed void of any of the celebratory feelings she had felt on her last morning swim there. Maybe she was too tired today to respond to the beauty.

She was out of breath by the time she had

hiked back up the hill and arrived in front of Dan and Irene's home. Kai's small SUV was parked in the driveway, and Irene was perched in the passenger's seat.

"I was hoping we would see you before we left," Irene said. "I put the key to the house inside the mail basket on your front porch. You know where we keep the key to the car, and you're welcome to use it as much as you like."

"Thank you. I really appreciate it. Is there anything you would like me to do while you're gone?"

"If you wouldn't mind, there's a corner of the garden that the sprinklers don't quite hit. If you could give that a good watering once or twice while we're gone, I know Dan would appreciate it. And be sure to help yourself to anything you would like in the garden. Some of the smaller watermelons are ready now."

While Irene was asking this favor of Carissa, Kai was in the driver's seat with the engine idling. She could feel his gaze on her.

He leaned over. "Sure you won't change your mind?"

"I don't think so. Hope you guys have a great time."

She stepped to the side, as he backed out of the driveway. Then, sticking his muscular arm out the window as they were driving away, he gave Carissa a wave of his hand with his little finger and thumb both sticking out. She didn't know what that particular gesture meant, but it was nice to have a little friendly attention from him. She hoped he had forgotten about the flying eyelashes. She was certainly trying to.

He hasn't exactly expressed an interest in me, but then I'm sure he knows I'm married. He must not be married. Divorced perhaps? I noticed he doesn't wear a ring.

Carissa made herself stop speculating. She had plans for the day, and the best way to occupy her thoughts was always to get on track with a list of tasks. First on her list, after shower and breakfast, was a trip to the town of Lahaina, where the whalers used to pull into port for winter.

She walked around the old, western-style town and toured the art galleries on Front Street. The tour brochure recommended a visit to the whaling museum in Ka'anapali, so she drove farther up the road and strolled around the shopping center where the museum was located. She stopped to watch an outdoor performance of a troop of little girls doing the hula in rustling grass skirts and long, dark hair that swished with the skirts every time the small girls turned.

Carissa had a coupon to ride the sugarcane train and a map to drive up to the coffee plantation. But after a short stroll down the beautiful beachfront walkway that connected all of Ka'anapali Beach, Carissa finally admitted defeat.

Her plan to keep herself so busy that she wouldn't feel anything was failing horribly.

Pulling out her cell phone, she strode back to the Whaler's Village shopping center and found a bench in the shade. She was going to call Richard. This had gone on too long. She didn't know what she was going to say, but the time had come.

He didn't answer.

She didn't leave a message. He was probably in the middle of a counseling session. Or he could be on his way to Denver for the conference where he was speaking this weekend. Carissa wondered what he had decided to do with Murphy when he went to Denver. He would be away too long to leave Murphy at home alone in the backyard. Most likely Richard would pay the boy who lived at the far end of their street to come down every day to feed Murphy and give the old dog some attention.

Then Carissa wondered what Richard was going to think when he saw that she had called but not left a message. Brushing away the thought, she pulled the brochure from her purse and flipped through the coupons in the back. Her eye caught on one for a free ice-cream cone at Whaler's Village. Perfect. She found the ice-cream shop listed on the coupon and walked in, feeling frugal and in the mood for something tropical. She selected a flavor called "Makena Mango" and asked for it in a waffle cone, as the picture showed on the coupon.

The end result was huge! More than she thought she could eat. She handed the coupon over and said, "Thanks."

"Wait," the guy behind the register said. "You didn't pay yet."

"I thought it was free with the coupon."

"No, you got the wrong one."

"The wrong one?"

"See, on the back of the coupon it says you can get a free *keiki* cone."

"What's a kay-key cone?"

"Kid's size. Like this." He held up a two-inch-high sugar cone that looked as if it would hold a scoop about the size of a golf ball.

Carissa looked at her monster-sized cone and back at the one the guy was holding up. The *keiki* was the one she originally had wanted. How was she supposed to know what a *keiki*-size was? Clever the way they put the picture of the waffle cone on the front of the coupon.

"I suppose I have to pay for this one, then."

He nodded.

"How much is it?" She could feel the "Makena Mango" drip out of the waffle cone's bottom.

He pointed at the sign above his head, and Carissa's jaw dropped. This one ice-cream cone was going to cost her the same price she would have paid at home for three cartons of gourmet ice cream.

At least it tasted good. That is, the ice cream she

managed to eat before it melted when she went outside. Tossing the remainder of the cone into the trash, Carissa went looking for a restroom so she could wash her sticky hands. Nothing seemed to be quite the way she had hoped it would be when she decided to try to turn her visit on Maui into a real vacation.

"I might as well go . . ." she muttered to herself. She hadn't finished the sentence, but the mystery followed her into the restroom. *Might as well go . . . where? Back to the cottage? Home to Portland? Or to the other side of the island where Kai and Irene are camping?*

The final option intrigued her the most. But that was crazy.

Carissa looked at her reflection in the washroom mirror and decided that what was crazy was the way she had been talking to herself, analyzing her life, or avoiding thinking about anything. In general, not acting normal but instead feeling desperately lonely. Being alone wasn't a good course of action for her right now.

If she were going to experience anything enjoyable from this trip before returning home to what she was sure would be a long, painful stretch in her life, then she might as well be adventuresome and go camping.

Driving back to Kihei took twice as long as it had taken to get to Lahaina because of all the cars on the two-lane road. At least the drive along the ocean was pretty. She spent the time listening to the Hawaiian music on the radio station set in Irene's car and feeling the lovely breeze through the open windows. Those two ingredients seemed to work as an elixir strong enough to dull her senses and make her feel as if things weren't quite so bad after all.

Once she was back at the cottage, she used the key to the house to look at the map on the dining room table where Irene had marked Kipahulu. Finding the same spot on the map in her island guide brochure, Carissa read what the brochure had to say about the waterfalls, hiking trails to the bamboo forest, and the pristine beauty of the Hana area.

She was convinced this was a good idea. What wasn't a good idea was leaving now, at four-thirty in the afternoon. It would be better to leave in the morning.

Carissa organized her clothes, trying to figure out what she should take and whether a few days' worth of items would fit in her carry-on bag. She was checking on her damp bathing suit hanging in the bathroom when her cell phone rang. It was Heidi.

"I know, I know, I said I'd wait until you called me, but you never called. I was worried. It's been a week, Carissa. Are you okay? What's going on?"

"Well . . ."

own course. Finding her way not only to the campground but also in life. She could do this. She could make herself strong.

As the road continued to climb, the views of the valley below were breathtaking. Stunning shades of rich red island dirt blended with a variety of greens right up to the shoreline's edge. There, etched in white from the foam of the waves, was the dividing line where the island stopped and the immense blue ocean began.

Carissa pulled over and took several pictures. She drew in a deep breath and enjoyed the briskness of the fresh air at this higher altitude. Even though she had been climbing for some time, the view to the top of the volcano seemed just as far-reaching into the heavens as it had from sea level. The guide brochure had given all the specifics of this twelve-thousand-foot dormant volcano known by the Hawaiians as Haleakala, or House of the Sun. Carissa tried to capture some of the grandeur of the colossal mount with a string of photos, but she had a feeling she didn't have just the right angle to convey its magnificence.

Steering the car back onto the quiet road, she remembered reading about a tour company that offered bike rides down the main road that led to the top of the crater. It sounded interesting. She would have to ask Kai if he had ever done that. He looked like the sort of man who liked to ride bikes.

She would also have to ask him about the half-day sailboat tours listed in the brochure. Several of them sounded good, but one of them promised to take visitors to a site where it was guaranteed they would see thousands of tropical fish while snorkeling. She guessed it was expensive, but she loved the idea of floating in the warm ocean and looking through an underwater mask at all the amazing fish.

She knew that was the one thing Richard would want to do for sure, if he were here.

"But Richard is not here." She stated the truth firmly, as if reprimanding a child in the backseat who was asking for something he couldn't have. "I'm going to ask Kai. That's all, just ask his advice."

Her mind might have engaged more in the now-familiar tug-of-war that had plagued her for the past week, but she realized she was coming up to some buildings. It was the first development she had seen for miles. All that had lined the road were stretches of rocky meadowland dotted with a few cows. She hadn't seen a single stand for fresh pineapple or shaved ice, like the photos showed. Those, she decided, were all along the other road. The long, winding Hana Highway.

Carissa slowed the car and pulled into a gravel parking area at the base of a lovely Victorian-era home with soaring trees providing opulent shade over a grassy picnic area. The signs indicated this was the Tedeschi Winery. Carissa remembered reading about how it was known for its pineapple wine and that the family that built the estate did so at great expense in the mid-1800s.

She also recalled that elk burgers were served in the general store across the road from the estate. The elk were raised on the ranch, and according to the reviewer, the burgers were "a unique Maui experience not many other than the locals are privileged to experience."

Despite her less-than-favorable experience with "the best taco bar on Maui," she was curious about the elk burgers and decided to go check out the deli. Carissa sauntered across the road and stepped onto the western frontier–style front porch of the general store. The porch came complete with benches and with painted, wood-carved figures in the shape of rugged ranch hands settled in relaxed poses with their cowboy hats dipped low and their wooden thumbs tucked into the tops of their wide belt buckles.

The interior of the store made Carissa feel as if she had entered a movie set for something out of the Old West. The rough wooden shelves artfully displayed a bounty of one-of-a-kind souvenirs, such as bandanas with silhouettes of hula girls and colorful children's books with paintings of whales and dolphins. Carissa took time to check out the assortment of island jams and syrups as well as barbecue and teriyaki sauces.

A round table in the center carried a bountiful array of tropical-scented lotions and candles. Their welcoming fragrance attracted Carissa's attention, and she helped herself to a sample squirt from one of the tester bottles labeled *pikake*. She rubbed her hands together and took a sniff. She smelled like a flower. A tropical flower.

Picking up the smallest bottle, she decided this would be her first souvenir. The wood floors creaked as she made her way to the back of the quaint building. She joined two men dressed in soiled jeans and long-sleeved work shirts, who were talking to an older woman behind the deli counter. Their conversation carried the same clipped and lyrical rhythm she had heard from Mano when they stopped to get the "pig."

The men stepped aside, checking her out. Carissa smiled at the woman behind the counter. "Do you have elk burgers?"

The woman smiled back warmly. Carissa felt as if she had entered a private club and knew the secret password. She congratulated herself for being brave and daring and coming to this off-the-beaten-path place. Also, she was ordering something she had never eaten before. Now all Carissa hoped was that the burger was better fare than the tacos had been.

She paid for the lotion and the food, including something called POG that she pulled from the refrigerated beverage case. It was what both the guys in front of her were drinking; so she reached for a carton as if this were part of her initiation into this up-country club. The small print listed the ingredients as passion fruit, orange juice, and guava juice; the initials formed the word POG. It sounded good.

And it was. So was the elk burger. The meat was tender, lean, flavorful, and satisfying. Carissa enjoyed her luau-for-one while sitting under an enormous tree on the front grounds of the grand manor across the road. A sign at the tree's base labeled it as a camphor tree. A few curious and daring birds hopped over close to her and begged for crumbs, which she gladly shared.

This is wonderful. So peaceful. I feel like a little girl being pampered.

A distinct thought hopped over to her as courageously as the birds. *That's because you're my daughter. I long to give you gifts like this, gifts of peace.*

Carissa didn't move. She knew where that tender impression came from. It rested on her with such subtle affirmation she knew it had to be God. In the seasons of her life when she deeply trusted him, this was one of the ways she sensed his presence, with calm yet piercing affirmations that went deep inside.

Her first reaction was to spring to her feet and run. She had been found when all she wanted was to be alone. But where would she go?

She looked around. No other humans were in sight. She was alone under the tree with just God.

Carissa didn't get it. Why was he being nice to her? She had closed him out. She had left God somewhere back in another season of her life. Why was he still here? She thought he had abandoned her long ago.

Then Carissa knew. She knew the truth. She could see it clearly. She was the one who had packed her bags and left, not God. She was the abandoner, not the abandonee.

A deep scowl crossed her face. The birds flitted away.

No.

Tiny breaths passed in and out through her nostrils. She pushed it all away. The peace, the possibility, the truth.

No.

Rising and tromping back to the car, Carissa turned her thoughts to the plan for the day. Waterfalls, camping, stories by the fire with Irene and Kai. That's what she had on the agenda. Not divine revelations from God.

Somehow repeating her agenda took her back to the fuzzy, hopeful place she had been earlier on her drive, when she was turning her attention to the possibilities that were ahead in her life.

Continuing on down the smooth road, Carissa fell back in sync with the energy that came from anticipation. She was looking forward to showing up at the campsite. She wondered what Irene, and particularly Kai, would say, or what sort of expression he would have on his face.

It's a beautiful thing to be wanted.

Those thoughts propelled her on into what waited ahead for her. That was the reality she chose to live in at the moment. Right or wrong, she was determined to move forward and not get stuck on trying to resolve the past or make sense of the present.

The road narrowed, and several small potholes appeared, causing her to focus on the road. Just then her cell phone rang. She pushed the speaker button and returned both hands to the wheel.

"Hello?"

"Carissa." It was Richard. She didn't know why his custom tone hadn't rung. If it had, she might not have picked up his call just then.

"Hi." Her voice quavered.

"I'm having problems with my cell phone. I saw that you called, but if you left a message, I couldn't pick it up."

"I didn't leave a message."

Silence.

"Well, I'm at the hotel in Denver. If you need that number, I can give it to you now."

"I can't write it down right now, Richard. I'm driving."

"Are you able to pull over?"

"No, the road is really narrow, and there's no

shoulder." She hit a small pothole. "It's not possible for me to pull over."

"Where are you?"

"On Maui!"

"I know you're on Maui, but where are you going on such a bad road?"

"I'm going to a campground."

The minute she let that detail out of her mouth she regretted it.

"Did you say campground?"

"Yes."

"You're going camping," Richard repeated.

"Yes." She knew nothing she said now would sound right or make sense.

He seemed at a loss as to how to reply.

"Can we talk later?" Carissa felt her throat tightening. "I don't know if I'll have very good phone reception where I'm going for the next few days. Your voice seems to be cutting out."

"Well, I'll be here in Denver until Sunday morning. Do you want me to call you then?"

"If you want. But I'll be home a few days after that." She almost added, "So we can bring out the hatchets then, and I'm sure you'll want to hack to pieces the flailing bits of our relationship that are left." But she didn't add any commentary on the future of their relationship.

"Carissa?"

"Yes?"

He lowered his voice. "Are you sure you're okay?"

The voice coming through her phone was the man she had married. This was Richard as his truest self. All the counselor was gone. All the impatient, irritated, hardened tones of the past year and a half were absent. This was just her best friend asking her how she was doing.

A shiver went up her neck, but she forced herself not to take it in. He couldn't call her like this and try to coax her back into a place of trusting him simply because he sounded concerned about her well-being. No. She was not okay, and she did not want to report her current condition to him, no matter how right it felt to let down her defenses.

"Carissa, are you still there?"

"I'm here." She clenched her jaw and told herself to hang up on him. She could always blame it later on poor phone service. But she couldn't bring herself to move her hand from the steering wheel.

In a low and uneven voice, Richard tenderly said, "Listen, I have to tell you. I . . . I'm sorry."

She knew he was speaking from his heart.

"I've thought a lot since you left, and you were right. I should have demonstrated more care and concern for you the night my client came to the house. I've thought about that and about a lot of other things that have been going on between us for quite some time now. I want to apologize. I haven't done a very good job of loving you or caring for you. I'm sorry."

Carissa slowed the car to a crawl and stared out the windshield, as a view of the ocean came into sight. She had nothing to say. She had no place to put his words. Never in her wildest dreams did she expect this. It had been years since Dr. Richard Lathrop had apologized for anything. Her tightened spirit kept saying, *No. No! You can't do this. You can't get off this easy. No. I don't want to have this conversation now. We can talk when I get back. After I've had time to order my thoughts. Not now. Not like this.*

"I really can't talk about this right now." She forced herself to find those few words.

"Is someone with you?"

"No. I just . . . I'm trying to drive on this narrow road and . . ."

"Ca . . . ssa?"

"Richard? I think my phone is losing service. We'll have to talk later."

"O . . . we'll . . . later . . ."

Their call cut off. She looked at her phone just to make sure she was the one who had lost reception and that he hadn't hung up on her.

Why did he have to call me? Why right now?

A car covered in dust passed her, uncomfortably close. She saw a small turnout and knew she could go back to where the phone had reception. She could find a place farther back up the road where she could park the car, and they could talk at length. But she was on her set course now and didn't want to turn around. Besides, she wasn't ready to talk more and couldn't imagine what she would say.

Around the next curve, the paved road turned into an uneven gravel road. The immediate change in the driving conditions caused Carissa to brace herself, as the car jostled from side to side on the precariously narrow road. Apparently this was the beginning of the remote side of the island and the reason the tour brochures insisted visitors take the paved Hana Highway.

Carissa's heart picked up its pace. She had no idea what she was getting herself into. The bumpy dirt road around the underside of the island continued for mile after weary mile. She had no space in her thoughts to process the call she had just had with Richard. All her concentration was on what she was going through at the moment.

Carissa felt bruises on her leg where the car jostled her against the door. She had to roll up her windows and turn off the air-vent fan because of all the dust flowing in from this arid portion of the island. The terrain had changed from the lush hillside of the winery and the huge trees to no vegetation and nothing but rocks and dirt.

The jostling wasn't nearly as frightening as the narrow road's trajectory along the rim of a steep cliff that plummeted to the ocean far below. No guardrails were in place. Only loose rocks. In some parts of the road, nothing separated her car from the edge. One bounce too far to the right, and she would be hurled down a three-hundred-foot decline before crashing headlong into the water that she could see stretch out to the horizon.

Carissa checked the speedometer. She was going less than ten miles per hour. How many more miles did the terrible road continue? She felt very much alone.

At one of the narrow curves, she heard a car horn sound. Oddly, the sound gave her a sense of cheer. She wasn't the only traveler on this road. If something did go wrong, she wouldn't be undiscovered for days.

However, a moment later, the oncoming car appeared around the blind curve and screeched to a halt only inches from the front bumper. Carissa slammed on her brakes and could tell that a ball of dust and rocks was spinning out from under the tires.

Terrified, Carissa stared at the driver in the other car. He appeared to be a local. His arm was hanging out the open window; his dark hair was a wind-whipped mess of curls. He looked reasonably carefree as he backed up his car. He kept going until he had disappeared around the blind curve like a sand crab, tucking itself back in its hole.

"What am I supposed to do?" Carissa said under her breath. Had he backed up into a turnout she couldn't see? Was she supposed to go forward and pass him? For miles the road had been only wide enough for a single car. She didn't remember any recent turnouts. How far would the guy have to go?

She heard the sound of his car's horn again. Slowly, trying to keep her hands steady, Carissa inched the car forward until she was around the curve. The other driver had backed up against the side of the hill in a precarious spot. He motioned for her to hurry up and drive past him. With her teeth clenched and hands gripping the steering wheel, Carissa eased her way along, clearing his car by inches.

He said something through his open window that she didn't catch since her window was rolled up. Then the driver gave Carissa the same sort of hand gesture Kai had given her when he was pulling out of the driveway yesterday. They were so close, Carissa realized that if her window were rolled down, they could have reached out and touched the other's face.

The next blind curve Carissa came to she sounded her horn just to be sure she had the right-of-way. She didn't usually get carsick, but then she had never driven on a road like this before. She was definitely feeling nauseous. The road continued without improvement and added several short bridges to the challenge. One of them appeared to be brand new, which gave her hope that she was coming closer to civilization. If she could have turned around and gone back to the cottage without having to navigate the stretch she had already driven, she would have done it.

I've gone too far now. I'm committed.

The word "committed" didn't sit well with her. But she had too many crucial driving challenges before her now to evaluate why the word bothered her.

Just when she was about to let out a wail of exasperation, she noticed the landscape change. Stretches of green grass spread out from the road on either side, and tall jungle foliage appeared. Then the road changed instantly. She went from clunky bumps and dips to a smooth, blessedly smooth, road.

Carissa felt her jaw relax. She had made it. The terrible, bone-rattling part of the journey was over. She had stuck to her commitment even in the rough spots, and she was almost at her goal.

Looking out the windshield over the top of her sunglasses, Carissa shot a sardonic glance at the sky above and then shook her head, eyes back on the road. "Yes, I see the analogy. All commitments go through rocky patches. I know that. Now, please, don't follow me where I'm going. Just let me be free, okay?"

Carissa drove slowly. On either side of the road,

wild vines wound themselves around the tall, tropical trees, using the stability and strength of the unmoving trees to reach ever upward toward the light.

Loosening her grip on the steering wheel, Carissa couldn't believe she had just talked to God as directly and frankly as if he were real and sitting beside her. Then the word that had come to her mind and her mouth several times over the past four hours came out again. "No. I don't want to talk to you right now. I don't want to think about all my problems."

It had worked with Richard because he knew quite a bit about honoring boundaries. When it came to God, Carissa wasn't confident her "no" would carry the same punch. If that were the case, then the way she felt right now, she would just have to punch harder. It was, after all, her life. She got to make her own decisions.

And it was her decision to block out everything else so she could focus on what awaited her at the campground.

Or was it *who* awaited her at the campground?

11

"He lepo makou, he po'e make no
Ia 'oe no na'e ka hilina'i mau
'O 'oe ka Makua, Ho 'ola pana'i
A nou mai ka pono, ka ho'opomaika'i."

"Thy bountiful care, what tongue can recite?
It breathes in the air, it shines in the light;
It streams from the hills, it descends to the plain,
And sweetly distills in the dew and the rain."

BY FOUR O'CLOCK ON the afternoon of her courageous solo drive to the rainy side of the island, Carissa was seated in a comfortable folding lawn chair. Beside her, in the shade of a grove of guava trees, was Irene. Both of them were balancing blue china teacups on blue china saucers.

Behind them, above the tall grass and strung between two guava trees, was a brightly colored mesh-net hammock. In front of them was a picnic table courtesy of the Haleakala National Park along with a standing charcoal grill, also part of the camp setup. The rest of the cozy items had been brought in by the group.

Three medium-sized dome tents were set in place on the anchored ground tarps, looking like three gray igloos transplanted from the tundra of the forty-ninth state to the lush green open space of the fiftieth state.

Beyond the tents, across the wide field of mown grass that comprised the extent of the primitive camping area, was a spot where the grasses had been left to grow wild. Through the tall jungle of waist-high grass were several trails that led to the volcanic cliffs. Beyond the rocks and cliffs, Irene informed Carissa, was the ocean. Several palm trees dotted the scene at unplanned intervals.

Carissa counted five cars parked on the grassy camping area. Three of them had tents set up beside them. At the far end of the wide stretch was the only facility, an outhouse. She had been warned the camping was primitive, but only a single outhouse? No running water?

What fascinated Carissa most was that Irene was in her happy place. That she had brought her china, carefully packed and lovingly presented to Carissa brimming with mild green tea, was evidence that Irene had a sense of hospitality about her no matter where she went.

"When the men return, they will be so surprised to see you," Irene said. She offered Carissa a plate of plein-air treats—slices of guava and small, round ginger cookies.

"I'm so glad you decided to come. They will all be eager to hear the story you told me about driving through Ulupalakua and around the back side. I wouldn't have recommended that route for you your first time here. It took you half a day!"

"I know. It was a spontaneous decision, as I said." Carissa licked the sticky, sweet guava from her fingers and sipped the cooled green tea.

Suddenly something darted out of the rustling grass under the guava tree grove. The long, fuzzy creature with short legs stopped two feet away from Carissa, picked at something in the dirt, and then dashed back into hiding.

"What was that?" Carissa involuntarily had lifted her feet.

"A mongoose." Irene named the creature without looking at it or batting an eyelash. "They were introduced to the islands to help curb the rat population that came ashore with the whaler and trader ships."

For a moment Carissa didn't move. Then she lowered her feet. "Curb the rat population? Oh, I feel better now about sleeping in a tent tonight."

"You'll sleep just fine. Kai will let you use the other air mattress."

Carissa tried to find a point of reference for everything she was feeling at the moment. The humid warmth of the tropical breeze, the pungent scent of the overripe fruit falling from the surrounding trees, and the visiting mongoose were all far stretches from anything she had ever experienced. A week ago she had felt unsafe in her own backyard, for valid reasons. Yet, here she was, surrounded by unfamiliar territory and about to spend the night in a tent. A tent that was pitched in a place so remote she didn't have cell phone service. More than that, she was here with people she barely knew while around her feet were marauding animals that belonged in a zoo.

From the dirt road that led into the camping area came the voices and laughter of several men. Carissa and Irene looked in that direction and saw Kai coming toward them with two others. Irene said earlier that they had hiked up to the bamboo forest and were going to swim in the waterfall pools.

Carissa felt all the funny little childish squirms and tingles she had experienced the first time she had seen Kai. She told herself she wasn't doing anything wrong. She was just feeling happy, and nothing was wrong with that after all the horrible emotions she had felt over the past week.

When Kai saw her, a look of pleasant surprise came over his face. At least that's what she liked to think she saw in his expression. Carissa rose to greet him, and he came to her the way Mano had at the airport, straightforward with a brush of a kiss on her right cheek and a warm greeting.

Inside, Carissa glowed. The two other men were introduced. To her surprise, they repeated Kai's gesture and greeted her with a kiss of aloha on her cheek and greeted Irene, calling her auntie.

Carissa noticed that one of the young men, Joel,

appeared to be about the same age as her son, Blake. Joel had round glasses and was wearing a long-sleeved shirt. He seemed the least comfortable with offering a kiss on the cheek. He was comfortable, though, with talking about the incredible photos he had taken during their hike through the bamboo forest. He reminded Carissa of Blake, and she wished her son could come here one day and experience all this. She knew he would love it.

In the twenty minutes or so that followed, they took turns relaying their tales of the day. Carissa told about her nerve-racking drive to the campground, and all of them acted impressed, even though she doubted they were.

She calmed her inner flutters as the guys talked about their hike. She reminded herself that Kai hadn't really "kissed" her, nor did the greeting mean anything other than a normal island-style hello. It was an expression of Hawaiian hospitality, not of favoritism or affection.

Dinner became the next topic for the five of them. Tony, the tallest, looked as if he were in his late thirties. He wore his long dark hair pulled back in a ponytail and fastened with a thin strip of leather. Insisting on taking over the details at the grill, he told Carissa he was a cook at a restaurant in a town called Paia, and if she came that way, she should stop in.

"If you're there for breakfast, order the

pineapple macadamia-nut pancakes with the coconut syrup. That's one of our specialties. For lunch, you have to go with the mahimahi sandwich but ask for the whole wheat bun instead of the kaiser roll. And ask for lettuce. That sandwich doesn't automatically come with lettuce, but I think it's better with it."

Carissa nodded but knew she would never remember anything he was telling her. She went to work helping with dinner preparations by following Irene's instructions on plates and flatware. No paper plates for this crew. Irene had packed her everyday dishes and even had votive candles in glass holders for the table.

"Is this the entire group?" Carissa asked, pulling out five of everything.

"For tonight," Tony said. "What do you think, Irene? Will we have about fifteen more tomorrow?"

"At least."

"How often do you guys come here?" Carissa asked.

"We try to come two times every year," Irene said. "We started as a fellowship group from church back when our children were young. Even though the group has changed dramatically over the years, a remnant always manages to come. Last spring we had thirty. That was the most we had had in a long time."

In a strangely detached way, Carissa had put

aside everything that was familiar to her. When the trauma hit last week, it was as if she started to separate herself from the familiar routines of her day-to-day life and had been set adrift, seeking a new shore. This island, these people, this new rhythm of life felt attainable to her in a surrealistic way. She could adapt. She could make this her new home. Here she would be safe.

Carissa found she couldn't eat much of the well-prepared dinner of chicken thighs and corn on the cob from Dan's garden. Thoughts of Richard and his heartfelt apology kept returning to her, but she pushed them back in the file cabinet where that topic belonged for now.

Tony stood and went to the ice chest for a bottle of water, asking if anyone else wanted one.

"I would," Carissa said.

Tony flipped his hand toward her with the same gesture she had seen first from Kai in the driveway and then from the driver she had passed on the narrow road.

"What does that mean?" she asked.

"This?" Kai reproduced the sign by turning the palm of his right hand toward himself and sticking up his pinky and thumb. Then he gave his hand an easygoing shake. "It means, 'hang loose,' 'take it easy.' "

Carissa tried to duplicate the gesture. "Like this?"

"You got it. Now say, *'Shaka.' "*

"Shaka."

"That's it. You're ready to go island-style now. *Shaka.* Hang loose."

Carissa smiled, and Kai smiled back.

The natural light around the campsite was dimming. New sounds emerged from the trees behind them. In the other direction, far across the water, a few glimmers of light flitted in the distance.

"Is that another island?" Carissa asked.

"Yes, that's the Big Island. Or the island of Hawaii, whichever you prefer to call it." Kai leaned back and stretched with his hand clasped behind his neck. "I'm sure my mom can talk story about something that happened there a century or two ago."

"I'll tell you something about Ka'ahumanu that happened right over there, on the west coast of the Big Island where those lights are coming from."

Carissa had forgotten the name of the six-foot, three-hundred-pound woman who made kites and surfed and had a tattoo on her tongue. But she remembered everything about the woman's verve.

"Ka'ahumanu had been intricately entwined with her husband, Kamehameha the Great, for thirteen years when she believed she was losing his love and favor."

Carissa felt an odd shiver go up her spine. It struck her that women everywhere, in every generation, must struggle with the same thoughts and feelings that were affecting her.

"Kamehameha went to Honaunau to be with another woman. Remember, Kamehameha had at least eighteen wives, so Ka'ahumanu was used to the competition for his attention and affection. However, this woman was different. This woman her husband was going to be with happened to be Ka'ahumanu's younger sister."

"Not cool," Tony said.

"That's exactly what Ka'ahumanu thought. In an act of perhaps desperation, perhaps passion, she jumped into the ocean and swam more than five miles in shark-infested waters at night just to be with him."

Joel laughed. "That's legend. Has to be. Five miles? At night? No way."

"Almost all my sources agree on that story as fact."

"What happened when she got there? Did she deck him?"

"I don't know. None of the historians included that detail." Irene lit the votive candles on the table and started in on another story. "When Kamehameha the Great died, Liholiho, the son of his sacred wife, became the king even though he was only a teenager. At the *makahiki* feast soon after Kamehameha the Great's death, Liholiho changed the course of history for these islands. You see, the ancient law prohibited women from eating with the men. They also weren't allowed to eat certain foods such as pork, bananas, or coconuts.

"So, when Liholiho arrived at the feast, all eyes were on him. Would this newly appointed king maintain the ancient traditions? Or would he give in and adopt the cultural changes that had come to the islands as a result of the outside world's influence?"

"I think we can all guess what happened," Tony said. "He caved, didn't he?"

Irene grinned. "First he sat with all the men, then he walked over to the group of women, and then back to the men, and then back to the women. The huge crowd grew silent, waiting to see what he would decide. They believed that if he ate with the women the gods would strike him dead. Suddenly he sat down between his royal mother and Ka'ahumanu and ate their food. Very quickly, I might add. Everyone at this huge gathering saw that he could defy the gods and live. That very night the burning of the tiki gods and the destruction of the *heiaus* began."

"What are *hay-ee-ows*?" Carissa asked.

"They were the holy places on all the islands where sacrifices were made to the gods—sometimes human sacrifices."

A debate ensued over whether the early Hawaiians actually performed human sacrifice, since some reports indicated they lived under a peaceful feudal system.

"I hate to say this," Tony said, "but all I've ever heard is that the missionaries came and messed everything up for the peaceful Hawaiians. They destroyed the ancient worship and traditions."

"But the Protestant missionaries weren't on the islands when the old system was destroyed." Irene rustled on the picnic bench like a pleased hen. "They arrived six months later, after sailing all the way from Boston, with no idea of the changes that had happened here during their journey. I believe it was God—*Ke Akua*—who took away the old ways to make room for the new truth."

Tony didn't look convinced. "So, when the missionaries arrived, who gave them permission to live here?"

Irene smiled. "Ka'ahumanu. I think she liked that the seventeen men and women missionaries arrived with five children. The whalers and traders didn't bring their women and children."

Tony stood and threw in one more antagonistic comment. "They may have started with only seventeen, but they ended up taking over the land. Isn't that when the Hawaiians started dying by the hundreds due to the missionaries bringing in diseases like measles and smallpox?"

Kai was the one who jumped in next. "Why do you attribute the diseases to the missionaries? What about the hundreds of whalers, sailors, and traders who came here and took in the young women who swam out to the ships? Not exactly a hygienic bunch. You really think it was the missionaries who brought syphilis to the islands?"

"All I know," Tony said, "is that during that time in history, thousands of native Hawaiians died because their immune systems couldn't handle the diseases. My *tutu* says it was a great loss from which the islands have never recovered."

"It was. No one would argue with your grandmother on that point." Irene lowered her voice and added, "I also believe that the shedding of innocent blood in ritual sacrifices for hundreds of years prior to any Western or Eastern contact was a great loss to the Hawaiian people."

The discussion ended there, and Carissa felt a sense of relief that the topic wasn't going to stay fixed on the spread of disease and human sacrifice. While they had lingered at the table, the sky had darkened, and she was feeling creeped out by the topic. It didn't help that a few persistent mosquitoes had come after her blood and kept landing on her bare legs in spite of all the jiggling she was doing under the table to keep them away.

"Not to change the topic, but by any chance does anyone have some repellent? These mosquitoes must think my legs are an open buffet."

"I have some." Joel headed for the van. "It's all natural. Good for the environment, good for you, but not so good for the mosquitoes."

Kai collected and stacked the dishes now that there was a pause in the after-dinner entertainment. Apparently he had a story he wanted to be added to the evening. "You do know that there weren't mosquitoes in old Hawaii, don't you?"

"Yeah, right." Tony wasn't in an agreeable mood about anything at the moment, it seemed.

"It's true. Tell 'em, Mom. This is one of her stories I've never forgotten."

"Then you tell it, Kai." She looked pleased that he remembered one of her stories.

"As I understand it, mosquitoes were introduced to the island by a crew of angry sailors. They wanted to get back at the missionaries in Lahaina for not allowing the young Hawaiian girls to swim out to the ships to be with them. They brought back a cask of mosquito larvae from Mexico and released it into the drinking water behind the Baldwin Missionary House. And here we are tonight. Swatting away their offspring."

"Are you serious? How idiotic could those guys be?" Joel had returned with a small pump-spray bottle and handed it to Carissa. "They upset the entire ecological balance of the islands."

Carissa stepped away from the group to apply the mosquito repellent without upsetting everyone's ecological balance.

After all the food was closed up and put away from any midnight snackers of the wildlife variety, Carissa asked to borrow a flashlight since it seemed like as good a time as any to make the dreaded trek to the outhouse.

She opened the creaking door, flashed the light around, and was quick. At least it was a well-maintained facility and as "nice" as such a place could be. Even a bottle of hand sanitizer was provided at the door. She stepped out into the darkness and hurried to the campsite, keeping her eyes on the earth just a few feet in front of her.

Kai was seated at the picnic table and appeared to be watching her. In the candleglow, she could tell he was grinning.

"What's so funny?" She quickly looked down to make sure she hadn't trailed any toilet paper back with her.

"You missed the best part of the walk to the outhouse."

"And what could possibly be the best part of that walk?"

He got up from the table. "Come on, I'll show you."

Carissa handed him the flashlight, and he led the way back to the center of the open field and then suddenly stopped. He turned off the light.

"What is it?" Carissa tried to adjust her eyes to the vast, shadowy field all around them.

"Look up." Kai said it as a command, and she obeyed.

Above them shimmered an astounding display

of all the twinkling starry hosts. There were more stars than Carissa had ever seen before in a night sky. Just behind one of the towering palm trees floated the moon. Tonight it was more than half a moon, fuller and brighter than it had appeared the other night above the cottage.

She blinked and tried to draw in the night's beauty. If Kai hadn't brought her out, away from the light, she would have missed this.

"Come on." Kai turned the flashlight back on. "You have to see the moon on the water. There's a path over this way."

Without hesitating, she followed him onto a narrow footpath that was hidden in the tall grass. It crossed her mind that this might not be a wise choice. But she ignored that thought and kept going.

12

"Mai hopo 'oe i na 'O nou,
Ke kia'i nei Ke Akua
Malalo o Kona mau 'eheu,
ana e ho'omalu mai."

"Jesus will answer
Whenever you call;
He will take care of you,
Trust him for all."

W ITH CHILDLIKE TRUST, CARISSA followed the flashlight's bobbing beam as
Kai held it above his head and lit the way for both
of them through the rustling grass. The moon rose
to the side of them, and as they neared the cliff,
the enormous boulders that gathered along the
coastline came into silhouetted view. Beyond the
rugged outcropping of boulders was the ocean. A
ribbon of moonlight stretched out before them,
trembling on the surface of the deep.

"It looks like a path, doesn't it?" Kai asked.

"It does." Carissa stood several feet away from
Kai. She had crossed her arms in front of her
stomach, as if she needed to hold all her feelings
inside and not let any of them tumble out of her
gut to go prancing off on the ribbon of moonlight.
Her mind played with the intriguing thought of

starting over. What would it be like to fall in love with someone new?

She knew she shouldn't think such things, especially in the wake of Richard's sincere apology earlier that day. If he was expressing willingness to start fresh with their marriage, why was she resisting?

Somehow the thought of taking control of her life and starting over held stronger appeal at the moment. A crazy image flashed through her mind. It was a picture of three-hundred-pound Ka'ahumanu in the driver's seat of the carriage charging through downtown Honolulu with her husband in the back.

I'm not doing that. I'm not her. That's crazy. I just wonder what it would be like to fall in love with a man like Kai. Would he ever be attracted to someone like me? He's so different from Richard. Would Kai be a good husband? A good lover?

An unexpected tha-thump echoed in Carissa's chest. She couldn't remember ever imagining herself being with another man. She probably had. She was human. But it was never like this before. This time the thought filled her with a rush of adrenaline, and with the adrenaline came a strange sort of desperation to hold on to the fantasy, embellish it, and carry it out to its exciting, forbidden conclusion.

"Would you jump in?" Kai's question came to

her in the depths of her private thoughts and startled her.

"Excuse me?"

"Like Ka'ahumanu. Would you do it? Would you jump in the ocean on a night like this and swim five miles through the shark-infested water to be with the man you love?"

"No." Her answer came out fast and firm.

Kai laughed. "You sure didn't hesitate on that one."

"I'm not a good swimmer. I could never stay afloat for five miles; so I'd be shark bait long before I arrived. What would I have accomplished?"

"I see your point."

"Would you do it? Would you jump in for the woman you loved?"

His answer came out as quickly as Carissa's and carried what sounded like deep conviction. "Yes. Absolutely. If that's what it would have taken to keep Bekah, I would've done it."

Bekah.

The single word doused the gathering of coals that Carissa's imagination had been fanning into a fire.

"Was she your wife?" Carissa asked the question before pausing to evaluate if she should.

"Yes."

Carissa didn't know what to say next. These were the sorts of stories Richard listened to all the time. She could hear in Kai's voice all the hurt and brokenness.

"What about you?" Kai asked. "How long were you married?"

"I . . . I still am married. My husband is giving a lecture in Denver this week so that's why he's not here."

"Sorry. I got the idea you were divorced."

"No, we're married." Defending her marital status was giving her an unexpected sense of conviction about her status. "We're going on twenty-four years."

Kai pulled back. "Twenty-four years? You must have married when you were a child. Like Ka'ahumanu."

"Not exactly a child. But I was only nineteen."

"Bekah and I married when we were twenty."

A pause lingered between them before Kai handed over a bit more information. "We lasted only six years, though. Not twenty-four, like you."

"I'm sorry to hear that."

"I'm sorry, too. It was rough. She's remarried now and back on the mainland. I think she's happy. I'm glad for that, I guess. Life doesn't always go the way you think it should, does it?"

"No, it definitely doesn't go the way you think it should."

"We should go back," Kai said quietly. They stood together in a shared silence, both staring at the moon. His voice carried a hint of depression.

As Carissa followed, Kai led the way with the flashlight overhead once again.

Why did I allow myself to entertain thoughts of being with Kai? He certainly wasn't thinking of me as we were standing there. He was thinking about swimming with sharks to be with his ex-wife. I have a husband. A strong-hearted, loyal husband. Why am I thinking all these wayward thoughts?

At the campsite, Irene had bedded down for the night. The plan was for Carissa to share Irene's tent, and everything had been set up for her in the sufficiently spacious dome.

"Do you need anything?" Kai asked, as he handed back the flashlight.

"No. Thanks. I'm ready to try out the air mattress. Thanks for letting me use it."

"No problem. Sleep well."

"Thanks. You, too."

She unzipped the tent and stepped inside. Her folding cot with the much-celebrated air mattress awaited her. Irene didn't say anything when Carissa entered so she guessed Irene was asleep.

Doing her best to get comfortable on the air mattress, Carissa pulled the lightweight blanket up to her chin. The appeal of leaving her marriage was still in her thoughts. She knew what was right. Staying with Richard was right. She had made a vow. A commitment. And yet . . .

Her sleep was rough. Not because of the mattress but because of the thoughts that crawled in on top of the air mattress and stayed with her all night.

Morning arrived before Carissa was ready to greet it. She rolled over and saw that her tent mate was up and gone. Unzipping the tent's opening, Carissa drew in a deep breath of the fresh morning air and watched Irene greet the day. She stood about 100 yards away in the open area under a bending palm tree. Facing the rising sun with her arms in the air, her words tiptoed on the breeze like a subtle whispering of the earth itself.

"Ke Akua Hemolele, ua piha ka honua i kou nani a ke ho'omaika'i nei ia 'oe."

Carissa stretched. She desperately needed to brush her teeth. Slipping into her flip-flops, which waited by the tent's door, she made her way to the picnic table area in search of bottled water.

"Morning."

Carissa jumped. She hadn't noticed Joel sitting in a folding chair off to the side. "Hi. I just need to find some water."

"You don't need to whisper. Everyone else is up. Kai went to the pools. Tony's in the tent, and Irene . . ." Joel nodded in her direction. "You know, I remember watching her do that when I was a kid when we first camped here with the group. There were three of them. Three aunties. They all stood together like that and offered up morning worship. It's a sight you never forget."

Carissa looked across the open space at Irene. She stood with both arms raised as she watched the sun inch over the Big Island and light the green world around them.

"Do you know what she is saying?"

"No. You'll have to ask her. It's a prayer. In Hawaiian, of course."

Tony emerged from one of the tents. "I could use some coffee. Anyone else want some?"

"Sure. Is there an espresso drive-through anywhere around here?" Carissa asked it with a subtle smile, but Tony seemed to take her seriously.

"I don't know. They might have espresso at the place across from Hasegawa's General Store in Hana. I know they have great ice cream. But it's about a twenty-minute drive from here."

"I was only kidding."

Tony pointed at her and grinned. "You got me there. That was a good one. I was going to start up the fire and boil some water. Irene has a French press around here somewhere."

Carissa set aside her teeth brushing need and helped Tony hunt for the French press. He started the fire, and soon the fragrance of ground coffee beans mixed with the smell of the wood smoke. Joel sliced up one of the round watermelons from

Dan's garden and pulled a box of cereal out of the back of the car.

"That's my contribution. Grape-Nuts."

"Well, here comes mine." Tony held the camping pot with both hands and carefully poured the boiling water into the French press.

Carissa could understand why some people liked camping. This was good stuff. Fresh air. Fresh coffee. No schedule.

Carefully sipping the steaming brew, Carissa took a seat at the picnic table. Irene rested her cane beside her reclining La-Z-Boy-style lounge chair.

"Hey, auntie," Joel said. "Carissa wanted to know what your prayer meant."

"It's a simple line of praise. *Ke Akua Hemolele, ua piha ka honua i kou nani a ke ho'omaika'i nei ia 'oe*. It means, 'Holy God, the earth is full of your glory and so we worship you.'"

Irene's hair was a glad tangle of unreliable strands. Her shorts and cotton shirt were terminally crumpled, and her bare legs bore the evidence of a lifetime of bumps, bruises, and raised blue veins. But her face bore a child's expression, trusting, sweet, and eager to share a secret.

Carissa sipped her coffee and thought how lovely and unpretentious Irene's ritual was. She was worshipping the Creator, not the creation, as Carissa had first supposed.

"I picked up a few guavas for us, there on the

204

table." Irene tapped the side of the picnic table with her cane. "And I've got my eye on a papaya for us. It looks about as ripe as it's going to get. How about it, Carissa? Would you mind being the one to gather our food from afar?"

"Sure. That will be my contribution to breakfast. Where is it?"

"Right there." Irene lifted her cane and pointed to a tall, skinny tree at the far end of the guava grove. Carissa could see the cluster of green, teardrop-shaped fruit clumped together at the very top under leaves that reminded her of large clovers. One of the papayas was plump and sunflower-yellow.

She laughed. "I don't think I'm quite tall enough to pick that papaya for you."

"You don't pick it. You shake the tree until it comes to you."

"Okay." Taking one final sip of her coffee, Carissa hopped up from the picnic table and strode over to the tree while the others watched.

"Give it a good rattle," Tony called out.

Carissa wrapped both hands around the slim trunk of the papaya tree and gave it a shake. Nothing fell.

"You've gotta give it more than that! We know you have it in you. Shake that papaya down!"

Playing along, Carissa pretended to spit in both her palms before rubbing them together and grasping the trunk with a more purposeful grip.

Then she shook it. And shook it. On the third momentous tremor, her efforts were rewarded. The ripe papaya succumbed to gravity.

"Catch it!" Joel yelled.

She wasn't quick enough. The tender fruit fell to the ground and split open on impact. Carissa bent down to examine the broken fruit. Dozens of slick, round, tiny black seeds like opulent caviar tumbled out. Even in its battered state it looked beautiful.

"Should I leave it?" she asked the others.

"No!" they responded as a chorus.

"Bring it here," Irene said.

Carissa carried over the two halves of the bruised fruit and offered it to Irene. "Is it okay?"

"Yes, of course. Everything is redeemable."

Irene's response struck Carissa as poignant and went deep inside, which felt strange at this particular moment. It was a piece of fruit, after all. She decided her emotions were far too out of whack to pay attention to anything she felt.

Tony took over cutting up the inner soft, orange part of the fruit and putting the irregular-sized chunks in a bowl, which they passed around, eating the warm, sweet papaya with their fingers. It was another one of the Maui moments on Carissa's growing list of things she loved about this place.

Kai strode back into camp with a beach towel

over his shoulder. "The pools are perfect this morning. The water is just right."

"I'm on my way," Tony said.

"Me, too," Joel said. Turning to Carissa and Irene he said, "Aunties? Do either of you want to come?"

So now I'm an auntie. I guess that's a good thing.

Irene smiled. "I'm content to stay right here. What about you, Carissa?"

"Sure, I'll go."

Kai stayed at the campsite with his mom as the three of them took off. Joel and Tony started out at a quick stride, leaving Carissa behind. She hurried to catch up and hoped she wouldn't regret wearing flip-flops, as they tromped along the dirt trail cut through the tall, thick grass.

They stopped to examine a huge spiderweb. Near the center of the web was the spider's tightly wrapped larder, filled with what looked to be a pudgy feast. Joel, the most eco-friendly of the bunch, studied the back of the spider that clung to the upper edge.

"Friendly," he declared.

Carissa smiled. She had never met anyone who knew enough about spiders to make an on-the-spot call on their sociability. She found all of this fascinating. Not only the curious bits of nature in the beautiful surroundings, but also the relationships between the people she was with.

"How far is it to the waterfalls?"

"Not far."

Joel pointed out the trees as they approached the spot where the narrow path connected with the well-trod, wider path from the parking lot. The trees were shorter than palm trees and had wider trunks. The long, narrow fronds were pointed on the ends like palm fronds.

"We call those the 'walking trees' because the roots come out of the trunk and look like a bunch of legs. The Hawaiian name for them is *lauhala*. You'll see them everywhere around here. The fronds are used for weaving baskets or making mats," Joel told her.

They came to a wide, open space that caused Carissa to stop walking and catch her breath. To their right, a grassy hillside curved down to the ocean that spread out in the morning sun like a shimmering blanket of rippled blue.

Directly in front of them the hill sloped to an abrupt, rounded curl that kept going down a cliff. The volcanic flow that shaped the cliff continued over the side and formed a garden of ominous boulders and irregular-shaped tide pools in a rugged cove. White ocean spray shot into the air as the waves rushed into the cove, and the salt water met the freshwater that tumbled from waterfalls Carissa could just see to her left.

"This is unbelievable."

"Wait until you see the pools." Tony led the

way down the trail to stairs that had been securely set in the petrified lava flow and flanked by steady metal handrails.

At the end of the steps they walked a few feet across the smooth, black boulders before Tony and Joel stopped. A large, shallow-looking pool stretched out and met with a rounded pool farther up. Into that rounded pool cascaded a twenty-foot waterfall encased in the black obsidian of ancient lava flow. Above that waterfall another pool appeared and high above, surrounded by trailing vines and tropical foliage, was a bridge.

"Not bad, is it?" Joel asked.

"I can't believe places like this really exist."

"Believe it. Hey, we're going to the upper pools. You staying here?"

For a minute Carissa felt like she wanted to follow the boys and check out the upper pools. But something told her they wouldn't want to be responsible for her if she slipped on the wet rocks in her flip-flops.

"I'll stay here. I can find my way back to camp, too; so when I'm ready, I'll just go back."

Tony gave her the "hang loose" hand sign with his thumb and finger extended.

"Shaka," Carissa replied.

"Hey, you remembered."

The two of them took off like mountain goats. They had no difficulty forging a trail where none existed along the side of the hill. Carissa made her way to one of the rounded boulders and sat down to take it all in.

She lingered for a long while, simply thinking. Thinking and breathing. It seemed to her as if time itself had tiptoed into this sacred pool and knelt to take lush, lingering sips of life, and now Carissa wanted to do the same. Her deep draughts of air were laced with mist and hints of ferns and fronds, a subtle scent of all things green and tropical.

The dream that had washed over her as she fell asleep in the backyard hammock at home now came to her. She remembered the image of floating on a wide ocean, heading for an inviting cove. An island cove, such as this one.

How could I have dreamed about an ocean and floating to a cove when I didn't know anything about this? I thought my job was secure that night. I thought my marriage was stable. I had no idea I was coming here.

In a lovely yet disturbing way, Carissa sensed that God had placed that image of drifting toward a safe harbor into her dream. He knew the future. He knew the past. And he was here in the present. She couldn't deny it.

The all-encompassing beauty around her in the midst of the fragile, broken world brought Irene's words back to her. *Everything is redeemable.*

13

"Malalo o Kona 'eheu malu wau la
Ke nou na 'ino a pouli ka po
Ia ia ku'u hilina'i, Nana e ho'omalu
Nana e ho 'ola, 'o wau Kona poki'i."

"Under his wings I am safely abiding,
Though the night deepens and tempests are wild,
Still I can trust him; I know he will keep me,
He has redeemed me, and I am his child."

WHEN CARISSA RETURNED TO the campsite, she carefully maneuvered into the makeshift hammock that hung between two palm trees a few hundred yards from the tents. She had seen Tony in it earlier, so she knew it could hold her weight. Once she was wedged in the hammock and balanced in the woven mesh, she was surprised at how comfortable it was. If anyone took a picture, she knew she would look like a plump fly, caught in a human-sized web.

But no one was taking pictures. Irene was reading, and Kai was talking to some people who had pulled in next to their campsite. They apparently knew each other. Two of the teenage boys with the group came over and greeted "Auntie Irene" and then took off for the waterfall pools.

As Carissa swayed in the unruffled morning

breeze and drew in the pungent scent of the ripening guavas, she thought about leaving in a few hours and driving back to the cottage. She didn't need to stay the whole time with the group, especially since it would soon be growing with the arrival of many more of Irene's friends, who were like family to her and to each other. As much as Carissa enjoyed pretending, this wasn't really where she belonged.

"If Dan were here, he would be painting right now." Irene had walked over to the hammock, standing a few feet away, balancing on her cane with a homesick look on her face. Carissa hadn't noticed her until she was right beside her.

"It's too bad he couldn't be here."

"Next time," Irene said. "He'll come next time. And next time, you'll have to come back, and your husband will have to come with you, too."

"Oh, I don't know." Carissa gave a nervous laugh. "He's . . . we're . . ."

"Now, now. You thought you weren't much of a camper, and yet here you are, as content as can be."

"Yes, but . . ."

Irene leaned on her cane and seemed to be waiting for more of an explanation. Carissa didn't want to open up to Irene. Not now. It wasn't her way of dealing with things. But the woman looked at her with such an expression of caring and wisdom that Carissa felt compelled to respond with the answer that shot out of her mouth.

"Richard and I . . . we're going through a rough stretch right now. I don't know what's going to happen. I'm . . . I'm conflicted." Carissa pressed her lips together, not willing to say anything else. She expected Irene to turn into a fountain of knowledge and spout helpful advice.

Instead, Irene looked sorrowful. Her empathetic expression made it clear that she had walked this road with many couples, and she grieved with Carissa in a deep place in her spirit. Irene opened her mouth and was about to say something when Kai charged toward them, holding up his cell phone.

"Hey, it's Dad. I told him the signal wasn't strong, but he wants to talk to you." Kai handed over the phone.

Irene shouted, "Dan? Where are you?"

"Mom! He can hear you fine. He can probably hear you on the mainland without the phone."

Carissa wanted to laugh, but she kept it in.

"What?" Irene yelled. "Well, I don't know what you should order. Is it lunchtime there? Okay, so then order breakfast since you're in a place like that." Turning to Kai, who was still only a foot away from her, she maintained her high volume. "Twenty-four-hour breakfast place. Have you eaten at one of those before? No, not you, Dan. I'm asking Kai."

213

Kai leaned over. "Tell him to order an omelet and ask for tomatoes instead of hash browns. He'll like that."

"Did you hear that? No, you, Dan. Did you hear what Kai said? He said to order the omelet and ask for tomatoes instead of hash browns."

Turning to Carissa with a grin, Kai said in a low voice, "My dad usually eats only what he grows in his garden and what he likes to order from places around here. He's a wreck on the mainland."

"No, tomatoes. I did not say potatoes. You did. Did you say potatoes, Kai?"

He shook his head.

"We both said TOE-MAY-TOES. You don't have to get it with . . . what's that?" She looked at Kai. "I don't know. Rye toast, then. Yes, you like rye toast. I've seen you eat it before. Dan? Hello? Dan?"

She held out the phone to Kai. "He hung up on me."

"He didn't hang up, *Momi*. It's the cell phone service out here. I never get good reception on this side."

"Call him back. He hasn't ordered yet."

Kai grinned. "I think he can take it from there. He'll be fine. You did a good job." He kissed his mom on the top of her head. "Listen, I told Mark I'd help him set up their tent and then we're going to the Kaupo Store for some water and ice. So, if you still want me to walk over to the pools with you, how about if we go later this afternoon?"

Just then Kai's cell phone rang again. He answered, listened a moment and said, "Okay, I'll tell her."

With another grin for his mom he said, "Dad ordered oatmeal."

Carissa had to cover her mouth so the two of them wouldn't see her swallowing her laughter. "That man," Irene said.

As Kai walked away, Carissa swung her feet over the edge of the hammock and said to Irene, "I understand the area gets really populated with visitors in the middle of the day. If you would like to walk over there now, I'd love to go with you. I didn't have my bathing suit on earlier, and I think I'd like to at least put my feet in the water."

Irene looked delighted. "Not just your feet, dear. You must get all the way in or it's not worth the journey."

Carissa donned her bathing suit and a loose cover-up, adding shoes that had soles designed to handle the slippery rocks better than flip-flops. The two women took their time along the trail, stopping to look at the immensely large spiderweb. The sunlight came through the vibrant green leaves at just the right angle to accent the intricate design. The "friendly" fellow wasn't at home to receive his late-morning audience, but he had managed to catch and wrap up a second insect not far from the pantry where the first pudgy, freeze-dried feast awaited.

They continued down the trail only a short distance before Irene stopped again and leaned in to sniff some tiny white flowers that were growing wild on a thin green vine. *"Pikake,"* she said. "Can you smell it?"

Carissa sniffed. "I think this is the same as the lotion I bought at the general store by the winery. What's it called?"

"Ulupalakua."

"No, the flower."

"Pikake. It's wild jasmine."

"That's what it is. I couldn't place it. I love this fragrance."

"So does my husband." Irene peeked at Carissa over the top of her glasses. "I used to wear wild jasmine in my hair. That is, back when my hair would let me keep something more than a tangle in it. Dan loved it, absolutely loved it. The night he proposed to me we were walking on the beach, and out of the blue he asked me to be his wife. Just like that! He was completely unprepared. He didn't even have a ring."

Carissa grinned.

Irene grinned back. "He always said it was the wild jasmine that made him propose like that. The fragrance made him fall in love with me. That was fifty-two years ago."

"Fifty-two years. Wow!"

With a mischievous grin, Irene added, "Sometimes it feels like 152 years; other times—most of the time—it feels like 2 years."

"Do you have any secrets to your success?" Carissa didn't like the way her question came out, but she figured this was her opportunity to address their conversation that had been cut off earlier. As if to qualify her question she added, "I mean, what the two of you have is rare. I haven't seen many marriages like yours that have lasted so long."

With a casual brush of her hand, Irene said, "I'm sure you can find better advice in books or at some of those marriage seminars they're always hosting at our church. But I'll tell you what I think."

She paused, seeming to make Carissa ask for it, beg for the sage advice.

"So, what do you think?"

"Stay."

"Stay," Carissa repeated.

"Yes, stay. That's my only advice."

They continued down the trail. Carissa tried to add meaning to Irene's simple answer. She assumed Irene meant to stay in love. Stay married. Stay *committed*. Something in her spirit was still bucking against that word.

"You know, sticking it out is hard to do sometimes," Carissa said. "People change a lot during a marriage."

"Maybe."

"Haven't you and Dan changed a lot over the years? He's not the same man you married."

"And don't I know it!" Irene grinned. "But in all the ways that really count, he is still who he has always been, and I'm still who I have always been. We just go through seasons that press us to behave differently. But deep inside we're still the same. Even along those rocky stretches of road."

"Like my drive here yesterday," Carissa said more to herself than to Irene.

"Yes, like that. But you stayed on the road and didn't go over the side. That's what I mean when I say, 'Stay.' Marriage is a covenant relationship. It's not just a promise you made to your spouse. The promise you made to stay together was a promise you made to God as well."

Irene lifted her cane, as if attempting to point to the sky. "And *Ke Akua* dearly blesses those who keep their promises, even when it's difficult. He knows. He hears. He cares."

They arrived at the stairs that led down to the pools. Irene paused. "And for those who cannot or will not stay, there is always grace. Extravagant grace. One of my own children is demonstrating in his life what that sort of grace looks like. That, too, can be a deep blessing from *Ke Akua.*"

Carissa assumed Irene was referring to Kai. She thought it was lovely the way Irene brought up the topic of his divorce without labeling him or giving away specifics. Her mother-heart was a place where confidences were kept.

As they reached the bottom of the stairs that led to the pools, they slipped out of their shoes, and the two of them carefully edged their feet over the slick stones. A handful of tourists were swimming in the deep pool ahead of them.

Carissa stopped short of the more difficult stretch of rocks that they would have to climb if they wanted to get into the upper pool. She assumed this would be as far as Irene could safely go.

"No, we must keep going," Irene said. "All the way to the upper pool."

They were already up to their hips in the water. To reach the next level they would have to put Irene's cane on the side rocks and do a bit of maneuvering to get up to the area where they could swim freely. If Irene was up for the challenge, Carissa didn't see how she could hold back.

Leaving her cover-up on the dry rocks along with Irene's cane and glasses, Carissa looked for the best entry route into the pool. Irene was wearing her baggy shorts and breezy cotton shirt as her swimming apparel. She kept a steady grip on Carissa's arm as the two of them helped each other over the next stretch. Irene had difficulty with the loss of clear vision as well as her loss of agility since she was able to use only the strength of one leg. Twice Carissa paused to ask if she wanted to stop or go back.

Irene's answer was "no" each time.

It came to Carissa in a fleeting thought that she had also been saying "no" a lot these past few days. Only Carissa was saying "no" to facing the difficult thoughts and relationships while this intrepid woman beside her was saying "no" to giving up.

With considerable effort, they reached the place where they could finally enter the upper pool. The dense jungle foliage cascading over the dark rocks gave the feeling that this was a hidden pool where they were tucked away from modern civilization. This area had been a feast for her eyes when Carissa viewed it from a distance earlier. Now that she was surrounded by the timeless elements of rock, water, and air and taking in the sound of the waterfall close-up, Carissa felt exhilarated.

She turned to Irene and saw tears rolling down her cheeks.

"Irene, are you okay?"

"Look at this! All of it! I love this place. I've always loved this place. I thought I might never return. When we came last spring it was too soon after my car accident and surgery. I couldn't get down here to the pools. I thought I would never do this again."

Irene's small confession made her noble effort that much more impressive. Carissa felt honored to be here with her and wanted to wrap the fragile warrior up in her arms in a big hug. If she did that, there was a good chance both of them would lose their footing and tumble into the pool. It was better to wait to give the hug.

"Shall we?" Irene's question came with a sense of triumph.

"I'm ready if you are."

In unison, the two women lowered themselves into the pool. They bobbed in the chilly water that came up to their necks, and they each made glad, shivering sounds. Irene stretched out her arms and became a lovely sight in the water. Her frame moved differently in water than it did on land. Here, she was unhindered by the challenges she had with her leg and hip. Here, she was weightless and free. And so graceful.

Carissa stroked her arms through the water right beside Irene, and the two of them headed to the center of the pool. There, in the full sunlight, Irene dipped all the way under the water. She came up radiant and glimmering, with the fresh water droplets clinging to her skin like stars.

Carissa wanted to grow up to be like Irene. She wanted to be radiant, with a face full of stars when she was seventy and not to be afraid to traverse rocky places so she could swim in an ancient pool. She knew deep inside that part of Irene's beauty treatment was to "stay."

They swam toward the rushing waterfall and yelled to hear each other over the sound of the unleashed fury.

"Come!" Irene called. She paddled closer and closer to the falls until she was right beside the monstrous flow. Then she disappeared.

"Irene!" Carissa swam quickly and found her companion behind the waterfall laughing her little heart out.

Carissa joined her, feeling the roar of the falls cascading in front of them and blinking from the constant spray on her face. The rush was like nothing she had ever experienced.

Irene pushed her way through the water and out the side. She kept stroking her way through the pool until she was back to where the two of them had entered.

Carissa couldn't stop smiling. The din of the rushing water was still reverberating in her ears.

"Deep calls to deep," Irene called out triumphantly.

"Yes," Carissa agreed, even though she wasn't sure what that meant. She did notice that Irene's teeth were chattering, which meant it was time to get out. But Carissa found it difficult to keep her balance on the underwater ledges around the pool's edge as she tried to hoist herself out. She couldn't pull herself up, nor could she push against the sides of the slippery pool enough to get a grip.

Two teenage boys, who had been jumping off the rocks, came swimming toward them calling out to Irene. Carissa recognized them as the boys who had arrived with their dad earlier.

"Do you need some help, auntie?"

"I do," Carissa confessed. Before she could make a suggestion of what they should do, the two boys swam up behind her and told her to pull herself up with her arms. Suddenly, four flat hands were firmly placed on her rear end, giving her a rousing boost up and out of the pool.

She flopped onto the rocks, feeling like a beached seal and almost certain she matched her own visual image in the eyes of the two teenagers.

The first thing she did was to reach for the bottom of her bathing suit and tug down the elastic leg opening so as to cover up the slippage of whiteness she could feel peeking out. Then she rolled over, sat up slowly, and did a quick scan to make sure other bits of personal white space weren't peeking out anywhere else.

One of the boys was already out of the pool on the other side. "You should come on this side, Auntie."

Irene scooted over to their suggested exit, and with more dignified assistance, the two of them helped her out.

"Oh, that was heavenly, wasn't it?" Irene patted the drips off her wrinkled cheek with the palm of her hand. She adjusted her balance and twisted the ends of her shirt to wring out the water. "How about if we get our things and then go find ourselves a bit of sunshine where we can sit and dry out?"

The boys were already back in the water, splashing each other. Carissa handed Irene her cane and glasses, and the two of them gingerly sloshed through the ankle-deep water. They had to go all the way up the stairs to the upper cliff before they found an open patch of sun.

"Did you notice the signs over there by the stack of volcanic rock?" Irene pointed to the left.

"No, what do they say?"

"This is an archaeological site. At one time a large village thrived here."

"If I were to live in Old Hawaii, this is where I would want to live, too." Carissa sat down on the velvety green grass that felt as soft as a tucked Berber carpet. Irene stood, leaning on her cane, her shirt flapping in the strong wind.

"Did I tell you that Ka'ahumanu was born not far from here?"

"Yes, you mentioned that the other night."

"Her father was a chief of notable rank. She may have come to this very spot as a child. She might have swum in the same pool we just paddled around in or sat right here and gazed at the sky."

Carissa looked around at the ancient ruins. Irene's nearly legendary superwoman seemed more real than ever.

"One of my favorite stories about Ka'ahumanu happened in Lahaina, on the west side of the island."

"I went to Lahaina the other day and had a look around."

"Then you'll be able to imagine what I'm going to tell you. Not far from where you saw the huge banyan tree was where the royal residence used to be. Ka'ahumanu was in her mid-forties when this happened, if I remember correctly. She had gone through a rough season with illness, great loss, and opposition from enemies on many sides. But she had returned to a position of strength. One sea captain who had known her for years wrote that her life showed evidence of a genuine conversion to Christianity."

Irene stepped over to a small, rounded boulder that faced Carissa, and Irene carefully sat down. She kept her chin lifted to the strong breeze.

"This is what happened. A priestess who worshipped the ancient gods came from the Big Island to hold an audience with Ka'ahumanu and the rest of the *ali'i*, the royalty. She brought with her an agitated entourage. A scholar who was there that day recorded the moment by saying that a priestess approached the *ali'i* with an intense expression. Her tangled hair stuck out in every direction. The edges of her robe were singed from the fires of Kilauea. The wild woman carried a spear and a feathered *kahili*—that's a tall pole with feathers in a circle around the top. It represented power. For her, it was the power of the ancient gods. Thousands of people gathered to see what was going to happen."

Carissa could imagine right where all this had occurred. What made the story even more vivid was the way the wind was drying Irene's hair, pulling it away from her face as she spoke. Even though she was sitting still, she appeared to be traveling at a great speed, taking Carissa back in time with her.

"Ka'ahumanu asked what message the woman brought. The priestess said that while she was in a trance, Pele, the goddess of fire, had come into her. The priestess demanded that the missionaries who had offended Pele be forced to leave the islands. If they didn't go, Pele would show her vengeance by causing the volcano and sending its death flow of searing lava across the island.

"Ka'ahumanu asked the woman to put down her spear and put down the *kahili*. The woman refused. Ka'ahumanu then commanded her to do so. Can you imagine it? Thousands of commoners watching this challenge. And the priestess complied. Then Ka'ahumanu spoke to her kindly, saying, 'You are not Pele. You are a woman, as I am a woman, both made by God. The volcano of

Kilauea, likc all the volcanoes around the world, was also made by the one, true God. Now give up your false gods. Go back to your island. Plant the sweet potatoes. Beat the *tapa* cloth, catch fish, and be responsible for your own provisions instead of living on the gifts you demand from the people on behalf of Pele.' "

"And with that," Irene gave her hand a flick of the wrist, "the priestess left. The thousands of observers saw once again that the old gods no longer held any power over them. It was an exceptional day."

With just enough panache to be endearing, Irene lowered her eyes, smiled at Carissa, and said, "And on that day, Ka'ahumanu demon-strated which woman carried the true strength and power. She was the one who stayed."

14

"Iesu e, ke Kumu mui 'o na pomaika'i o'onei
Kahe mau na wai aloha paipai ia'u e ho'omaika'i
E a'o mai ia'u la e memele me lakou ma kela ao
Hapai au i kou aloha kou aloha 'oia mau."

"Jesus sought me when a stranger,
Wandering from the fold of God;
He, to rescue me from danger,
Interposed his precious blood."

FOR THE REST OF the day Carissa thought about Richard. She thought about what it would look like for her to "stay." Where would they live? What would she do for a job? Would Richard adjust his schedule so the two of them would have more time together?

She checked her phone twice, just to see if she could pick up a signal. No success.

Returning to the hammock, she pretended to take an afternoon nap. What she was really doing was formulating a plan. She always did better when she had a schedule to follow. Here, everything was unscheduled. Uncharted. If she was going to at least attempt to be a courageous, strong, and determined woman who had chosen to "stay," she needed to know how to start the process.

Richard had taken the first step with his apology. It was her turn to respond, but she didn't quite know what to do.

She decided to stick with her plan to drive back that afternoon. She would have phone service and could start to talk through with Richard some of the things that she saw as big problems between them. That way, she reasoned, she could finish out her vacation on Maui without this restless, not-knowing sense of foreboding following her around. When she got home, they could work at things together.

Or not. That remained to be seen. At least she wouldn't be stuck here in limbo, and she could rest and enjoy the time she had left.

Sliding out of the hammock, she went over to the newly formed circle of fifteen lawn chairs that had been set up by the others in the group who had been arriving all afternoon. Irene was conversing with another woman when Carissa interrupted as politely as she could.

"I've decided to drive back to the cottage this afternoon."

"Not this afternoon!" The other woman's eyes grew wide. "Either direction it will take you forever. That's why we came as early as we could today. Wait till the morning. You'll have the road to yourself, if you leave early enough."

Irene nodded, and Joel, who had joined the group, agreed.

Carissa gave in to their persuasiveness, and when Joel asked if she wanted to go with some of them to buy water, she agreed so she would have something to do.

"I thought Kai went for water this morning," Irene said.

"He did. He bought drinking water. We need to go to the church and fill up the containers from the spigot so we have water to wash up."

"You have a waterfall to wash up in," Irene said.

The other woman chuckled at Irene's comment as Joel and another young woman led Carissa over to a minivan.

"How far do we have to go for the water?" Carissa asked.

"Not far. A couple of miles. There's a spigot available for public use next to an old church. I walked to it one time, but you know, carrying twenty gallons of water back to camp is no fun."

She was about to climb into the car when Kai appeared from one of the neighbors' campsites. "Did I hear you say you guys are going over to Palapala Ho'omau?"

"You mean the old church? Yeah, we can. Why?"

"I thought Carissa might be interested in seeing it. She's never been there before."

"Okay, sure. You wanna come too?" Joel asked.

Kai thought a moment. "Sure. Why not." He

hopped into the backseat and slid over. The young woman climbed in next to him, leaving the front seat for Carissa.

Carissa tried to remember the young woman's name. It was Hawaiian but it didn't seem to stick even though she'd heard it several times.

They drove back through the entrance of the Haleakala National Park and saw a lineup of cars waiting to enter. Three large tour vans led the pack.

"Are all those people coming here to camp?" Carissa asked.

"Probably not," Kai said. "They all drive over for the day to see the waterfalls. That's why we come here and stay. It's no fun to drive four or five hours to get here and then, after one swim, turn the van around and drive back."

Carissa was glad she was in on the camping experience. She had loved going to the pools early that morning and then again with Irene before many visitors had arrived.

"Have you been camping here before?" Carissa asked the young woman in the backseat.

She had short, bleached-blonde hair and wore a clunky, ornate cross necklace that hung down to the middle of her stomach.

When she didn't reply to Carissa's question, Joel looked in the rearview mirror and said, "Maile, Carissa asked if you've been camping here before?"

"Oh. I didn't know you were talking to me. No, this is my first time here. These guys invited me. I met them at church in the addicts' class."

Carissa thought she misunderstood her or maybe that she was kidding. But then the expressions all three of them shared made it clear Maile was serious.

"Addicts?" Carissa repeated.

"We don't call it that," Kai said. "It's the 'New Life' group."

"He's one of the leaders," Maile said. "All of us are overcoming some sort of addiction."

Carissa glanced at Joel. He placed his hand over his heart and said, "Drugs. Twenty-seven months clean."

"Good for you," Carissa said.

"Mine's alcohol," Maile said. "Just three months sober. But I'm really trying, and the class is helping."

"That's great." Carissa knew a little about what it meant for them to make their declarations to her. She applauded their bravery and honesty.

Maile turned to Kai. He seemed pained the most to name his addiction, even though the two others apparently knew what it was.

"You don't have to say anything," Carissa said.

"Does it make you uncomfortable talking about this?" Maile was looking at Carissa when she asked.

"Me? No, not really."

"My mom says I should never talk about it,

especially to people I hardly know, but that's part of how I got where I am. Or, I should say, where I was."

"I'm sort of used to it," Carissa said. "My husband is a counselor. He specializes in addictions. Well, specifically, he counsels men who struggle with sexual addiction." Carissa couldn't believe she was rolling that piece of information off her tongue as easily as she was. She usually worked hard to hide it from others, especially strangers.

Years ago, when Richard did mostly premarital counseling, she loved telling people what he did. Who doesn't enjoy hearing about plans for a wedding? But when his clientele changed, her bragging about him changed, too. She hadn't seen that fact until this moment.

Is that part of the reason Richard feels I don't honor him?

Maile broke into Carissa's thoughts. "My boyfriend says sexual addiction isn't really an addiction. It's just the way guys are."

"My husband would disagree with your boyfriend. For some men it is an addiction. Not for all men. But for some. The cycle is triggered a little differently than with drug or alcohol addiction." She paused, but all of them had their eyes on her, waiting for her to go on.

"A lot of people don't realize that during arousal the body produces chemicals that induce a high that's as powerful as some narcotics."

"Endorphins, right?" Maile asked.

"That's one of them. Also, dopamine and adrenaline. With an addict, instead of experiencing all that naturally in the marriage bed, as my husband says, they use the chemical high to medicate the pain in their lives."

"Like any other drug of choice," Joel said.

"I think it's more complicated than that, but I know that to continually experience that high, men and women fall into cycles of looking at or participating in whatever they need to release that mix of chemicals in their bodies and use the high to medicate."

Carissa realized again that she was speaking boldly about something she never wanted to talk about at home. Whenever Richard used those terms in casual public settings, she felt uncomfortable and wanted to change the subject. She couldn't remember a time when she was the one reciting all this information, but obviously she had been listening when Richard gave his lectures.

Since they were still staring at her, she added a bit more information she had heard Richard deliver in talks over the years. "There's one other part to it. As with any addiction cycle, the addict believes he needs the high, the drug, to feel normal. It becomes a daily focus. A basic need. So when the original, entry-level high isn't enough, he looks for ways to intensify it. That's when a lot of perversion enters, and well, I'm sure I don't need to say any more. It's all around us and getting worse."

Carissa tried to think of how to put the lid back on this can of worms and conclude the subject so they could move on. "It can be treated. That's what my husband does. The cycle has to be broken and new cycles put in place. That's why it takes so long to recover. Usually five years. Old lies have to be replaced with truth. Some of my husband's clients have issues in their past that have never been addressed, and the pain from those issues is often what they're medicating."

"We know all about that," Joel said.

"Richard says the recovery process begins with forgiveness and healing. That's where he always starts. He's seen marriages restored and men's lives put back together after years of addiction."

Kai had been staring at her the whole time she was speaking. "He's right on. Forgiveness and healing. It has to start there. Your husband must be an extraordinary man."

"He is." Carissa didn't realize what she had said until the words were out of her mouth. It felt like a breakthrough moment for her, accepting her husband for who he was and what he did—and honoring him.

"May his tribe increase," Joel added.

The van had turned down what looked like a rarely traveled dirt road that cut through the middle of a grove. An abundance of tall, slender trees shaded the path, and exotic-sounding birds called to them as the van slowed and pulled up in front of a surprisingly well-maintained, white-washed chapel with a green, pointed roof. It felt as if they were entering a place that time had forgotten. Carissa noticed the scent of mold mixed with a lingering faint sweetness that hung in the air when they stopped and got out.

"This is the church Kai wanted you to see. Do you guys want to go inside?" Joel asked.

"Sure," Maile said.

Kai headed for the front door down the short path. "I'm sure my mom could tell you the entire history of this church and the names of the missionaries who came from New England and built it more than 150 years ago."

He tried the door. It was open. The four of them entered. The rows of wooden pews were painted deep green, and the simple altar at the front appeared not to have changed over the decades.

Kai took a seat in one of the pews, as if they had arrived for a special service. Maile and Joel sat in a pew across the row from him. Carissa quietly slipped into the row behind Kai and waited for whatever was supposed to happen next.

The silence inside the cool chapel covered them in the same way the soft air and the birdsong had covered them when they stepped out of the van. Around her, it seemed the others were resting their spirits in contemplation and quiet prayer. Carissa sat comfortably with them, settling into a long-forgotten place of reverence in her spirit.

She thought of how simple all this was: wooden benches, whitewashed walls, a roughly hewn pulpit. This be-still-and-know-that-I-am-God moment of quiet contemplation struck a sharp contrast to how complex church had become for her over the past few years.

Blake was young when they found a church all of them liked. Carissa and Richard became involved and helped on many levels to build up the small congregation. Blake made some close friends, as did Carissa and Richard. It was a good place for them to be for many years.

Then for a dozen small reasons it became exhausting to go to church. They were volunteering in too many areas. A new pastor came, and the church grew to three services, five on Christmas and Easter. Carissa and Richard withdrew from their volunteer commitments after Blake left home. They found they could go to any one of the services and not see a single person they knew or feel as if they received anything personal out of the message.

Their church stopped being a place of worship for Carissa. It was different here in this humble chapel, covered by the silence. No pictures flashed on large screens. No jokes were being told into lapel mikes. Here, the simplicity gave plenty of room for a worshipper to focus on God alone.

Reaching for the book resting on the uneven wooden shelf on the pew's back, Carissa discovered it wasn't a Bible but rather a hymnal. All the hymns were in Hawaiian. The English titles were listed in small print under the Hawaiian title on each page. Carissa thumbed through the pages, reading the English titles:

Abide with Me
God Will Take Care of You
Softly and Tenderly Jesus Is Calling
Safe in the Arms of Jesus
Savior, Like a Shepherd Lead Us
What a Friend We Have in Jesus

In the same way that she had felt God nudging her yesterday while she was having her luau-for-one under the camphor tree, she felt as if he was trying to show her, here in the hymns' titles, that he was with her. Right beside her. He wanted to be close. He wanted her to come close to him and to trust him.

She didn't want to deal with any of those thoughts at the moment. She still was processing her feelings about Richard and trying to understand what it meant that she had felt honored to talk about his occupation. Maybe the ongoing stresses in their marriage hadn't been Richard's doing. Maybe she had pulled back in small ways over the past few years that had added up to significant distance between them.

The others rose and filed out reverently. Carissa left the hymnal in the pew rack along with her thoughts on God's gentle nudgings. She followed the others out into the warm sunshine.

"There's a grave you might want to see," Kai said.

The extensive grounds were well maintained and felt alive with flowering trees and freshly mowed grass. Many of the stone grave markers were old and tilting, due to the expanding tree roots underneath them. The wide, grassy area where Kai led her was distinguished by a mound of gathered lava rocks. The memorial space was larger than other graves around it, and the flat marker was embedded in the mound of black rocks.

Kai dipped his chin as if indicating that she should read the marker and draw her own conclusion.

CHARLES A. LINDBERGH
BORN MICHIGAN 1902
DIED MAUI 1974

"IF I TAKE THE WINGS OF THE MORNING
AND DWELL IN THE UTTERMOST
PART OF THE SEA . . ."

"Charles Lindbergh? The famous aviator? He's buried here?"

"You've heard of him, then?"

"Of course."

"He came to Hana to live out his days in peace. My mom always says she wished that whoever put this verse on the grave marker would have finished the whole verse."

"Do you know the whole verse?"

Kai nodded. "I took it on as my life verse about five years ago. It's from Psalm 139. 'If I take the wings of the morning, and dwell in the uttermost part of the sea; even there your hand shall lead me, and your right hand shall hold me.'"

They could hear Joel and Maile laughing from where they had wandered over to the far side of the grassy expanse. A picnic table awaited revelers under a gathering of palm trees. Joel and Maile were acting out a sword fight with two dried palm fronds that had fallen to the ground. Beyond the picnic table was a chain-link fence that marked where the property apparently took a plunge to the ocean below. All that was visible from where Carissa stood was the expansive blue sky smeared with a few long, pale white clouds.

Kai kicked at the small rocks at the base of the grave marker. "I didn't tell you what my addiction is."

"You don't have to. I think it's really brave of Joel and Maile to speak up the way they did, but my husband says it's not always helpful for a person to let his struggle name him."

"Well, I don't let the addiction I've struggled with name me, but I also don't have any problem naming it. It's sexual addiction, your husband's area of expertise." Kai held up his hand. "And before you get embarrassed or try to cover up anything you said back in the van, you should know that everything you said was dead on. I wish I had known your husband about twenty years ago. I think I would have had a different life. I know my wife and daughters would have had different lives."

Carissa felt like she should say something, but she was too stunned and trying hard not to show it. It was the same feeling she had when she first watched Irene offer up her morning worship and Carissa realized she could be considered a Peeping Tom. It was also the way she had felt when she had sat in Dan and Irene's car in the empty church parking lot and she realized she had been the one who had abandoned God, not the other way around.

This time the chagrin was over the fear she felt when she thought about being around Richard's clients. On the night of the prowler, those deeply embedded fears had exploded and left her afraid to be alone at home, even though the house was equipped with alarms, locks, security lights, and a husband who vowed he was protecting her.

Yet here she was, by herself, in a remote area of a faraway island, and she had willingly traipsed off into the dark last night with a man who just told her he struggled with sexual addiction. For all she knew, Kai could be a predator. A pedophile. A convicted sex offender. He was the very sort of man she had insisted Richard protect her from.

Yet part of the reason she had made the journey all the way to the campground was because she was allowing herself to play with the idea of leaving her marriage. She had let herself consider "what if" she fell in love with Kai.

Carissa felt the need to sit down. She knew she had to say something in response to all that Kai had shared with her. Oddly, the only thought that came to mind was Irene's words: "Everything is redeemable."

Kai nodded. "That's what my mom likes to say, too. If it weren't for God and his extreme grace, I don't know what my life would be like now. I've been clean eight years. No convictions for inappropriate conduct, but all the stuff that's out there, so easily accessible, it's poison. But you know that. When I hit a really low point, I caved and started using it just like your husband said, as a drug. My wife wouldn't forgive me. She left, took our girls, and I just got worse after that."

Carissa wondered if Irene's wisdom to "stay" in a marriage had come from watching her son go through so much pain.

Kai drew in a deep breath and rounded back his shoulders. "Like I said, eight years clean. Your husband said it takes five to break the cycle, right? I think I'm there. I'm doing well. Really well. But I'm doing life without my wife and girls. I wish I hadn't messed up so bad, and I wish she could have stuck it out."

Carissa nodded. She was taking all this in—Kai's words, his pain, his humbled heart. For the first time since Richard had begun counseling men who struggled with sexual addiction, Carissa understood. Men like Kai were worth saving.

15

"Hola maika'i e pule ai!
Nau wau e hoohauoli mai
E mau me au a hiki mai
Ka hola a'u e waiho ai."

"Sweet hour of prayer! Sweet hour of prayer!
Thy wings shall my petition bear
To him whose truth and faithfulness
Engage the waiting soul to bless."

THAT EVENING THE CAMPGROUND was packed with weekend revelers. Their group now consisted of twenty-six people and three dogs and had turned into a carnival, complete with kites, horseshoes, and children's contagious laughter. Music blared from the campsites to the right and to the left of theirs. The dogs scrounged between the lawn chairs where the aunties were all lined up, chatting and calling out directions to the boisterous children and the circle of men, who stood around eating the spread of food that appeared on the picnic table.

The experience was completely different from the night before when the five of them had gathered at the table and talked story by candlelight. Tonight the meal was an ongoing feast, with interesting dishes that kept appearing.

Carissa tried a little of everything. Her favorite was the pulled pork, or *kalua* pig, as everyone called it, like the kind Mano had picked up at Da' Kitchen that first day. She tried some of the pungent bits of pink salmon that Joel told her was *lomi lomi,* and of course, Tony insisted she try some of the poi his wife brought in a small plastic bag.

"Like this." Tony opened the bag, inserted his first two fingers, quickly drew the gray, pastelike glob to his mouth, and said, "You try it."

She repeated his actions, only retrieving a dab of the goo and swallowing it before her mouth could ask what she was doing to it. With a long swig from her water bottle, she nodded her head and let her eyes convey to Tony that she thought it was "grrrrr-eat!" even though she could think of nothing in her life that had ever felt or tasted like that. She wasn't sure she needed to try any more.

As it grew dark, several camping lanterns were lit, and everyone pulled up a chair to fill in the circle. The stories that unfurled were mostly personal recountings. Everyone seemed to have a memory about someone else in the group, and each person took delight in telling the story with humor while the object of the tale took the friendly roasting in stride. The group had a great feeling of warmth and closeness. Carissa could see why Irene would want to come here twice each year to keep up this tradition.

For a while Carissa thought she had managed to remain invisible in the wide circle, but then the two teenage boys from the pool decided to talk story about their escapade that morning, and how they had to push one of the aunties out of the water.

"Like this." One of the skinny boys stood and used both hands with his palms open and his face demonstrating heroic exertion. "And we pushed and out she went."

The chuckles around the circle were good-natured.

Carissa decided she didn't mind being included in the story-telling. No names were uttered, no fingers were pointed. A young boy got to brag about his manners and his prowess. It was a good evening all the way around.

The trek to the outhouse was a different experience that night as well. While Carissa waited her turn for the facilities, two guys invited her to join their party at the far end of the campground. They told her they had lots of beer.

Carissa wanted to laugh. Obviously they were either too drunk to get a good look at her, or she was standing where it was too dark for them to see how old she was. All she said was, "Thanks for the invitation." They went on their way, apparently in search of more agreeable fellow revelers.

It took longer to fall asleep that night because of all the merriment going on around them.

"Are you still thinking of leaving early in the morning?" Irene asked from her side of the tent.

"Yes. Is that okay?"

"I'd like to go with you. Kai wants to stay longer, but I have to go back tomorrow because I travel to Oahu Monday."

"Is that for your lecture at the school?"

"Yes. I'm so tired tonight I can't imagine going to Oahu. But I didn't want to miss this."

"I can see why you would say that."

Irene didn't say anything for a few minutes. Then Carissa heard her name being called out softly from Irene's cot. "Carissa, would you consider something?"

"Okay, what is it?"

"Well, I was thinking how much I enjoyed the

swim with you today. It was such a lovely moment, wasn't it?"

"Yes, I loved it."

"I was wondering if you would consider coming with me. I'll buy your plane ticket. It's only for the day. You can see another island, and I would very much enjoy your company. You're a lovely woman, Carissa."

Carissa wasn't sure she wanted to give up an entire day to travel with Irene. Maybe Irene couldn't travel well alone and needed an assistant.

What am I thinking? I watched this woman navigate her way to the waterfall today! That was something even I wasn't sure I was brave enough to try.

"Sure," Carissa said. "I'll go with you."

"Good. You sleep on it. If you change your mind, perhaps I'll ask Mano."

Carissa smiled in the darkened tent. Now the little dearie definitely was playing her. Both of them knew that Mano wouldn't make the ideal traveling partner in a small plane to a school filled with teenagers. He would look like her personal bodyguard or bouncer.

"Good night, Irene."

The clever auntie giggled. "Good night."

The two of them were up at first light. Irene was joined by one other auntie in her contemplative morning praise with arms outstretched to the heavens. Carissa started to pack up Irene's belongings, but then Kai emerged from his tent, ready to head to the falls for a morning dip and convinced her to leave everything. He said he would take it all back for Irene.

With his voice low so as not to disturb the others in their camp who had stayed up far too late under the stars, he said, "Thanks for taking my mom back."

"It's no problem. I was planning to leave this morning anyway."

"It's been good having you here. I'm glad you came."

"Thanks for inviting me. I can see why all of you love it here. I would have missed so much if I hadn't come."

Kai leaned over and brushed an aloha kiss across her cheek. "Next time you come, bring your husband. I would like to spend some time with him."

So would I.

Carissa raised her palm to wave as Kai turned and headed toward the trail to the waterfalls. She realized the truth of her thought. She missed Richard.

Carissa had lots of time to sort and organize her thoughts about Richard on the long drive back to Kihei. Irene convinced Carissa to return the way she had come rather than go the longer and winding way.

"I'd prefer to go that way. We'll stop at the Kaupo Store to see Linda."

The Kaupo Store, similar to the ranch general store across from the up-country winery, was smaller and seemed to double as a museum for a variety of old items. As Irene chatted warmly with the shop's owner, Carissa took a self-guided tour of the shelves that displayed dusty old radios, vintage photographs, and rusted cooking utensils. If she hadn't felt like she had been in old Hawaii already, this stop would have done the trick.

Irene bought several fresh papayas, a faded postcard, some cans of iced green tea, and two frozen candy bars. Carissa selected a lei-style necklace made from delicate tiny shells and two paperback novels from the rack of books pertaining to local interests.

Linda hugged both women and sent them on their way with *"aloha nui loa,"* which Irene said meant "much love."

As Carissa hit the gravel road, she said, "You really can feel the love and closeness of friends here. At least I feel that way around you and everyone you know. Everyone shows such a sweet respect for each other."

"That's the aloha spirit." Irene's voice came out jiggly on the bumpy road. "Dan says it wasn't their idea first, though. The blueprint is right there in the book of First Corinthians. 'Love is patient and kind.'"

Carissa was familiar with the chapter. "We had that portion read at our wedding."

As if Irene hadn't heard Carissa, Irene kept quoting what were apparently her favorite parts. " 'Love does not demand its own way. Love is not irritable, and it keeps no record of when it has been wronged.' "

Carissa ventured another, "Yes, I know the verses," in an effort to stop Irene, but she kept going. " 'Love never gives up, never loses faith, is always hopeful, and endures through every circumstance. Love lasts forever. There are three things that will endure—faith, hope, and love— and the greatest of these is love.' "

Then, because Carissa didn't know any other way to respond to Irene's triumphant conclusion, she added a spontaneous, "Amen."

"Yes. Amen and *amene.*"

Those were the last words Irene spoke until they arrived back in Kihei, as if she didn't want to distract Carissa from her driving. Carissa navigated the bumpy terrain with less anxiety just having Irene silently keeping her company. Once they reached the smooth road, Irene nodded off, and Carissa drank in all the parts of this area she had enjoyed on her drive up the side of the volcano the other day. Maui was certainly an island of contrasts. She loved it here.

They were back at the house by noon, after leaving the campground shortly after sunrise. It felt luxurious not to have to unload or clean up any of the camping gear. Carissa made her way to the quiet little bungalow waiting for her, tucked away behind the banana trees. Instead of going inside, she sat in one of the high-backed rocking chairs on the front porch and eased her way into civilization.

When she had first arrived, Carissa had pictured herself spending long hours sitting in a rocking chair on the front porch reading or stretched out for days on end on one of the chaise longues on the back patio. So far she had read only a few chapters in one book out of her stack. She hadn't done nearly as much napping as she had expected. Now, with only a few days left, she wished she hadn't agreed to go to Oahu in the morning with Irene.

Pulling her cell phone from her purse, she saw the battery had gone dead. No surprise. Unlocking the front door and going inside, Carissa plugged in her phone and went around opening all the windows to let in the welcoming breeze. She drank a tall glass of iced tea from the refrigerator and went to the shower, where memories of the waterfall shower from the day before came back to her when she closed her eyes.

As she lathered up the shampoo, she thought through all that had happened since she had arrived. Everything seemed purposeful. Directed.

What was it that Dr. Walters said when he told me to come? Something about how God would meet me there or that God was already here.

She thought about how Dr. Walters's words had been accurate. Back at home she had dreamed in the hammock that she was drifting toward a desirable haven. Now, during her visit here, she knew her shipwrecked life had floated toward a place of peace in her own spirit. She wasn't there yet, but she could see the desired cove more clearly than last week, when everything seemed to capsize at once.

Fresh from the shower, dressed in clean clothes that didn't smell like organic mosquito repellent or smoke from the grill, Carissa made a bite to eat and took her partially recharged phone out to the back patio. She stretched out on the padded lounge chair and listened to her voice messages.

The first one was from her mother. "I hope you know that Heidi and I are trying very hard not to be too jealous of you. We wished you had let us know about this free condo you were given for the week because she and I would have come with you."

Carissa bit into a baby carrot and murmured, "And what a different trip this would have been!"

Her mother's voice concluded her wee-bit-woebegone message with, "Before you leave I hope you have one of those fruity drinks with a little paper parasol. As you drink it, think of your mother, who hopes she gets a chance to go to Hawaii someday."

"Sorry, Mom. I do hope you get to come. But I'm so glad you didn't come this time."

Carissa deleted the message. She noted that her mom didn't say anything about Carissa's job loss. Somehow her conversations with her mother focused more and more on what her mother needed or was going through and less and less on Carissa's life. She didn't know when that life shift had happened. Probably it had come gradually, like most of the other shifts in her life.

At least she didn't tell me I needed hormone therapy, the way Heidi did.

Her next voice message was from the dentist, reminding her of her six-month cleaning appointment on Monday. Carissa returned the call and left a message that she couldn't make it and would have to reschedule. It took everything within her not to add: "Because I'm in Maui and won't be home by then."

The next message was from Richard. "Hi. I'm at my hotel now and was hoping you could talk. I know you said you might not have service. Listen, Carissa, I have to say, I'm not quite sure what to do with our situation. I'm not tracking with you. The fact that you said you're camping . . . it's not adding up for me. That isn't like you. So I guess I just need to ask the hard question.

Did you go to Maui to meet up with someone? Are you having an affair?"

Carissa dropped the bowl of carrots and watched them roll across the cement.

"I'll wait for you to call me back. If you don't want to talk about this until you get home, then I guess we'll have to wait to talk it through then. I'm just pretty much at a loss as to what's going on with you."

Carissa couldn't believe her husband's message. How could he have reached such a conclusion?

She called him back immediately and listened to the greeting on his voice mail. "Richard, listen. I didn't have phone service for the last few days, but I'm back at the cottage now, and everything you were imagining isn't true. I'm not with anyone. I didn't meet anyone over here. And about the camping trip, it wasn't that unusual, really. It's something I wanted to do. If you were over here, it would have made sense to you. Everything is okay. Or at least I hope it's okay. It is with me. I hope you're okay. I think we can get through this. I think we can work things out."

The allotted message time ended, and Carissa hung up. She pictured Richard in Denver, trying to give important presentations yet all the while wondering if she was being faithful to him. She felt horrible for him and felt guilty for having even entertained those fleeting unfaithful thoughts about Kai.

Why did I seek the attention of a man—of Kai—when I felt so unsettled with Richard? Did I think Kai could somehow comfort me? I guess I wanted to know that, if my marriage was over, I would have someone who would be there for me. Not just someone. A man. A caring man, whose broad shoulder I could cry on.

Aloud, Carissa spoke a truth she hadn't let herself ever admit before. "I want my father."

A lifetime of longing was wrapped up in that statement. But the truth was, she couldn't have what she wanted.

In the midst of that poignant reality came an unexpected assurance that rested on her. The assurance made no sense. It was simple. She could name the desire, even if she couldn't have it. She could acknowledge the loss and know that it never would be fulfilled by the earthly human who had abandoned her.

However . . .

Ke Akua. The Hawaiian name for God came to her clearly, as if she already knew him by that name. She couldn't have what she wanted, but she could have God, and he would be to her the Father she longed for.

"Ke Akua," she whispered.

That was as far as she got in her prayer. Her phone rang the customized ring she knew was Richard's.

16

"Mamua ke ku nei ka pae pu'u
He kino mai ka honua
Mai kino hi 'oe e ke Akua
A mau loa ano."

"Before the hills in order stood
Or earth received her frame
From everlasting thou art God
To endless years the same."

CARISSA REACHED FOR HER phone and noticed her hand was trembling slightly. "Richard?"

"Hi."

"Hi." Carissa switched the phone to her other ear so she could hear better. "How are you doing?"

"I've been better."

Her heart fluttered nervously.

"Did you get my message?"

"No. I just saw that you called. I have to be on a panel at a workshop in ten minutes."

"I won't keep you then. I just wanted you to know that I didn't come here to be with anyone. What you said in your last message, there's no truth to it. I'm not having an affair. Not at all." Carissa wished she could see his face. She would know what he was thinking. Moreover, he would be able to see her face and read all the hurt and uncertainty she had been struggling with. He would know that while her heart had been confused and wobbly, she had been true to him.

"I appreciate your telling me that." His voice turned tender. He sounded relieved. "Everything has been so unlike you lately—the secretiveness, the lack of communication. I haven't been able to figure out what's going on."

She knew it drove him crazy when he couldn't diagnose a lineup of symptoms. To help him out, she said, "I'm struggling with some stuff. I'm not sure I can even explain what it is exactly, but I'm working on it."

As vulnerable as she wanted to be with her husband, she would prefer to say these deeper things when they were together, face-to-face.

"I've been working through some issues as well. Listen, like I said to you a few days ago before your phone cut out, I'm sorry I wasn't more sensitive to you the night the police came to the house. You were right. I should have thought of you first and done what I could to make you feel protected."

Her eyes teared up. "I know. I'm sorry I shut you out and stopped communicating. I shouldn't have pulled back the way I did."

"I understand. You were hit with a lot all at once. I don't think I did a very good job of being there for you. I wasn't very patient. Will you forgive me?"

"Yes. Will you forgive me for shutting you out?"

"Of course."

Carissa swiped at the tears that were now trickling down her cheeks.

"I know you and I have a lot more to talk through . . ." He paused, and she could picture him checking his watch. "I have to go. I hope you believe me when I tell you that I love you. I've always loved you."

"I love you, too. I wish I were with you right now. Better yet, I wish you were here with me on Maui."

"Believe me, I do, too. I have to go. I'll call you later."

"Okay. Love you."

"I love you, too."

Closing her phone and leaning back in the lounge chair, Carissa released a deep breath. She felt lighter. Calmer. Happier and more at rest than she had been the whole time on the island. She felt loved.

Under that covering of returning contentment, she closed her eyes and settled into the sort of slumber she had hoped to experience since the day she had arrived. When she woke from her nap, the first thing she saw was a small brown bird with a bright red face and top feather, pecking at one of the carrots on the patio. She didn't move. The bird twisted its head, looking at her, then back at the carrot, then back at her.

With a flit, the bird left, apparently disinterested in the carrot now that Carissa was awake.

"I have a few goodies that might interest you more than a carrot," she said.

Going inside the cottage, she plugged her phone back in to let it recharge and went through her food stash, pulling out a piece of bread as well as some cookies. Back to the patio she went. From the lounge chair, she crumpled up the bread into crumbs and tossed it near the carrot.

"I have cookies." She crumbled up the cookies and sprinkled them on the ground.

Three birds came hopping in from the shrubs and poked around at the crumbs, nibbling their treat.

I wish I could write a poem about how it feels to be on the mend with Richard, to be in Hawaii feeding the birds.

She tried to compose a few lines in her head but didn't get anywhere. She couldn't think of a flattering word that rhymed with "birds." Settling instead on reading one of the books from her to-be-read stack, Carissa went back inside. She gathered up the books, more iced tea, and a plate of cookies, which she planned to share with her new fine-feathered friends.

A text came through on her phone while she stood in the kitchen. She checked and saw it was from Ruthie. She hadn't told her friend from work that she was going to Maui, either. Instead of calling back now and trying to explain everything, she sent a text promising to call her in a few days. The best part about Ruthie was that she would understand the simplicity in the message and know that Carissa was doing okay.

When Richard called back two hours later, he sounded much better than when he had phoned earlier.

"How did the panel discussion go?"

"Much better than I expected. One of the specialists for the NWCA was in the audience. Afterward, he asked if I could meet him in the morning for coffee before my flight goes out."

Carissa assumed that was a good thing. She had given up long ago trying to decipher what all the abbreviations stood for in Richard's long list of organizations and associations.

"I'm so glad you called me before I had to go up on that panel," he said. "What you told me took a heaviness off me."

"I feel the same way. I know we have a lot to figure out, but I don't ever want to go into that deep valley again."

"We need to communicate," he said adamantly.

"I know."

"So, can you explain this camping trip to me? That part still has me mystified."

Carissa relayed the highlights to Richard,

starting with why the adventure appealed to her. She told him about the elk burger and the difficult drive over the rocky road and how the stars looked at night. She told him what she loved the most was swimming in the pools with Irene. She talked about Kai, Tony, and Joel and about the visit to Lindbergh's grave.

Then, because her heart was so open to her husband at that moment and she felt it was best to tell him everything, she did something she couldn't remember ever doing before. "Richard, you know how sometimes over the years you've told me when you're struggling with inappropriate thoughts toward another woman?"

"Yes."

"You've said in the past that you tell me what you're thinking so that it diffuses the potential of what might happen if those thoughts went unchecked."

"Right."

"Well, I don't think I've ever made the same sort of confession to you, but I need to do that now. When we were camping, I opened my thoughts to the possibility of what it would be like to be romantically involved with Kai."

Carissa paused. She couldn't believe she was saying this to her husband. But as she spoke it, the already withered fantasy turned into dust and dissipated with a puff. She understood why Richard had made that sort of confession to her in the past. Honesty and transparency were powerful dragon slayers.

All the potential went out of the possibility when the truth was pulled out of the darkness and set up in the light.

"And did anything happen between you and Kai?"

"No. Nothing happened. And I'm certain the fleeting attraction was on my part only. The crazy thing was that the next day, after I had some of those inklings, Kai shared with me that he helps lead a recovery group at his church. He said he struggled with sexual addiction and had been clean for eight years."

"He offered that information to you?"

"Not right away. I was talking about you, about what you do, and I kind of got going on some of the stuff you talk about in your lectures. He came to me privately afterward and said that everything I was quoting from you was right on. Kai said he wished he had met you twenty years ago. He would have had a different life."

Richard's end of the phone was quiet for a moment before he asked, "What did you tell him?"

"He said you must be an exceptional man, and I said that you were. And Richard? I felt really proud of you. Proud of who you are and proud of what you do."

Again his end of the phone was quiet.

"Are you still there?"

"I'm here." His voice was softer. "I can't

remember hearing you say those sorts of things for a long time, Carissa. Thank you."

"I meant what I said."

"I believe you. Now I need to confess something to you. I had a hard time my first night here with the options on the television in my hotel room. I rented a movie, thinking that it would be okay, but it turned out to be pretty vile."

"What did you do?"

"I turned it off and ate all the salty food in the minibar. I have to tell you, I paid way too much for a bunch of peanuts and a candy bar."

Carissa smiled. "I love you."

"I love you, too. I've really missed you."

"I've missed you, too."

Their conversation continued another ten minutes as they exchanged sweet verbal affections before her phone beeped. "My battery is running low. I think I'm going to need a new phone battery pretty soon."

"Call me later if you can."

"Okay, I will. I love you."

"I love you."

When she hung up, she felt a small ache of separation that she hadn't experienced since she was a teenager and her mom had put her on phone restriction. Her mother had decided during Carissa's senior year that Carissa and Richard were spending too much time on long, "moonie" phone conversations.

According to her mother, that was the time for Carissa to focus on her studies and pull up her grades as best she could. Even though Carissa's plans were to go to community college, and her grades had been just fine to sail her through admissions, her mother was on a kick to prepare her children for lucrative careers so they would never be dependent on a man for their livelihood the way she had been.

What Carissa's mom didn't know was that Richard and Carissa had privately promised themselves to each other. They attended different high schools; so every evening during those long, moonie conversations they were planning their engagement announcement and subsequent wedding.

Carissa thought about how hard it had seemed back then to wait until they could be together fully, as man and wife. They had promised each other they would go no further than kissing while they were dating, which felt like torture at the time. All further expressions of intimacy, they decided, were saved for marriage.

With no encouragement from either set of parents, Carissa and Richard's track record stayed commendably on target. They reached their goal and entered their honeymoon with an innocence and fulfillment of pleasure that was far beyond their hopes.

That choice so many years ago seemed to be

more significant now than she had ever realized. She and Richard had never been with anyone else. That single-hearted focus might have helped both of them during this brief season of separation to remain faithful to each other.

Carissa was about to return to her book when her phone rang again. Richard's ring. She grinned and hurried over to the counter in the kitchen where the phone was plugged in.

"Hello. So it's you again," she said in a playful voice.

"I miss you."

She laughed. "Is that what you called to tell me?"

"Yes. I miss you. Are you sure you don't want to come home tomorrow?"

"I don't know how much it would cost to change my flight. Besides, I agreed to go to Oahu tomorrow with Irene. Did I tell you that?"

"No. What's that all about?"

She reviewed the details about Irene and her love of Hawaiian history and that Dan was on the mainland so Carissa had agreed to accompany Irene.

He had one question for her after she went through the specifics. "Is Kai going?"

"No. Seriously, Richard, you don't have to worry about him. Not at all."

"He's struggling with the same issues my clients wrestle with. I know what goes on in his mind.

You're a beautiful woman, Carissa. I would never forgive myself if anything happened to you."

Inwardly she felt the embers of her love for Richard warming into a nice glow. Those were the words she had longed to hear from him during the time of their disconnection. For him to give them to her now meant that they were in his heart, even if he hadn't expressed them when she needed them most. In her heart, she felt the stirrings of new love.

New love with an old husband.

"So what are you going to do tonight?" he asked.

"I need to check with Irene and see what time we have to leave in the morning. I also thought I might walk on the beach."

"Then I hope you take advantage of it and enjoy your final days. Take a picture of the sunset for me."

"Okay, I will."

Carissa decided to do more than just walk on the beach at sunset. She changed into her bathing suit, borrowed Irene's car, and drove down. The beach was filled with groups having picnics. She slid past all of them and went in the water at the same place she had gone in earlier that week for her morning swim.

The water felt different at dusk. It was warm and languid, as if even the waves were slowing down just a bit at the end of the day. Ducking all the way under and stretching her arms and legs, Carissa swam with renewed vigor.

Hope is a wonderful thing. And love. Love is so powerful. I can't believe how different I feel since Richard and I talked. I wish he were here.

As soon as the sun began to make its exit, Carissa emerged from the water and sat on the shore, wrapped in a beach towel, and took pictures. She wouldn't call it a stunning sunset. There were so many clouds on the horizon the sun seemed to disappear without turning them into the mauve and tangerine shades that she expected would mark every tropical sunset.

When she pulled Irene's car back into the garage, the gas tank was filled. She had also run it through a car wash.

Entering through the back door into the kitchen, she called out a hello.

Irene was seated at the table, busily writing with a pen, copying something from one of her many history books.

"I wanted to check to see what time we need to leave in the morning."

"Five."

"Seriously?"

Irene turned and looked at Carissa over the top of her glasses. "Do you want to change your mind about going?"

"No. I just didn't expect it to be so early. I'll be ready."

Carissa noticed a pan of water on the stove that had boiled down to almost nothing.

"Did you want to have this pan on the stove? The heat is still on."

"Oh dear, I completely forgot. I was going to make some noodles." Irene started to get up, pressing both hands on the table and appearing to have quite a bit of difficulty standing.

"Why don't you let me do this? You can finish up whatever you need to do there."

Irene lowered herself back into the chair. "That would be wonderful. I'm afraid I got caught up in trying to track down a missing detail in Ka'ahumanu's life."

Irene shuffled her notes as Carissa filled the pan with fresh water and went to work making some dinner for both of them.

"I'm trying to conclude the account of what happened at the end of her life," Irene said. "She had spent her final years traveling around the islands with the missionaries, assisting them by preaching her little heart out. After she came to faith in Christ, Ka'ahumanu's efforts for good among her people were tireless. She changed laws, cared for the sick, and fought to keep seamen from taking young Hawaiian girls off with them when they left port."

"Is it okay if I use these vegetables in the sink?" Carissa asked.

"Yes. I picked them from the garden to go with the noodles. Have you eaten yet?"

"No."

"Please join me. I have plenty."

"Thanks."

"Now, with the story, when Ka'ahumanu knew she was dying, she was carried to her house in the cool Manoa Valley. There she was placed on a bed made from fragrant maile leaves and ginger, covered with a piece of velvet cloth. One of the missionaries, Hiram Bingham, came to her with the first copy of the printed Hawaiian New Testament. It took twelve years to complete the translation because the Hawaiian language had never been transposed into a written language. The missionaries had to start by composing an alphabet. In the end, the Hawaiian alphabet consisted of only twelve letters—a, e, i, o, u, h, k, l, m, n, p, and w."

Irene looked over at Carissa. "I got off track, didn't I? What was I saying?"

"Ka'ahumanu was dying, and someone brought her a Bible."

"Yes, that's right. The first New Testament translated to the Hawaiian language. The work had just been completed. She examined it carefully and then wrapped it in her handkerchief. She clasped the Bible to her chest and pronounced it *mai ka'i*, which is the most tender way of saying 'good.' She was asked her dying thoughts and she said, 'Oh, my friends, have great patience, stand firm on the side of the good way.' Then a little later she raised her hands and in a clear voice she repeated two lines from a native hymn. *'Eia no au, e Iesu, E. E nana oluolu mai.'"*

"And what does that mean in English?"

"It means, 'Here am I, O Jesus. Oh, look this way in compassion.' " Irene had tears in her eyes. "Such a tenderness from such a strong woman who had started her days with a haughty spirit."

The water was boiling. Carissa put the flat, long noodles in and stirred them slowly. "That is remarkable."

"Yes, she was a remarkable woman. Now, if only I could find this one missing piece."

"What's that?"

"I can't find the hymn she quoted anywhere. I found that it was based on Psalm 51 and was an original Hawaiian hymn, not an English hymn translated into Hawaiian. But I can't find the source."

"I'm not sure it will matter to the students tomorrow," Carissa said cautiously. "They'll just want to hear the stories. That's what they'll remember."

Irene put down her pen and leaned back. "You're right. All the exact details are important to me. The students will just want to hear the stories. Yes, thank you."

Carissa had chopped the fresh vegetables and had them steaming now as she strained the noodles and poured them into bowls. "Are you feeling nervous about tomorrow?"

"A little." Irene smiled shyly at Carissa. "I'm glad you're coming with me."

Scooping the steamed vegetables over the noodles, she carried the two bowls over to Irene and sat beside her. "You'll do great tomorrow. I know you will."

"And if I don't do so well, you might hear me crying out, 'Here am I, O Jesus. Oh, look this way in compassion.'"

Carissa smiled, and the two of them enjoyed their simple meal.

A short time later, Carissa cut through the Garden of Eatin' on her way back to the cottage. Around her echoed the lush night sounds of the garden. She stopped beside the banana trees and looked up to see how the pudgy-fingered bananas were coming along. She was thinking about making some banana bread tomorrow night when they returned from Oahu.

What she saw made her stop and catch her breath.

17

"Ho 'ola nani
Haku o na lahui
He Akua no na kanaka pu."

"Fair is the sunshine,
Fairer still the moonlight,
And all the twinkling starry host."

THE PLUMP MAUI MOON hung overhead, looking fuller and closer than ever. It wasn't like the half-moon that had stared unblinkingly at her when she had first arrived. Nor was it the mysterious floating moon that had cast its waving ribbon of light on the ocean when she was camping.

This moon was stronger and brighter and was beaming at her. Carissa lingered under the glow. If *Ke Akua* was looking down tonight, she wanted to make sure he saw her. And somehow, she knew he did.

Carissa felt as if her relationship with God had returned to its most elemental level. She was a child. His child. It was like the sign on Dan and Irene's front door: "Two of God's Children."

A lulling trade wind rustled the shaggy palm fronds and played with the loose ends of Carissa's hair. She drew in a deep breath. A faint sweetness floatcd on the air. Taking off her sandals, she sunk her bare feet into the damp grass. Lifting her arms as she had seen Irene do not far from this same spot in the garden, Carissa raised her head and softly cried out, "Here am I, O Jesus. Oh, look this way in compassion."

If she had known how to say Ka'ahumanu's final words in Hawaiian, Carissa would have. All she remembered was how to say God's name in Hawaiian so she repeated it to him as a starting point of her reconciliation with her heavenly Father. *"Ke Akua, Ke Akua."*

It sounded to her as if she were calling out, "Daddy, Daddy," and waiting for him to gather up her spirit and hold her close to his heart. Then she realized he had never let go. She knew he had always been with her. He hadn't abandoned her, as she had realized earlier that week. She had abandoned him.

Now she wanted to come back. She didn't know exactly what to say or do next, so she stood there, staring at the moon, caught up in the sense of holiness that pervaded this garden. Was it enough that she had expressed her thoughts to him, or did she need to pray?

Her reflections drifted off on the trade winds and slipped through the fronds of the palm trees overhead. She felt pulled toward the moon. Drawn closer, like the tides. She wanted to sleep here, in the garden, under the watchful, protective glow.

Maybe tomorrow night, when I don't have to set the alarm to wake up so early. I could pull one of the padded lounge chairs out here and sleep under the silver moonlight.

Softly padding her barefoot way back to the cottage, Carissa got ready for bed. She called Richard from under the comfy covers while the ceiling fan slowly stirred the air above her.

It was very late for him, and he had been asleep, but he listened patiently as Carissa told him about the moon and the impressions she felt. It had been a long time since she had shared anything with Richard about her relationship with God. She could tell Richard was listening carefully.

He responded with kindness and affirmations about everything she was expressing to him. It was the most intimate talk they had shared in months. Maybe years. She wished he were beside her in this big, beautiful bed and not far across the sea. She wanted him close to her.

She tried to go even deeper and express how she saw that she was the one who had abandoned God. He had not abandoned her the way her father had.

Then, for the first time, she recounted to Richard what had happened the night her father left. How he had pulled his clothes from the closet and never even looked back at her or Heidi. She told her husband how it made her feel and all the fears from that moment that she had carried these many years.

Richard was a gentle listener. His responses drew the last drops of the deepest poison from her soul. He understood. She took her time crying through all her feelings from that long-ago moment. And she knew she would never need to cry about it again. She felt cleansed. Once she got it all out, she felt free.

Exhausted but feeling lightened, Carissa exchanged several "I love you's" back and forth with her husband, and their night rendezvous came to a close. Carissa turned off the light, snuggled under the covers, luxuriating in a surrounding sense of peace.

She fell asleep easily enough, but it wasn't so easy to wake up when her alarm pierced the darkness at 4 A.M. She had such a limited wardrobe with her that it made her choice of what to wear easy.

Irene was ready when Carissa entered by the sliding patio door. They drove to the airport without much conversation and not much traffic in either direction. Carissa parked the car, carried in their things, and had no problems checking in or boarding for their short, interisland flight.

Carissa took the window seat, from which she had a great view of the water and islands, as they soared over them. She thought of Charles Lindbergh and what it must have been like to be a pioneer in aviation and to be among a small number of observers who viewed such sights from a small plane.

Irene tried to reach for her tote bag, which was tucked under the seat in front of her. She wasn't having much success.

"Here, I'll get it for you." Carissa pulled out the bag and handed it to her. "Are you going to do a last-minute review of your notes?"

"Yes. Can you hand me the binder? I want to make sure I have everything in order. I didn't recheck it last night."

Irene took the binder from Carissa and opened to the first page. "What's this?"

"Is it the right binder?"

"Yes, but . . . oh, that man!"

Carissa looked at the paper that occupied the first-page position in Irene's binder of history notes. While Carissa didn't want to pry, she saw writing in the form of a poem, which made it doubly difficult for her to not want to invite herself to read it.

Irene held the binder closer and read slowly, her lips moving as she read through the poem.

"Oh, that man," she repeated. Then she patted her moist cheeks with the palm of her hand. "When did he manage to slip that in there?"

"What is it?"

"It's a poem. He started it years ago and never finished it. He apparently found the ending that had eluded him all these years. When I wasn't looking, he put it in the binder. Oh, that man."

The tears came back in a steady stream, as Irene held out the binder to Carissa.

"Are you sure?"

"Yes. You'll appreciate it."

Carissa felt as if she were being offered a glimpse of what two hearts look like after sharing life together for fifty-two years.

A Touch of Paradise

A touch of paradise is all I ask
To lift my spirit high.
A trade-wind breeze about my knees
A gray dove's gentle cry.
The push of a swim, the burning sun
Fish beneath the sea
Love was there and friends were there
To keep me company.

Sun-flecked blue, fishnet globe,
Buoyant in the ocean's foaming swell
Awesome breakers consuming coral reefs,
A story long to tell.
Starlit nights with tropic song
That dances to its grace
The strings of life come pulsing back
To show my Father's face.

And when it's gone my heart will ache
For Islands' perfumed air
May I walk with you again,
Wild jasmine in your hair?

Now Carissa was teary-eyed, too. She reached over and slipped her hand into Irene's. Such love. Such a beautiful reward for a lifetime of faithfulness. She could picture Irene as a young woman with wild jasmine in her hair. She could see Dan walking with her on the beach hand in hand.

"It's beautiful," Carissa said quietly.

"I know."

As the plane was coming in for a landing in Honolulu, Carissa thought of Richard. She wanted to believe their marriage could be A Touch of Paradise after fifty-two years as well.

The two women waited for most of the plane to empty before Irene got her cane in place and started down the aisle. They were greeted at the exit by a petite blonde woman who was wearing a beautiful purple floral muʻumuʻu. She held two intricate yellow leis and presented the first one to Irene with hugs and kisses and much aloha.

Irene introduced Carissa to Catherine, and the sweet woman presented Carissa with the other lei. Catherine's warm greeting was followed by a kiss into the air next to Carissa's cheek.

"I'm so glad you were able to come, Carissa." Catherine was already in motion, walking toward the parking lot. "This is going to be such an honor for our students. I don't know if Irene explained to you that I'm a teacher at the school. I met Irene at a luncheon for an organization we belong to, the Daughters of Hawai'i. That was several years ago. I have been so eager to have her come talk to our students."

Carissa tried to slow down the pace because she was sure Irene was having difficulty keeping up.

"We'll meet with Kahu Kalama first. He's our chaplain. He'll offer the invocation for the chapel and introduce you, Irene. You'll have thirty-five minutes for your presentation. If we have time afterward, we would love to have questions and answers, but if there's not time, that's okay."

"Did you receive a copy of my notes?" Irene asked.

"Yes. I gave copies of the summary to all the teachers, and they were very appreciative. It looks like it's going to be a fantastic talk. I can't remember anyone ever coming to talk about Ka'ahumanu. The students are in for quite a treat, I'm sure."

"How many students will come to the assembly?" Carissa asked.

"We have two assemblies with about 450 to 500 students in each. You'll have a twenty-minute break in between." She unlocked the door of her car with the remote keypad and opened the front passenger's door for Irene.

As they drove away from the airport, one of the first big differences Carissa noticed between Maui and Oahu was that Oahu had freeways with overpasses and on-ramps. It felt like a different place from Maui, even though the terrain and foliage of the two islands were the same.

"Do you need anything?" Catherine asked. "We'll have water for you up at the podium. And we have some snacks in the back room. But let me know if either of you would like anything else. Kahu Kalama wanted to meet with you first. We start right on time at the school so it's great that your flight was on time."

The approach to the school grounds was breathtaking. The campus was spread out across a deep green hillside with amazing views all the way to the ocean. When they drove past the guard booth, Carissa felt as if she were being invited onto the private grounds of an expansive resort. This wasn't the sort of school ground she had ever seen before. Catherine explained how the land, more than six hundred acres, had been donated by a member of Hawaiian royalty, Princess Bernice Pauahi Bishop. Her request was that the land be used for a school for native Hawaiian children and that children from all the islands board at the school.

Kahu Kalama, an older man with glasses, was warm and friendly and expressed his appreciation to Irene for coming. As the four of them crowded into his back office, the dark-haired chaplain said, "Irene, I have a special gift I want to give you." He picked up a rectangular-shaped box from his desk and handed it to her.

Before she opened the box he said, "When I started here as a chaplain almost thirty years ago, this was given to me. I was told that one day I would pass it on to another who would bring light to our people. Please, open it."

Irene lifted the lid on the box and took out a lei made of what looked like shiny black nuts strung with faded yellow ribbon. Strung in between each black nut was a very small box that looked as if it were made from woven grass.

"The boxes represent gifts, and of course, as you know, the *kukui* nuts were the source of oil for ancient Hawaiian lamps so the nuts represent light. Irene, you are using your gift of story to bring light to our people. One day you, too, will pass this lei on to another."

He held out his hands, and Irene gave him the lei. In turn, he placed it over her head. For the second time that morning Carissa watched as the demure woman received a gift that touched Irene's heart and caused her to cry. She looked radiant. Radiant and ready to give the students a beautiful story.

Carissa felt honored to be part of all this. They were ushered into the front of the Bishop Chapel that was built in the heart of the campus in 1988. The huge chapel was like nothing Carissa had ever seen. The walls and the pews were made of dark wood and polished to such a shine it almost looked as if they were wet or covered with a coat of clear gloss. The rounded shape of the chapel gave Carissa the feeling of being safe and covered. Held in the hollow of God's hand.

The students were arriving with surprisingly hushed voices. Their respect added to the feeling of sacredness inside the chapel. All of them wore uniforms.

When the chapel was full, the chaplain stepped to the podium and said something in Hawaiian. Immediately all the students stood, making very little noise. Carissa helped Irene up, and they stood with their hands folded in front of them. The chaplain spoke again in Hawaiian, and one of the students, a young man, came and stood beside him. Squaring his shoulders, the young man raised his voice and spoke several lines in Hawaiian, projecting the words over the heads of the other students.

They responded by chanting back to him in unison. It was beautiful. Like a wave of words rushing forward and then receding, waiting for the lone call of the young man onstage. A second time the students spoke together in harmony, pressing their response forward to the front and pulling back on the last few words.

Carissa felt her heart beating faster. It was as if the words had covered her, like the ocean, pulling her all the way into this moment and immersing her in a sense of being drawn in and welcomed to this experience.

Kahu Kalama spoke again, and everyone was seated. Irene was introduced, and with only a little help, she made her way up to the front. Earlier she had been fitted with a lapel mike, which Carissa now saw was a good idea because, since Irene was so petite, the podium would have hidden her completely, if she stood behind it. This way she could stand next to the podium and keep her hand on it for support.

Without hesitation, Irene made eye contact with the students and submerged herself in her story the way she had lowered herself into the waterfall pool—fearlessly. Once she was in, she moved about with grace and agility.

"I want to tell you the story of a surfer girl who was 100 percent Hawaiian. She learned to surf the long boards off the Kohala Coast and was known as a graceful and agile surfer. She was called a flirt and had elegant tattoos on her legs, left palm, and even one on her tongue. One night she swam five miles in shark-infested waters to be with the man she loved."

All the students had fixed their attention on Irene.

"This surfer girl was six feet tall. Her name was Ka'ahumanu."

The students quietly murmured and exchanged glances. Carissa guessed that they thought at first Irene was talking about a modern surfer girl, but they definitely recognized Ka'ahumanu's name when they heard it.

For the next twenty-five minutes, Irene held them spellbound as she rolled out story after story about this amazing woman. Several of the stories Carissa hadn't heard yet. The students were transfixed as Irene told them how Ka'ahumanu changed the old laws, forbade the young girls to swim out to the ships, and outlawed the killing of babies.

Every eye was on Irene, as she talked about the showdown with the priestess, who came to Lahaina with the message from Pele.

One story that caused the students to laugh was when Irene described how Ka'ahumanu resisted the missionaries' teachings at first and how she deliberately went surfing on Sunday morning while church service was going on.

"One Sunday, after the proper missionaries returned to the main house after service, Ka'ahumanu came by for a visit. Still dripping with salt water, she draped her large frame all the way across the missionaries' upholstered settee. The missionaries didn't know where to look because, as Lucy Thurston wrote of the experience, 'She came as if from Eden, in the dress of innocence.' "

The students quickly caught on as to what that meant and exchanged naughty looks and giggles.

"Her relationship with the missionaries changed, though. At one church service she attended, Charles Stewart was preaching on the passage, 'Thy Word is a lamp unto my feet.' Suddenly Ka'ahumanu wailed in the tradition of ancient Hawaiian mourners, *'Auwe!'*"

The sound that came from tiny Irene surprised the students, but it especially startled Carissa. It was a sound of despair and deep loss.

"Pastor Stewart had to stop the service. He asked her to tell him what was wrong. This is what she said." Irene turned, as she had a number of times, to the pages in the binder and read in a powerful voice, as if she were demonstrating the force of Ka'ahumanu. "'We were all in thick darkness. We wandered here, and we wandered there, and stumbled on this side and on that side and were hastening to the dreadful precipice down which our fathers have fallen.'

"Charles Stewart later wrote that he began to see changes in her such as a softened state of feeling, in her countenance, manners, dress, and whole deportment."

Looking up from the papers she was reading, Irene said to the students, "I believe that was the beginning of Ka'ahumanu's conversion to Christianity. She learned to read and write the Hawaiian language. One day during lessons she wrote a message on her slate and read it aloud."

Irene paused. She shifted her weight on her cane and seemed to be catching her breath. Carissa realized Irene had been going strong for a long time, standing with her cane. It seemed as if she were looking for a quote to read from her notes but couldn't locate it.

Instead, rallying her strength and heading for the conclusion of the story, Irene picked up with the details she had relayed to Carissa the night before about Ka'ahumanu being on her deathbed and receiving the first New Testament and then reciting the words of the native hymn.

With perspiration glistening on her forehead and her voice fading, Irene held up her notes and concluded with an admirable push of strength. "David Malo wrote of her passing, and these are the final lines of his chant:

" *'Lilo aku la I ka paia ku a Kane,*
I ke ala muki maawe ula a Kanaloa,
Keehikulani aku la ka hele ana.' "

" 'She has gone from us, to the courts of Kane,
Treading royally the red-streaked path of the
    rosy dawn
the misty, broken road to Kanaloa.
An ebbing tide flows out.' "

Looking out over the gathering of students with a calm and steady gaze, Irene said, "Ka'ahumanu is a woman of your history. She was born in a cave on Maui and died on a bed of maile leaves not far from where we stand right now. She . . ."

Irene seemed to have lost her train of thought.

She glanced at her papers and then back at the students. "This is . . ."

Carissa thought Irene didn't look well. Her coloring had changed. She seemed confused, as if she had more to say, but she couldn't remember what it was.

Quickly getting up from the front pew, Carissa went to the steps at the side of the stage and motioned for Irene to come that way. She came toward Carissa, her feet shuffling. Carissa offered her a hand to steady her as she walked down the three steps.

The chapel suddenly filled with applause. As soon as Irene was down the last step, Carissa looked over her shoulder and saw that all the students had risen to their feet and were clapping for dear Irene.

"Do you need to sit down?" Carissa noticed that Irene's arm felt cold and clammy.

"Yes."

Catherine was right beside them and ushered them around the back to where a small room was prepared for them with snacks and a couch. Carissa helped Irene to sit down and then brought her a bottle of water.

"Are you okay?" she asked after Irene took a sip of the water.

"My heart pill. I forgot to take it this morning. Dan will be so upset."

"Do you have any with you?" Carissa reached

for Irene's tote bag that Catherine had brought when she ushered the two of them to the back room.

Instead of answering, Irene tried to take another sip of water. It dribbled out the side of her mouth.

Carissa reached for the water bottle just as Irene was about to drop it. Irene lowered her eyes. Her head fell forward.

"Irene? Irene!"

The lovely dove of a woman didn't answer.

18

"E ha maluna o'u
I ola au a mau
Noho a pa'a wau me 'oe
Iloko 'ka maha la'i."

"Breathe on me, breath of God,
Fill me with life anew,
That I may love what thou dost love,
And do what thou wouldst do."

CATHERINE CALLED FOR AN ambulance while Carissa checked Irene's wrist for a pulse. It was faint but still there. Catherine then phoned the doctor in residence on campus while Carissa tried to position Irene so she could breathe properly.

Grabbing Irene's tote bag, Carissa dumped out

the contents on the table beside the couch. Inside a plastic sandwich bag were two prescription bottles.

"Does she take both?" Catherine asked.

"I don't know." Carissa reached for her cell phone. "I'm calling her husband."

The on-campus doctor, who had been in the assembly, entered the back room and assessed the situation.

"Dan, it's Carissa. I'm with Irene on Oahu, and she said she forgot to take her heart pill. I found the two prescription bottles in her bag. Does she take both?"

"Yes, one of each. She knows that. She should have taken them this morning."

"Okay. I'll call you right back." Carissa handed the bottles to the doctor and relayed Dan's instructions. She then stepped to the side, thinking of how Dr. Walters always wanted space when he examined a patient.

Two other people from the school staff entered the small room, their expressions full of questions and concerns. Catherine suggested all of them leave to let the doctor have room. Carissa's cell phone rang, so she slipped out with the others to talk to Dan.

"Is she all right? What happened? Where is she? I'll come right now."

"The doctor is with her. We're at the school on Oahu. The doctor has her pills, and we called an ambulance; so if there's a need, we can get her to the hospital."

"What happened? Did she faint?"

Carissa gave Dan all the details and promised to call him back the minute she knew anything further. She then returned to the room.

Irene was stretched out on the couch with her feet raised. Her eyes were open, and the doctor was talking with her, holding her wrist and checking her pulse. Carissa hung back. The door opened and two EMTs entered. As the on-campus doctor gave an update, one of the EMTs pulled a stethoscope from his bag and went to Irene.

During the next ten minutes, the emergency scenario changed to one of mixed assessments. In the end, Irene had her way and chose not to go to the hospital. Carissa had Dan on the phone while the decisions were made, and he agreed with Irene's choice.

Before Carissa hung up, Dan said, "Promise me you'll take good care of her for me. The woman can be stubborn."

"I'll take care of her. Don't worry."

By the time the EMTs were on their way out, Irene seemed herself and was offering them gracious smiles and thanks.

Now that the crisis had passed, the next dilemma was what to do about the second gathering of students, who were now entering the chapel.

"We can cancel," Catherine said.

"I might be all right to go a second round. Just give me a minute."

Carissa had kept quiet in the middle of all the diagnosing and decision-making, but as she looked at Irene, she knew the woman needed more than her indomitable spirit to keep her going onstage for another thirty-five minutes.

"No," Carissa said plainly. "You don't need to go for a second round, Irene. I promised your husband I would take good care of you; so I'm making the decision for you. For all of us."

Irene's gentle brown eyes appeared large through her round glasses. A winsome expression touched her lips. "What a good idea! You can tell them."

"Okay. I'll tell the students the assembly is cancelled."

"No, no, no." Irene pointed a determined finger at Carissa. "I want you to tell them about Ka'ahumanu. You have heard everything before. You have all my notes. You can do this for me."

Carissa swallowed quickly and shook her head. "I don't think I can. No. I'm not a storyteller like you. I'm uncomfortable speaking in front of crowds."

"They aren't a crowd. They are a little flock. This is their story. Please, give them their story." Irene lowered her head, and with both hands she removed the *kukui*-nut lei, lifting it over her matted-down hair and handing it to Carissa.

Not knowing what else she could possibly do at the moment, Carissa reached for the lei, watching Irene's weary arm fall to her side. She smiled at Carissa and said nothing. The message was clear.

Carissa didn't remember placing the *kukui*-nut-and-woven-gift-box lei over her own head, nor did she remember the introduction by Kahu Kalama as she sat in the front row frantically scanning Irene's notes.

But she did remember what the faces of the "little flock" looked like when she took her place behind the steady wood podium. They were curious. Open. Perhaps even a bit expectant.

Clearing her throat and hearing it resound in the fixed microphone, she leaned back slightly and began with the same opening Irene had used. "I want to tell you the story of a surfer girl who was 100 percent Hawaiian. She learned to surf the long boards off the Kohala Coast and was known as a graceful and agile surfer. She was called a flirt and had elegant tattoos on her legs, left palm, and even one on her tongue. One night she swam five miles in shark-infested waters to be with the man she loved."

She could feel the engaged stares from all the students. They appeared eager to sip from whatever this cup was that she had just offered them.

The rest of the half hour she felt the same way she had years ago when trying to drive a stick-shift car for the first time. Lunge, stall, restart, pop the clutch. It was a jumpy, bumpy journey, but the students stayed with her for the most part. Then she arrived at the final destination, the close of Ka'ahumanu's life.

While reading from the notes, Carissa reached the part where Irene had seemed to lose her place in her earlier presentation. Ka'ahumanu had become softened toward Christianity. She had learned to read and write and had written a message on the slate board that was read aloud. Since Carissa could see the message from the slate included in the notes, she read it to the students, trying to employ the same powerful voice Irene had used when she was quoting Ka'ahumanu. "This is what Ka'ahumanu wrote and read aloud: 'I am making myself strong . . .'"

Carissa felt a catch in her throat. Those were words she had thought a number of times this past week, but usually they referred to her intention to become strong apart from any sort of dependence on Richard or God.

Quickly pulling herself back into the moment, Carissa continued to read Ka'ahumanu's words. "'I am making myself strong. I declare in the presence of God, I repent of my sin and believe God to be our Father.'"

The words seemed to fly like an arrow, straight into Carissa's heart. She, too, had made such a declaration, such a commitment, when she was a teenager at summer camp. Now, in this vivid moment, she felt compelled to reaffirm that commitment. To repent of her sins and believe anew that God was her Heavenly Father, and that her salvation was through him alone.

Carissa adjusted the papers, as if she had lost her place. The truth was, her heart was finding its proper place, there in the presence of God and hundreds of waiting witnesses.

It took only a few seconds for Carissa to silently whisper her inward recommitment. She didn't imagine any of the students knew they had just seen a very private, sacred ceremony. With a sense of childlike faith and a tone of wonder in her voice, Carissa heard herself say to all the students, "I, too, believe God to be my Father."

Glancing at the windows in the back of the chapel, Carissa noticed it was raining. The rain came down in a fine sheet of mistlike droplets. It was the first time she had seen it rain since she had been on the islands, and it looked to her as if the building were being covered with a sheer veil. She felt safe. Protected.

Carissa concluded by reading directly from Irene's notes regarding the details of the final years of Ka'ahumanu's life. " 'She circled the islands, teaching alongside the missionaries and exhibiting the transformation Christ had created in her attitudes and actions. Everywhere she went the people looked on her with awe and reverence. The haughtiness of her youth was gone. She cared for the sick and elderly, communed with commoners, and shared with each of them her growing love for *Ke Akua* and his Word.

" 'Ka'ahumanu died just before dawn on June 5, 1832. In many ways it was a new dawn for the Hawaiian people. She had exerted her influence to put an end to the worship of the ancient idols, changed the laws to protect her people, and openly expressed her abiding commitment to Christ and the way of salvation. Within the next two decades, Hawaii became the most literate and most Christian nation per capita in the world.' "

Carissa was at the end of Irene's notes, but she didn't know how to end the talk. She looked out at the students. They were a beautiful little flock. Tenderness filled her heart. Extending her arms out and opening her palms to the students, she said, "This is your story. A story of one of your women. I give this story to you today with much aloha."

She could think of nothing else to say. Lowering her arms, she picked up the binder and stepped down from the stage. The moment her foot touched the first step, the room filled with applause, just as it had for Irene. Carissa felt overwhelmed, seeing the students rise to their feet as they continued to clap.

Instead of going to the front row and sitting down, she went out the back to the room where Irene was resting. Tears clouded her eyes. She couldn't believe how she felt in that moment. She had participated in something powerful. More than that, God had come close, very close to her, and drew her heart back into the hollow of his hand.

Feeling buoyant and incredibly free, Carissa entered the back room and smiled when she saw Irene sitting up, sipping a cup of tea. Her color was back, and her eyes had their clear glow once again.

Catherine was beside Irene, and the campus doctor sat opposite her.

"We heard the applause," Catherine said. "I'm sorry I wasn't in there to show you my support."

"No, you were in the right place, here with Irene. You're looking much better."

"I'm just fine. Quite embarrassed, but just fine. Dan is not a bit happy with me at the moment. I promised him we would try to catch an earlier flight back, if that's all right with you. He insisted on flying home today as well."

"Of course. Yes. Anything you want." Turning to the doctor, Carissa asked, "It's okay for her to fly?"

"Yes. All her vital signs are good."

Carissa removed the *kukui*-nut lei from around her neck and placed it back on Irene, who started to protest but was quickly silenced. "I was only the substitute teacher. This belongs to you."

A tap on the door was followed by the entrance

of Kahu Kalama. His face was beaming. "I'm glad to see you sitting up and looking so well."

"I am well."

"What a wonderful gift both of you have brought to our students. Three of them came up to me and said they wanted to research other important people in Hawaiian history and write stories about them. You have started something here today. Both of you. This is a strong catalyst for our next generation."

With a growing smile he said, "One of the young men said to me, 'Why is a haole woman from the mainland telling me my stories? I want to learn the stories and tell them.'"

Irene, Catherine, and the doctor chuckled. Carissa guessed the reference to her being a haole meant she was a foreigner or a "white" woman, which she was. If that fact alone prompted someone of Hawaiian blood to take up the torch, then she felt even more exhilarated about having delivered all of Irene's carefully prepared notes to these students.

Within an hour, they had said their good-byes, exchanged hugs, and were back at the airport. Irene resisted Carissa's suggestion that they ask for a wheelchair, but once they found out how far they had to go in this international airport to reach their gate, Irene acquiesced.

"This is the way to go," Carissa whispered to her after they were taken from the back of the security lineup to the front. "I'm glad you agreed to the wheelchair because now both of us get to enjoy a little upgrade in service."

Irene looked up at Carissa and grinned. "Well, then, we'll just say that I did this for you."

"Fine with me." It was also fine with Carissa when they were allowed to be among the first to board the flight to Maui. Their seats were at the bulkhead so they had more legroom. Carissa pulled out her phone and was about to turn it off for the flight when she noticed she had several messages. Since passengers were still boarding, she listened to voice mails.

The first message was from Blake. She smiled a mama smile from her heart when she heard her son's voice. "Hey, Dad told me you're in Hawaii. What's up with that? Good for you, Mom. So, I called him this morning, and he told me to call you and tell you what I told him. What I told him is that I've met someone. She's great. Really great. I'm pretty much smitten. Is that the word for it? I don't know. She's just great. Really sweet and pretty, and she's funny and . . . well, just call me back when you have time. Love you. Bye."

Carissa saved Blake's message. She knew she would want to listen to that message over and over. It made her laugh because, in all his gushing, he hadn't mentioned the woman's name. Carissa had a feeling she would find that out soon enough. This was really wonderful news from her man-child. She would always remember that he had used the word "smitten."

The next message was from Richard. He told her he was praying for her and that he would be eager to hear all about her time on Oahu. He also said in a lowered voice that he missed her and couldn't wait to see her and added, "I had a dream about you last night. It was a very, very good dream."

She felt her face warming as she listened to him, even though she knew no one else could hear. She saved that message, too.

The final message was also from Richard. He said a few more mushy things to her that caused her to blush even more. Then he told her to call when she could, and even if he wasn't able to pick up, she should leave a message because he missed the sound of her voice.

Carissa thought about the mushy things she wanted to say back to him and liked what she came up with. But she didn't want to call him now while everyone around her could hear. Instead she sent a text, telling him they were leaving Oahu early and that she would call him as soon as she could.

Irene napped on the flight and still seemed slow-moving when they reached the car and drove back to the house. It was almost three o'clock when they arrived. Kai was in the front yard cleaning out the camping gear. He offered his mom a hand as she extricated herself from the car.

"You brought her back in one piece, did you?" He was grinning, but his concern showed in his nervous mannerisms.

Carissa tried to keep the conversation light. "Yes, she's in one piece, and I'm afraid there might be no living with her now that she's a bit of a rock star with all the students at the Kamehameha Schools. You should have heard her presentation. The students ate up every word. They gave her a standing ovation."

Irene leaned on her cane and looked into her son's face. "What are you doing back from the camping trip so soon?"

"Dad called me."

"He overreacted. I'm fine. You shouldn't have come back."

"Well, I did." Kai resumed cleaning out the ice chest and acted as if he were ignoring his mom. Out of the side of his mouth he playfully added, "So deal with it, Rock Star."

Carissa left the two of them and went around the side of the house to her little cottage. She made herself something to eat and settled on the front porch, enjoying the peace and shade, as she rocked in one of the plantation-style, tall-backed rockers. From her lovely spot she watched the afternoon sun warm the clump of bananas, toasting them to a nice golden shade of yellow.

They would be ready for eating in a day. Two days at the most. Carissa hoped she wouldn't be gone before they were ready to be plucked and peeled and mashed in one of Irene's large mixing bowls to be turned into banana bread.

Pressing Blake's number on her phone, she left a message for her son. "I got your message. Smitten, huh? I can't wait to hear all the details. Isn't love just the best thing ever? Call me, honey. I love you."

She drew in a deep, fragrant breath of the jasmine-scented air and smiled. In two days she would be home and back in her husband's arms. She wondered if she could find a way to tuck some of the wild jasmine in her hair and if it would stay fresh all the way home.

She knew it was worth a try.

19

" 'Oe ke Kokua aloha
Hope 'i 'o o Iesu
Ike launa a ho'ola
Ho 'oma'ema'e la ia makou."

"Jesus, thou art all compassion,
Pure unbounded love thou art;
Visit us with thy salvation;
Enter every trembling heart."

STILL FEELING ENERGIZED AFTER the rousing time she had had on Oahu with Irene, Carissa decided that instead of snoozing the rest of the day away, she would venture down to the beach. She could read or sleep there, if she felt so inclined. For sure she could catch some photos of the sunset, as Richard had asked.

He had been sending text messages to her throughout the day, letting her know that he was forced to reschedule his flight, but he was leaving Denver that morning. His last text said his flight was on time. He didn't say what time he would arrive in Portland, but she sent a message back telling him to call her once he landed. She couldn't wait to tell him what had happened today at the Kamehameha Schools.

Around four-thirty, Carissa took off for the trek

down the hill to the beach. Instead of going directly to the sand, though, she decided to explore some of the stores in the shopping center across the street. The variety of fluttering gauze skirts and beach cover-ups hanging in front of one of the shops looked worth a peek.

One dress in particular caught her eye. It was a long, flowing white dress with white embroidery across the top. Carissa had a "flower child" dress like that when she was young. As she slipped into the dress, she found it made her happy, so she bought it. She located a few more souvenirs to take home—a beaded bracelet and some tiny seashell earrings. Heidi and her mom would appreciate those little remembrances. As she checked out some coasters with a bird of paradise design and pondered buying them for Irene, Richard's ring tone buzzed in her purse. She left the items on the counter and stepped outside.

"Hi." His voice sounded rich and warm.

"Did your plane land?"

"Yep. Just a few minutes ago."

"I'm glad you got home safely. I'm doing a little souvenir shopping at the moment. What would you like me to bring home for you?"

"The only thing I want you to bring home for me is yourself."

She smiled at his sweet words. "Okay. That's what I'll bring you then."

"I'll look forward to unwrapping my gift."

"Oh, you will, will you?"

"Yes, I will."

"Well, I'll look forward to that, too."

"Good."

A playful sort of invisible glow seemed to hang between them in the short pause. Even though the flirty words were being exchanged with her husband, Carissa still felt as if she were a teenager once again, with all the trembling, heady sort of feelings of first love causing her heart to rush.

"So, what are you doing after you finish your souvenir shopping?"

"I'm going to the beach. I plan to take some pictures of the sunset for you."

"I appreciate that. You remembered."

"Of course, I remembered. You know what I'll do? I'll call you while I'm taking the pictures. That way you and I can sort of be together for a walk along the beach at sunset."

Richard laughed.

"Don't laugh. I know it sounds like one of those cheesy personal ads you used to make fun of. 'Must love long walks on the beach at sunset.' It's just that if you were here you would see that it fits. It's so beautiful. So romantic."

"If you're feeling romantic, then you'd definitely better call me."

"I will. I promise."

Carissa purchased her souvenirs, impulsively adding a few hair clips, and then headed for the beach. After weighing down her shopping bags with her sandals, she strode into the salty waves. As she swam, a song played in her head. It was a hymn.

The hymn came from her high school days, when she, Richard, and their friends would all go to evening church service on Sundays and sit together in the back row. The big draw was each other, and the excuse was to go out for ice cream afterward. They could stand close during the singing and sit even closer during the service. Without realizing it, she and Richard learned many hymns as they shared a hymnal with their arms rubbing together.

Not all the words had remained in her memory, and she was pretty sure they weren't in the correct order, but enough were there to keep her singing silently as she swam.

"Great is thy faithfulness, O God my Father,
There is no shadow of turning with thee.
Thou changest not, thy compassions they fail not
. . . Summer and winter and springtime and
    harvest
Sun, moon, and stars in their courses above
Join with all nature in manifold witness
To thy great faithfulness, mercy, and love
. . . Great is thy faithfulness, Lord unto me."

305

Carissa felt as if she were beaming when she emerged from the water. It had been a long, long time since she had felt this happy.

Wringing out her hair and walking back to her beach towel, Carissa thought she heard her name. She heard it again. Only a few people on the whole island knew her. She wrapped up in the beach towel and looked around. From across the sand, where a large group had gathered, Carissa saw a man waving at her. She recognized him as the Australian who had sat by her on the plane the day she arrived. She smiled and waved back.

He took the hand of the woman beside him, and the couple came walking in her direction. "I thought that was you. Looks like you've been enjoying your vacation here on Maui."

"It's been perfect. Really perfect."

"This is my wife, Teri."

The two women exchanged friendly hellos.

"She just arrived yesterday, and we were able to fit in a birthday party with some old friends."

"Looks like fun."

"You're welcome to come join us," Teri said. "We have plenty of food. We always do."

"Thanks, but I have a phone date coming up with my husband."

"How sweet," Teri said.

Gordon gave her a nod. "Well, if you change your mind, come on over and get in on the grinds."

"Thanks. I might do that."

306

Once again, Carissa was amazed at the hospitality of the people she had met on Maui. She finished drying off and spread the beach towel out in the warm sand. Reaching into her shopping bag, she pulled out her new gauze dress and pulled off the price tag. This seemed like the ideal time to put it to good use as a bathing suit cover-up. She stood, slipped it over her head, and smoothed down the sides.

Carissa loved how she felt at that moment. Her new dress seemed like a cross between a Bohemian gypsy dress and an angelic choir robe. Pulling her still-wet hair up into a twist on the back of her head, she used one of the last-minute souvenirs. It was a long clip with a white silk flower attached. A few stray tendrils fell loose on the sides, but that was typical for her hair. Richard always liked it when she wore her hair up. She couldn't remember the last time she had twisted it up like this. It usually all fell out within the first five minutes, but the salt water seemed to help it stay in place this time.

She took a short stroll down the beach but had walked only a few yards when her phone rang.

"Hey, I thought I was supposed to be the one who called you."

"I couldn't wait. What are you doing now?"

"I just started to walk along the beach, and the sun has just dipped behind a long row of thin clouds on the horizon."

"Is the sky pink?"

"It's just starting to turn pink. More orange, actually. Light orange, like sherbet. There are a few rosy streaks. The top of the clouds look like ruffles, with the sunlight coming through the openings and shooting shafts of silver out on the ocean. It's really beautiful."

"I feel like I can almost see it with you. Are you taking pictures?"

"Oh! I almost forgot." Holding the phone to her ear with her left hand, she held up the camera with her right hand and tried to keep it steady as she lined up the shot.

"Hey, move!"

"Are you talking to me?"

"No. Some tourist in a big beachcomber hat just walked right in front of me as I tried to take the picture."

Carissa took several steps through the sand to the left. "What's the deal, buddy?"

"What happened?"

"I moved, and he moved, too. I had a perfect shot of the sunset, but he blocked it."

"Is he really large or something?"

"No, he's not large. He does have pathetically white legs, but then I'm one to talk. There. He's out of my viewfinder. Hang on. Let me take a few pictures here."

She snapped two pictures before the guy was back in the shot.

"You have to bc kidding me!"

"Is he back?"

"Yes." Carissa lowered the camera and kept talking to Richard. "I can't believe this guy. He has the whole beach, and he keeps . . . uh-oh."

"What's wrong?"

"He's coming toward me." She lowered her voice. "I hope he didn't hear me."

"Does he look mad?"

"I can't see his face under the hat. He's coming right toward me. What should I do?"

There was no response.

"Richard?"

The annoying tourist was now only ten feet away and was headed right for her.

"Richard!"

No answer.

The man took three long strides forward and removed the beachcomber hat.

Carissa's jaw dropped. Her heart pounded with wild surprise and deep delight.

"Richard?"

"So, what is the guy doing now?" Richard asked.

Carissa closed her phone. "He's standing right in front of me, and I think he's about to kiss me."

"I think you're right." Richard dropped his hat in the sand, pressed the remote phone receiver in his ear and reached out to Carissa. With both arms, he encircled her and dipped her back as he gave her the sort of kiss she hadn't tasted for many years.

Carissa felt the warm breath from her husband's mouth as he whispered, "I love you."

She drew in the smoldering words, swallowing them, and feeling the deep fires igniting. "I love you." She returned the truth to him with a kiss laced with tears.

Drawing back, they grasped hands and gazed at each other.

"I can't believe you're here." She loved the look of satisfaction on Richard's face. He found great pleasure in pulling off surprises. This was definitely the biggest one.

"I couldn't wait to be with you. That's why I was forced to change my flight out of Denver this morning." He kissed her again. "I had to be with you."

Pulling back, he touched the curve of her jaw. "You look absolutely amazing. I mean, really, truly stunning. You are so beautiful. I want to marry you. Right now."

Carissa laughed and touched the side of his face. Richard used to say that line to her during the last year of their dating and engagement, as they counted off the days to their wedding. He would say he wanted to marry her right now, and she would say, "Then I'll go find us a minister."

A crazy thought struck her. Tilting her head she said, "Do you really want to marry me? Right now?"

"Yes, I want to marry you. Right now." Richard kissed the tip of her sun-freckled nose.

"Then I'll go find us a minister." She released his hands and walked away from him.

"Carissa?"

"Wait right there. Don't move. I'll be right back." Hiking up her long skirt, she hurried through the warm sand and approached the large birthday party gathering. Gordon waved as she entered the party area and called out, "You decided to join in, did you? Good deal."

"No. Actually, I have a question for you. This might be the most bizarre question you've ever been asked."

His wife laughed. "I doubt that. My husband tends to be a quirky-experience magnet."

"Well, then, here's my question. You said on the plane that you're a pastor. I wondered if you would consider performing a vow-renewal ceremony for my husband and me. You see, he just surprised me and showed up. He's down there by the water. The one with the white legs, looking perplexed."

Gordon grinned. "This is why I always carry my Bible. Come on, Teri. Grab my backpack. We shouldn't keep them waiting."

The three of them arrived in front of patient Richard with breathless introductions. "This is Gordon and Teri. He's a pastor. He's willing to marry us again, if you have no objections."

Richard laughed. "Are you serious?"

"Completely serious."

"Then my answer is the same now as it was the first time you asked me to marry you. Yes, please."

"I did not ask you to marry me. You asked me." Carissa linked her arm in Richard's and gave it a squeeze. Grinning up at him she said, "Or are you getting too old to remember such details?"

He playfully squeezed her back, adding a rib tickle.

Gordon had his Bible out and open and appeared ready to begin before they lost another moment of the sunset. "All right then, you, Richard, you stand right here. And you, Carissa, the beautiful bride, you stand right there. Yes, just like that, with the sunset behind you. What a couple you two make. Are you ready?"

Carissa and Richard exchanged fond glances and both turned to face Gordon. Teri had picked up Carissa's camera and motioned that she was going to take pictures.

"Dearly beloved, we are gathered here in the sight of God and some of his children to ask his rich blessing on Richard and Carissa, as they reaffirm their sacred vows of marriage."

Gordon opened his Bible. Carissa thought he was going to read from 1 Corinthians 13, the familiar love chapter Irene had recited earlier and that had been read at their wedding twenty-four years ago. Instead, he started with a passage from 1 John: " 'In this is love; not that we love God, but that he loved us.' "

He gave a brief, off-the-cuff talk about how God's love is unending, unstoppable, and unfathomable. "We are given the privilege of entering into that love and sharing it with others. No place is the picture of God's love demonstrated more clearly than between a man and wife."

Then Gordon chose a heady passage from the Song of Solomon for the close. "So 'kiss me with the kisses of your mouth! For your love is better than wine.' "

With a broad grin, he asked the important questions of each of them that signified the renewal of their vows.

Looking into each other's eyes and clasping hands, they each replied on cue with, "I do."

"Then to signify the recommitment of your union, I invite you as husband and wife to kiss again. And again. And again."

Carissa looked into her husband's strong face as Richard took her face in his hands, tilted her chin up and kissed her deeply. They drew back and gazed into each other's eyes, smiling.

"All right," Gordon said with his lighthearted voice returning. "That should do it. See if that doesn't hold for another couple of decades. If it doesn't stick, I'll let you know where to find me, and we can give it another go."

Teri gave Carissa a wink and a grin as she handed back the camera. "God bless, you guys."

"Thanks," Richard said. "I think he has."

Gordon and Teri said their good-byes and headed back to the birthday party. Richard wrapped his arm around Carissa's middle, and the two of them strolled barefoot down the beach. They whispered flirty little tendernesses to each other, laughed, kissed, and lingered on the beach as the final fading hues of pink, orange, and plum faded from the sky. Together, they spotted the first evening star.

"So where do we go from here?" Carissa asked.

"I don't know exactly. But we're going to go there together. And I think we need to start by extending our time here. How do you feel about spending another week, but with me this time?"

"I would love it!"

"Good. Because it's all arranged."

He kissed her. She kissed him. The trade winds began to undo her hair.

"Come with me," Carissa said with a beguiling smile.

Hand in hand they returned to where they had left Richard's beachcomber hat and Carissa's towel.

"Nice disguise, by the way."

"You like that? I bought it at a shop across the street along with this snazzy shirt." Richard led her to where he had parked his rental car, and Carissa laughed. The two of them had shopped in the same store, only she was there an hour before him. They slipped into the car and headed up the hill.

Twilight had come quickly. With quiet steps around the side of Dan and Irene's home, Carissa led the way past the verdant garden and approached the cottage.

"This is where you've been staying? Wow, this is amazing."

"I know." Carissa smiled. Everything she had experienced and loved about the island she could now share with her husband and so much more.

They were about to step up onto the porch when Richard let go of the handle of his suitcase and said, "Wait. Put your things down."

She complied, standing in front of him empty-handed.

"Do you have the key?"

"It's in the mail basket, right there."

Richard unlocked the front door and propped it open. With a boyish grin, he came toward her. She knew what he was about to attempt and immediately protested. "If you try to pick me up and carry me over the threshold, you're going to hurt your back."

"No, I won't."

"I'm not the same girl I was twenty-four years ago."

"Yes, you are." Richard paused and grinned. "There's just a little more of you to love."

Carissa took no offense at his words. She tilted back her head, playfully laughing along with him. The sight that caught her eye made her reach for his arm. "Oh, Richard, look! Do you see it?"

Peeking between the languid leaves of the banana trees was the fullest butterball of a moon Carissa had ever seen. The shadows of the craters across the face of the moon gave a strong impression of a pleasant grin.

"It's the face of *Ke Akua*," Carissa said, looping her arm around Richard's neck and resting her head on his shoulder. "I think he's smiling on us."

Richard kissed her on the temple and peered with her at the grinning moon. As they watched, a silver jet stream appeared just beneath the golden orb, etching a smudged line through the illuminated night sky. To Carissa, the airplane seemed to be swimming through the foreboding midnight blue, determined to reunite some other woman with the one she loved.

Carissa drew closer to Richard. He was the one she loved. He always had been. He always would be. She knew they still had a lot of adjustments to make and problems to solve once they returned home. But now Carissa knew they would be working through everything together. And as he always had been, God was with them.

He kissed her again, first on the cheek, and then warmly on her upturned lips. With both his arms flexed and ready for the task at hand, Richard scooped up his bride and held her tight. Carissa smiled. She leaned in as Richard carried her over the threshold and shut the front door with a backward kick of his heel.

She had a pretty good idea the next chapter of their love story was about to begin right here, in this blessed hideaway, tucked in under a Maui moon.

Benediction
The Queen's Prayer

Nolaila e ka Haku
Ma lalo kou ʻeheu
Ko makou maluhia
A mau loa aku no.
Amene.

And so, O Lord
Protect us beneath your wings
And let peace be our portion
Now and forever more.
Amen.

From the Author's Notes

Our family has camped a number of times here at Haleakala National Park campground. During our last trip, I peered from my tent our first morning and captured this sunrise. I knew one day I'd write a story about a woman who would come camping here and be stunned by the beauty.

Kipahulu, near Hana, is the setting for where Irene and Carissa took their leisurely swim in the waterfall pools. This is a popular spot for tourists, but my favorite time to come here for a swim is always at first light before anyone else arrives. Ka'ahumanu was born in a cave not far from this area.

The walk from the campground to the waterfalls provides lots of time and space for pondering. When we were there I could just "see" Carissa taking this stroll and thinking about how her life challenges would begin to untangle.

The graveyard where Charles Lindbergh is buried is a beautiful, sacred space. On one of our visits here with another family and their grown children, all nine of us entered the church and sang together, hymn after hymn. The sweet sound filled the small chapel and drew all of us closer together.

Ahhh, the Pacific Ocean that surrounds the island of Maui! Throughout the story Carissa took leisurely swims in this vast, blue body of balmy bliss.

The interior of the Bishop Memorial Chapel at the Kamehameha Schools on Oahu is crafted of native koa wood and is breathtaking. Just like Carissa and Irene, I had the privilege of speaking to the students here in 2008. What did I talk about? The life of Ka'ahumanu, of course.

Interview with
Robin Jones Gunn

Is it true that you've always been a storyteller?
Yes. And I have proof! A few years ago my mom gave me a box filled with childhood mementos including my grade-school report cards. The teacher's note on my report card from first grade said, "Robin has not yet grasped her basic math skills but she does keep the entire class entertained with her stories at rug time." How's that for early evidence? And I'm still challenged when it comes to math.

When it was clear that you were a storyteller, did you naturally decide you wanted to be a writer?
No. I wanted to be a missionary. I thought there was no higher calling than going to an unreached people group in some remote corner of the world and telling them about God's love. A long time ago a good friend told me that telling stories is simply what God created me to do and I shouldn't fight it. I didn't like their conclusion but I did like telling stories so that's what I put my heart into doing. Now, almost three decades later, I've discovered that exactly what I longed

for has happened—my books have found their way to remote corners of the world and through the stories many people are hearing about God's love.

What does the writing process look like for you?

I start by dreaming up a main character. She becomes a compilation of real-life friends as well as some of my own faults and foibles. Once I can "see" her in my mind's eye and feel as if we are truly "imaginary" friends, then I ask her quite candidly, "What is your biggest problem right now?" As soon as she tells me I start spinning all the possibilities of what could happen along the way as that problem gets resolved. I don't usually know the ending of the story or the way her problem gets resolved. That seems to happen organically as the story unfolds.

This process often feels as if I've started out standing on a riverbank observing the scenery and tossing a few pebbles of possibility into the story to see what happens. Then I put my toes in and start writing. At some point I find I've waded in deeper and deeper until I'm immersed and can easily swim around inside the story. At that point the story seems to move me along on its current and I just keep my head up and type as fast as I can.

Aside from your strong love for Hawaii, what other parts in *Under a Maui Moon* were inspired from your own life?

Well, to be quite transparent, I'll tell you that my husband is a counselor. He specializes in counseling men who struggle with sexual addiction. Like Carissa, I experienced a frightening situation one night when I was home alone and because of my husband's line of work I did not feel safe in my own home. My similarities to Carissa's experience end there but that one event planted seeds in my imagination for this story. I wanted to see what would happen when a woman like Carissa started to believe that "everything is redeemable" and that men who struggle with this prevalent problem are worth going after and helping through to the other side of the addiction. For helpful information on understanding sexual addiction, please visit www.skyview counseling.com.

Do you receive a lot of responses from your readers?

Yes, I do. It's always a happy day when I hear back from a reader.

One of the most curious things to me is hearing what readers take away from a story. Many times readers will say that a certain part of a book was just what they needed to hear. However, what they got out of the book wasn't at all what I was thinking when I wrote that part. Sometimes my favorite parts never receive comments while other parts carry deep meaning for the reader. It's such a lovely mystery the way that happens. I've come to believe even more humbly in the power of fiction. A story that comes from the heart will most certainly touch another heart. If that is how you felt as you read this story, I would love to hear from you. You can contact me at Robinsnest@robingunn.com or go to my website, www.robingunn.com, to sign up for my Robin's Nest Newsletter.

Discussion Questions for
Under a Maui Moon

1. Carissa is bitter and disheartened early in the story. What "external influencers" feed her emotional reaction? What "internal influencers" feed her emotions?

2. When you, like Carissa, are overwhelmed by life, where (or what) is your "Island Hideaway"?

3. How do these verses apply to Carissa's story and to our lives? Psalm 32:7, Psalm 61:1–8, 1 Peter 5: 7–10.

4. Carissa's emotional baggage from her father's departure affects her marriage. Jot down emotional baggage you might be carrying that is affecting relationships in your life. Share this with the group or with someone you trust if you think it might help you to have accountability in giving the past, present, and future to God. How does 1 Peter 5:7 apply to our baggage?

5. A number of marriages are depicted in this story. List and describe each. What can be

learned from each one about successful or less than successful ways of relating to a loved one?

6. What changes took place in Richard and Carissa that caused them to renew their love for each other?

7. Kai represents a temptation in Carissa's life. What temptations or fantasies do you hold on to rather than appreciating what you have?

8. How does the moon and its various phases as Carissa sees them represent her relationship with God?

9. What insights to relationships does Carissa gain from Irene?

10. Which of the hymns at the opening of the chapters meant the most to you? Why?

11. Kai, Carissa, Joel, and Maile discuss addictions in Chapter 21. What did you learn about addictions in this chapter that you hadn't realized before?

12. During Carissa's lecture in front of the students, Ka'ahumanu's life becomes linked to

Carissa's life. What insights does Carissa gain about her relationships with God and her husband during her talk? What leads her to recommit herself to God?

About the Author

A T MY FIRST WRITERS' conference more than twenty-five years ago I was given this advice:

Write about what you know.

Since my husband and I were involved in youth ministry at the time I knew a bit about teens and began writing the still-popular Christy Miller series. Over the years I've come to know what a gift it is to have close friendships and so I wrote about love and friendships in the Glenbrooke series and the Sisterchicks® series.

Then three summers ago my husband and I were on the island of Maui celebrating our thirtieth wedding anniversary and I asked God, "What should I write about for the next twenty-five years?" The answer floated to me on the gentle trade wind.

Write about what you love.

Ahhh. Yes. Write about what I love. At the top of my "What I Love" list are the Hawaiian Islands. Our honeymoon was on Oahu and our family lived on Maui for a year in the 1990s. Even though we've called Portland, Oregon, our home for many years, and love it here, our family returns to the islands every chance we get. Our *aloha 'aina* (love of the land) grows with each visit.

While we were living on Maui I picked up a Hawaiian history book in the reference section of the Lahaina library. Never would I have guessed how that book would ignite a passion in me for the people and places of Old Hawaii. I joined the Calabash Cousins of the Daughters of Hawai'i and began making trips to the Mission Houses Museum in Honolulu to research original documents held in the archives.

What fascinates me the most is that everything the women on the islands felt and struggled with one hundred fifty years ago are still common issues for women today. In my research of Ka'ahumanu, I found her to be a woman of great strength who used her influence and power to change the course of a nation. I love seeing women who get their strength back after a rough season. I call it "getting their heart back." I can relate. I've been through such seasons. I'm guessing you have, too.

As I was writing *Under a Maui Moon* I felt so sympathetic toward Carissa. Everything came at her at once and she could have made some decisions that would have changed the course of her life. But, as in real life, God had His hand on her. He was relentless in His pursuit of her and I think once she caught a glimpse of how Ka'ahumanu "made herself strong," Carissa began to get her heart back.

If this story could come wrapped in a *pule* (prayer) for each of you readers, my prayer would be that you would make yourself strong and that you would get your heart back.

I'd love to keep in touch. Would you like to receive my Robin's Nest Newsletter? You can sign up at www.robingunn.com. You can also connect with me through Facebook on the Robin Jones Gunn fan page or on Twitter via RobinGunn.

Additional Copyright Information

ROBIN JONES GUNN IS the bestselling, award-winning author of more than seventy books, with combined sales of more than 4 million copies worldwide. She is a sought-after international speaker and serves on the Board of Directors for Media Associates International and the Board of Advisors for Jerry B. Jenkins Christian Writers Guild. She and her husband have two grown children and live near Portland, Oregon.

Center Point Publishing
600 Brooks Road ● PO Box 1
Thorndike ME 04986-0001 USA

(207) 568-3717

US & Canada:
1 800 929-9108
www.centerpointlargeprint.com